Sister of a Sinner

by

Lynn Shurr

A Sinner's Legacy, Book Three

Sister of a Sinner

Cover Art by *Diana Carlile*

The Wild Rose Press, Inc.
PO Box 708
Adams Basin, NY 14410-0708
Visit us at www.thewildrosepress.com

Publishing History
First Fantasy Rose Edition, 2017
Print ISBN 978-1-5092-1401-3
Digital ISBN 978-1-5092-1402-0

A Sinner's Legacy, Book Three
Published in the United States of America

From the sidelines,
the man with the thin mustache glared at them with his dead black eyes.

Xo turned in Junior's arms. "Time to go home."

She insisted on remaining in the barroom while waiting for her favored driver despite the noise and dimness rather than out in the balmy May night where knots of men and women stood smoking and chatting on the broken sidewalk. When the taxi pulled up in front of Paco's, Xo bolted for its door and flung herself into the backseat. Junior joined her and carefully placed one arm around her shoulders, held her tight. She trembled, and he swore he could feel the frantic beat of her heart fast as a frightened dove against his chest.

"Did I do something wrong? Was the lift too much for you? Or was it the kiss?"

"No, no, nothing you did, Junior. The lift, the kiss is part of the dance. That man who wanted to be my partner, he is one of the dark men I've been seeing lately everywhere I go. Soulless men with auras so black they seem to make a hole in the universe. New Orleans is a big city, often a sinful city, and I've seen them before, but never so many or so close to me."

"I'll protect you, Xo. You know I'd give my life for you."

"Don't say that! No one should have to make that choice."

Praise for Lynn Shurr

"Shurr is a wonderful storyteller."

~*~

"Lynn Shurr's sinfully delightful New Orleans Sinners series is sure to please both non-sports fans and sports fans alike. Do yourself a favor and dive into the world of the Sinners."

~*~

"Very easy reads, well written, combined with conflict, believable plots and secondary characters that make the story come alive."

~*~

"The author has crafted a family full of surprises with the Billodeaux bunch. After reading just one book, I am eager to read more about this colorful family."

Dedication

For my friend, Jo Minvielle,
talented quilter and artist

A SINNER'S LEGACY

The Children of Joe and Nell Billodeaux who fulfilled the prophecy that they would have twelve offspring, this way, that way, all ways.

Dean Joseph Billodeaux—Joe's illegitimate son by a one-night stand with a woman who planned to shake him down for money. He is adopted by Nell, who believes she cannot have children of her own. Current Sinners quarterback. (*Wish for a Sinner*)

Thomas Cassidy Billodeaux—a redheaded son who enters the family through an open adoption with a teenage mother. His birth father is Joe's no-good cousin. He is a kicker for the Sinners. *(Wish for a Sinner* and *Kicks for a Sinner*)

Jude Emily Billodeaux—twin of Ann, conceived by in vitro fertilization using eggs purchased from Nell's sister, Emily. (*Wish for a Sinner*)

Ann Marie Billodeaux (Annie)—Jude's quiet twin. *(Wish for a Sinner)*

Lorena Renee Billodeaux (Lori)—First of Nell's little frozen babies to be born, one of the triplets. (*Kicks for a Sinner*)

Mack Coy Christopher Billodeaux—Second of the triplets to be born. (*Kicks for a Sinner*)

Trinity Billodeaux—Youngest of the triplets and named for the Father, Son, and Holy Ghost, smallest of the three and in need of a powerful saintly help to survive. (*Kicks for a Sinner*)

Xochi Maria Billodeaux—child of Joe's no-good cousin by a young Mexican woman. She is Tom's half-sister and is adopted into the family after the terrifying deaths of her parents. Her name means "blossom" in Aztec. (*Kicks for a Sinner*)

Teddy Wilkes Billodeaux—a child with spina bifida abandoned by his mother at Nell's health care center and adopted by the family. He believed himself to be Joe's natural son. (*Paradise for a Sinner*)

Anastasia Marya Polasky (Stacy)—daughter of Nell's sister, Emily, and a bogus Polish prince. She becomes a ward of the Billodeauxs upon her parents' deaths, but is never adopted by her own wish. She arrives on their doorstep the same day as Teddy. (*Paradise for a Sinner*)

Edith Patricia Billodeaux (Edie)—a normally conceived child, twin of Rex. (*Love Letter for a Sinner*)

Rex Worthy Billodeaux (T-Rex)—Edie's twin brother and future Sinner's quarterback, maybe. (*Love Letter for a Sinner*)

Chapter One

Junior Polk sat enthroned in one of the legendary Joe Billodeaux's oversized leather recliners surrounded by that great man's game balls, his trophies, his vast collection of football memorabilia. In other words, the family den of the Tara-like mansion. He remembered the days when he and the Billodeaux triplets could all fit into that chair and played fearlessly among the priceless artifacts. Now, Junior filled the space fairly well all by himself. Joe's son, Mack, occupied the other recliner because this was their day as candidates for the NFL draft.

The huge Billodeaux family filled the room, crowding the long sofa and sprawling on the floor. Friends filled every available form of seating from dining room chairs to beanbags dragged from the kids' bedrooms. The small towheaded Billodeaux grandchildren clamored over each and every one and moved from lap to lap like brightly flitting fireflies. Both had given Junior a hug, and nearly everyone else shook his hand or patted him on the back and wished him luck. While he appreciated their regard, he sought to impress only one person in the room, and that wasn't the famous Joe Billodeaux.

Joe's adopted Mexican daughter, Xochi, came up behind him, placed her hands on shoulders that had widened each year as they grew up together, and kissed

1

the top of his head. He felt her warmth flow through him, expanding his heart and rushing through his veins like game day adrenaline. "I know the Sinners will choose you," she whispered, giving him some added confidence.

Only the family and their most trusted friends knew Xochi saw auras. Some equated that with seeing the future, which she declared untrue. But, this gift did allow her to read people exceptionally well. Junior wondered if she could see his fear of being chosen last or not at all by a team like the chubby boy he'd once been. How he wished he could take Xochi on his lap and hold her like a prized talisman throughout the ordeal.

She withdrew, her long dark curls caressing the sides of his face. He wanted to grab her soft brown hands to keep them from leaving his body, but Xo took a seat behind him somewhere, probably in the cluster of her many sisters. He could pick out her voice—low and musical—but not exactly what she said. Stupid to believe she might be saying, "Junior Polk, he grew up to be *muy guapo*." He knew he did not qualify as handsome, not like her brother Mack, who could get any girl he wanted. Junior desired only one.

Junior's mama, the Billodeaux's cook and housekeeper, shouted for people to make way as she claimed her seat on the sofa within hugging distance of her son. She carried a huge, brightly decorated clay bowl of guacamole and set it beside a crystal punch bowl holding her fresh, spicy salsa. The family's butler followed like a minion with a tray full of small bowls to be filled and passed around with handfuls of tortilla chips. The audience had already made inroads into the platter of crispy baked chicken taquitos placed on the coffee table earlier. Ordinarily, Junior would have filled his plate, but his stomach couldn't handle it at the moment.

That did not stop his mother from taking a larger bowl from the bottom of the stack and filling it with dips, chips, and a garnish of half a dozen taquitos. "For my son who has grown so *grande.* Soon, he will graduate from college. Soon, he will play for the Sinners."

Junior accepted the bowl and managed a smile. Maybe the guacamole would soothe his roiling innards. He dipped a taquito and raised the green glob to his lips. His mama beamed. "*Excellente,* Mama." His mother's cooking, his desire to make her happy, had equaled a childhood body round as a basketball, a sport he was too fat and slow to play.

At the far end of the couch, Mack Billodeaux, lean and fast as a whippet in his time trials, stoked up on baby carrots dipped into hummus from the vegetable tray his Mama Nell always insisted upon serving no matter what the occasion. A woman so petite and fairy-like, she'd earned the nickname Tink, Nell also sat next to her son. Mack appeared discontent, and Junior knew the reason why. When he'd said he wanted to watch the draft at home with his family, Mama Nell had turned her big doe eyes on Mack and waited for him to say the same, so he did. Her son really wanted to be in the thick of things at the actual draft, striding on stage to be swathed in the jersey of the team who chose him. He'd confided that to Junior and blamed him a little for not wanting to go to the big time and have some kickass fun together.

Joe Billodeaux, king of the remote, pointed the device at the huge flat screen set up in front of the fireplace for the occasion. His wife turned on the somewhat smaller television over the mantel so that all could see. Of course, they might have used the home theater room attached to the house for the showing of movies, but this arrangement was cozier. Yes, cozy, Junior liked cozy. He ate some more guacamole as ESPN materialized onto the screens. The audience sat through the usual introductions and explanations of the process, but once the actual draft began, the players selected came out fast with only seven minutes each allowed for a pick. Not ready, lose a turn.

The most likely among the college quarterbacks went first, one, two, three, to the lowest ranked teams. Dallas with the fourth pick and badly in need of receivers called out the name of Mack Billodeaux. A cheer went up in the crowded den. Somebody dropped a paper crown upon his shaggy, long black hair, another small rebellion since Joe and his quarterback brother always wore theirs cropped short.

Mack, son of the awesome Joe, brother of the current Sinners' quarterback, Dean, had been crafted into the best wide receiver they could make him, and was guaranteed to be a top ten pick. He'd broken with family traditions every way he could by choosing to attend Alabama instead of LSU and refusing to be molded into a quarterback who had to compete with his brother. Junior suspected his secret though. Mack hated being hit on the football field. He would run like a cat with a tail afire carrying the ball and go out of bounds when the hounds of the defense neared. If Junior as a cornerback ever caught up with Mack in a game, he'd hit him hard and pop that ball out, not with malice, but because he wanted to do his job well.

Mama Nell said, "At least you won't be far from home." Joe leaned over her and shook Mack's hand. "Not everyone gets to be a Sinner. Do your best and wait for free agency." Good advice, but Mack had wanted to enter the draft last year as a college junior which would have put him one year closer to that free agency. While his dad might have wavered, his mother did not. All Billodeauxs finished college. Period.

Junior didn't even ask his parents if he could quit school early to go pro. Each one of them owned a Super Bowl ring presented for courageous services rendered to the Billodeaux family. The rings, earmarked for his education, sat in a safe deposit box to be sold if necessary to pay the fees. No need as it turned out. An LSU sports scholarship came through, a good thing because he wouldn't have gotten an academic one. His grades were decent, but not brilliant, primarily because Junior Polk cared more about three other things: food, football, and Xochi Billodeaux, but not in that order.

"You," said his mama, grasping his cheeks, "will be the first in my family to graduate from university." His dad had suggested military service if football didn't work out, an idea that made his mother cry. He'd craft a good sports career, absolutely he would, and then move on to his carefully considered retirement plans.

The numbers went up and up. No one called for Junior Polk as they had for Mack, now absent, talking on the phone in another room. The Sinners chose twenty-ninth out of thirty-one. Damn Dean Billodeaux for being such a hotshot quarterback that his team always got into the playoffs and won their conference last season. What if they didn't want him either? He'd go into the second night of the draft after everyone went home from the party. Junior clutched both sides of his snack bowl so tightly it might have snapped. A small hand he knew and loved took it from his grip and set it aside on the coffee table.

Xochi squeezed his fingers and warmth flowed up his arm. "Don't worry. Everything will be all right."

Did she remember the last time she'd said those words to him as a girl twice his age? Yes, really, since he'd been five and she'd turned ten when a gang of bullies cornered a pudgy Mexican kid with a cone of pink cotton candy grasped in one hand and a caramel apple in the other. They took his treats and shoved him behind one of the trailers at the street fair celebrating the sugar cane harvest. He had twenty dollars from his mother for rides and food. Mostly, he'd spent his on corndogs and sweet stuff.

His dad had his eyes on the horde of Billodeaux kids, the ones he got paid to protect, and no easy task either since they tended to scatter in all directions no matter what his commands. But, Xochi noticed. His attackers, probably six-graders from the public school who didn't know him, street kids who came without parents or money to spend, shoved him down into the dirt and damp straw covering a mud puddle. Emptying his pockets of what change remained, they landed a few kicks to his sides and pummeled his soft belly until he barfed up his corndogs and fries, his orange drink, and the deep-fried Twinkie. Then, Xo was upon the bullies like an avenging Aztec goddess, her black curls flying from the scarlet ribbon that bound them, her small fists balled tight and hard. She went right for the head, blackening more than one eye and splitting lips, a fierce fighter whose name incongruously meant blossom. "You leave Junior alone!"

The cowards ran. At first, he thought the sixth-graders were terrified of a girl nearly their age and very sturdy, but a tall shadow belonging to his father blotted out the hot September sun and cast him into shade from his place on his back, wiggling limbs like a helpless turtle. If the bullies didn't know him, they did recognize his dad, the ex-Special Forces warrior who guarded the Billodeaux children. "Get up, Junior. Stop blubbering if you haven't broken anything. I've told you not to get separated from the troop. Stick around Dean and the older kids."

Junior sat up. His snot mingled with the vomit on his cheese yellow T-shirt with the LSU tiger roaring on the front. He wasn't a tiger, never would be. Xochi squatted beside him and wiped his face with a handful of paper napkins and a bottle of water she took from her small red backpack. "Don't worry. Everything will be all right," she said as she scrubbed at her own bloody knuckles, skinned on the enemy's teeth.

Xo didn't see auras as a child. If she had, his would have glowed with adoration. Junior became a tiger, not for his loving mother or his stern father, but for her. If the Sinners didn't draft him now, he might have to live far from Xochi. *Dios mio*, let them choose him!

"Number twenty-nine. The New Orleans Sinners have selected Knox Polk, Junior."

Chapter Two

What to do about Junior? Xochi sat in a lawn chair in the shade of one of the ranch's numerous live oak trees. Her redheaded half-brother, Tom—a kicker for the Sinners—and his lanky, blonde wife, Alix—the team's punter—lounged on a blanket at her feet. Married not quite a year and still clearly honeymooning, Tom spooned behind Alix and fed her tidbits of pineapple and kiwi from a paper plate. Their intimacy made Xo a little uncomfortable, but she did love the way Tom's glowing yellow aura blended with Alix's bright blue to form a lovely shade of turquoise where their heads touched.

Over by the barbecue pavilion, Junior Polk stood in the place of honor next to the Sinners' retired Samoan cornerback, Adam Malala a master of the umu oven. The celebration of Mack and Junior's university graduation pig roast quickly became a three swine affair with both the football teams from LSU and 'Bama attending in addition to Sinners players old and new, their families, and a bevy of friends—an outsized affair as always. Adam, using his hands to make a point to Junior, nodded his head. The sun glinted off a few silver strands in Adam's wild, frizzy mane. They discussed football or maybe cooking while waiting for the pork extravaganza to emerge from the pit. Junior stood by prepared to lift the pigs from the oven, which took some muscle. Not that there wasn't plenty of that around.

On the other hand, Mack had gone off to the swimming pool with his pals who cavorted in the water, showing off for and ogling his sister and womb-mate, Lorena, who made up the second of the Billodeaux triplets and sat in the lifeguard stand. Long limbs toned from playing volleyball, Lori took a tan like no one else in the family. Her black hair flowed halfway down her back when not bound into a braid like today and had less curl to it than most of the family, only lovely waves. Her eyes were what the people in the nearby town of Chapelle called Billodeaux brown, a particularly rich, dark chocolate shade surrounded by thick lashes. She wore a bikini as if she'd created that style, not too brief and not spilling out of it anywhere, a problem that troubled Xochi with her abundantly curvy body. If Xo spent more time gazing into mirrors, which she did not, she'd see the same eyes, similar hair, but a different kind of beauty.

The LSU guys played shirtless volleyball on the sand court near the pool hoping to lure Lorena into a game. Knox Polk, Sr. prowled between the LSU Tigers and the Crimson Tide in the pool making certain no brawls occurred since the Tide had beaten LSU again this year. Lorena stayed on the stand, blowing her whistle occasionally if the horseplay got too rough and telling the college guys to stay in the deep water and let the little kids have the shallow end. She had no intention of taking sides no matter how the overgrown boys tried to attract her. Having grown up with football players, they failed to impress. Not a problem for Xochi as she was five years too old for this batch of young men. If only Junior thought so, too.

He glanced her way. His vast chest heaved. His violet aura flared around his big, round head like a crown. Not deep purple, not lavender, but the color of juicy ripe plums so sweet you could almost taste them, very becoming with his brown skin, lighter than his mother's and darker than his father's almost white complexion. He owned Corazon's round, brown eyes, puppy dog eyes, or maybe only Xochi thought of them that way since Junior had trailed after her like a pitiful stray from the day she'd punched his tormentors in the face.

Now as the leaves were raked from the earth oven, Junior sent his wide, appealing grin with the small space between his two front teeth her way and flexed his muscles playfully. They were nicely revealed by the purple jersey with the sleeves and tails ripped away. It rode up to expose one row of his six-pack abs. Cutoff jeans with frayed edges flattered his thick, muscular legs. He wore heavy sandals like Adam who motioned for him to help raise one end of the pig and place it on a plank. No tats and closely shorn hair showed his father's military influence. A lot to like there Xochi admitted to herself as she answered his smile—but young, way too young.

Junior and Adam hefted the pig, took it into the pavilion, and came back for the next. The third piece of pork went by a different route. Raising the plank to their shoulders, they carried it off toward the swimming pool and volleyball court. Children slid down the rock wall and left the bouncy house to follow. Adults joined the procession. Adam began a Samoan chant soon picked up by the crowd. No one had any idea what it meant and didn't care. Xo couldn't help herself. She tagged along as Junior once followed after her.

The Crimson Tide stopped splashing. The volleyball game ceased as the two brown men trotted the roasted pig once around the pool and back to the pavilion. As Xo passed Mack, he shouted to her, "What was that all about?"

If only his aura weren't the dull orange of ambition. If only Junior's violet crown didn't indicate love. "I think they are announcing that your graduation dinner is about to commence and to get your butt out of the pool and dry off." Sure enough, she heard Joe Billodeaux banging on an old-fashioned iron triangle over by the pavilion.

Lorena blew a shrill whistle. "Pool closed until an hour after dinner. Be sure to wash the sand from your feet in the outdoor shower." She left her perch so fast not a single guy got a chance to grab her around the waist and swing her down. Xo helped Lori herd the small children, buckling sandals, slipping flip-flops onto their feet, and wrapping them in big, white pool house towels before escorting them out, leaving all that gorgeous man flesh to dry off without a female audience.

By the time the sisters arrived at the pavilion, a long row of guests snaked through the grounds like a hungry anaconda. The new grads and their families had been shoved to the front of the line and already sat behind heaping plates. Junior cupped his big hands, making a pretty good megaphone, and shouted, "Let Xo and Lori cut in."

A tall, lithe light-skinned man with striking green eyes behind wire-rimmed glasses made a gap for them right in front of the pavilion door. Xo smiled her appreciation. "So, Connor Bullock is back in town. Have you finished your medical studies?"

Eldest son of the Reverend Revelation Bullock, the famed cornerback, and the one who didn't go into football, nodded. "Almost. I start my residency in orthopedic surgery at Ochsner next week. I hoped you might show me around New Orleans when we both have some free time. Johns Hopkins is a fine place to get medical training, but I missed Louisiana—words I never thought I'd say."

"The people, the food, the total lack of snow, the state does have its charms."

"Its women," Connor added. "I hear you sometimes act as a translator at the hospital. If you are over there, have me paged. We might be able to catch a cup of coffee together."

"As my partner in the interpreting service, Stacy still does most of the medical interpreting, but I take over when she's busy. Mostly, I do the business and police work."

"Must be interesting."

"Not so much. Too many dark auras." Xo moved her eyes away from his penetrating green gaze.

Connor lowered his voice. As a member of the family closest to the Billodeauxs, he knew her secret. "I still think you suffer from a neurological condition that could be cured with drugs or surgery."

"Drugs were tried early on. No thanks on the surgery. The only thing that made sense to me were the words of Rosemarie Leleux, our local faith healer. As a Cajun *traiteur*, she said I had a gift from God and to use it wisely."

Connor twisted one of her black curls around a slim finger. "I admit it would be a shame to shave your hair to get inside your head. Tell me what you see when you look at me."

"A brilliant orange halo—pride, ambition, self-confidence. Not necessarily bad attributes."

"I'm a surgeon so an easy guess."

Letting Lorena go first, they bumped along in the line and reached the stack of plates. Conversation ceased as they made their selections. Steaming roast pork of course, rice dressing, baked beans and French bread, potato salad, even some taro—Cajun barbecues tended to come down heavy on the starches. Xochi made sure half her plate held fresh fruit and green salad. Her curves didn't need to get any curvier. She'd have to dance off today's feast.

Puberty had knocked her down like a Mexican *lucha libre* wrestler. She started early, blossoming out at age eleven, developing a full womanly figure by thirteen, much to the envy of tall, flat-chested Stacy, the Billodeaux's ward and now Dean's wife who had turned out gorgeous in the end. Xo's full breasts wobbled and got in the way of most sports participation. Her rounded hips seemed to sap her speed on the soccer field. She stopped growing at an even five-foot-five, not tiny like some of the Billodeaux girls, but she'd never play volleyball like Lorena or basketball for sure. Then, the auras appeared, and she learned to recognize the hue of lust and sometimes even perversion when men stared at her.

Xochi pulled her mind back to Connor Bullock who had his father's height, but not his bulk, and definitely his physician mother's medical brains. He'd never be a candidate for CTE, chronic traumatic encephalopathy, the scourge of football players, especially ones like Junior who played defense. Junior caught her eye as she exited the pavilion. "Saved a seat for you!"

Indeed, he had by hooking his big sandaled feet around the around the chair opposite him so that no one could pull it out, childish but sweet. Xo headed his way followed by Connor and Lorena.

"Have room for me?" Connor asked politely enough.

Not seeming at all sorry, Junior shook his head. "Your folks are sitting right down there. They can put a chair on the end of the table for you."

Young Dr. Bullock, a very bright man, didn't push the point but made one. "Congratulations on your graduation and playing for the Sinners. I'll be able to put you back together again when you tear that first ACL. Xo, I'll be in touch. Looking forward to having you show me the sights." He ambled off to join his parents.

"Hey, what about me?" Lorena asked her triplet brother.

"Didn't think about it. I'm sure the 'Bama guys will fit you in," Mack said.

The hooting began like two troops of jungle apes trying to dominate each other. "Over here, Lori, right beside me!" "Hey, LSU rules. Sit with us, Lorena." The tables for the two teams had been prudently spaced far apart to prevent conflict. Short, brainy, bespectacled Trinity, the third of the triplets, saved the day. "Plenty of room at the geek table, Lori." She chose to take the space between the non-athletic brother and Teddy

Billodeaux in his wheelchair. Problem solved. More chest beating averted.

When the clamor desisted, Junior leaned across the table toward Xochi. He covered quite a distance. Puberty had done a job on Junior Polk, too, a very good job. From butterball child who played lineman in Pop Warner football because his dad, Joe Billodeaux, and even the Reverend Bullock thought that would toughen the boy, he'd grown up and up topping his father at six-foot-four yet retaining a solid, square body that somehow turned all that fat into two-hundred-thirty pounds of muscle. Yet, Junior still possessed those brown puppy dog eyes of his early years with not a hint of meanness in them.

"Adam says a boy becomes a man when he can build an umu oven and roast a pig for his family the way I did today. Mack didn't help at all."

"Yes, that trot around the grounds carrying a whole roasted pig was pretty impressive."

"You think so?" He gave her that hopeful, charming gap-toothed grin again.

She knew what answer he craved. "Absolutely."

Maybe she gave Junior too much encouragement because the next thing he said was, "I was thinking I might stay at your place until I can get my own space in the city." No lust in his aura, only love.

"Wouldn't you rather room with Tom and Alix? They have a much bigger place right on the edge of the Quarter."

"You're kidding me. Look at them. Tom says they still do it everywhere, both bedrooms, the sofa, the kitchen, the dining room table."

Xochi did look. The couple still lay on their

15

blanket far from others, plates of food in front of them, but feeding each other like mating cranes, so in love. She allowed herself an inward sigh of envy. "I guess I see what you mean. How about my dad's condo? He doesn't come into the city that often, and you'd have plenty of space with all those bedrooms."

"I only need one bedroom, Xo, and yours, I mean your guestroom, is closer to the action."

"Like you couldn't afford a cab with that signing bonus."

"Hey, I can walk to Mariah's Place and all over the Quarter from your location. You can show me your favorite spots."

"You were in New Orleans all the time when you played for LSU and hardly need a guide. Besides, my guestroom is pretty frou-frou. Stacy decorated it. Why don't you stay in the Garden District with her and Dean? Plenty of room there, and I bet they'd have a king-sized bed for you rather than a queen."

Junior's big brown eyes rolled sideways in the direction of Dean and Stacy. "She's not drinking anything alcoholic. You know what that means."

Xochi knew—because Stacy had told her, pregnant again not so very long after she'd given birth to her daughter. Stace simply wanted her childbearing over and done since she suffered terribly from morning-noon-and-night sickness as she called it.

"I mean I wouldn't want to be underfoot while Stacey isn't feeling well," Junior continued, all sincere consideration.

"Okay, okay. Stay with me, but put your mind to finding your own place."

Her concession lit his face even more than the *Tres*

Leches cake his mama carried toward him blazing with candles that spelled out his graduation year. Mama Nell followed with chocolate iced in chocolate for Mack. As the cakes were placed, the fathers pulled up in front of the table in matching Escalades, black with the Sinners' winking red devil mascot on the rear for Junior and white with the Cowboys' giant star logo in blue for Mack.

Junior's broad brow wrinkled with worry. "Mama, I hope you didn't sell one of the Super Bowl rings for this. You know I got a nice signing bonus and could buy my own."

"We did sell a ring! Back to Mr. Joe where it belongs. Me and your *Papi* want to do this for you."

Xochi noted Junior didn't ruin the surprise by protesting too much. Instead, he reached his big arm around his plump, gray-haired mother and gave her a squeeze. "You are the best. Now I can give Xo a ride back to New Orleans in style. I'm going to stay with her until I get a place of my own."

Corazon's round, brown face, mostly free of wrinkles despite her age, did crease now. "You don't make extra work for Miss Xochi, Junior."

When had she become Miss Xochi and not simply Xo, the little girl who yearned for someone to understand her Spanish? This kind-hearted woman had been glad to fill the role of Mexican *abuela,* a grandmother, in her life with Mama Nell's complete approval. Both had wanted her to feel as accepted and loved and protected as possible after the murders of her parents.

"I won't. You and *Papi* trained me well. I don't make a mess—and I can cook."

"You are a good son." Corazon ran a hand over his close cut hair as if he still had a little boy's curls to ruffle.

Xochi heard Mack grouse, "I wanted a sports car."

Mama Nell, never a pushover despite her small size, slapped down the cake extinguishing a few candles in the breeze, and answered, "Then buy one with your bonus." She leaned close to her third son's ear, but both Xochi and Junior heard the message she delivered. "You will not ruin today for your father. He is so proud of you."

Mack stared down at the cake with its guttering blue candles. "Yeah, sure." At least, he had the grace to be a little ashamed.

His orange aura, duller than Connor's, flared a little under his mother's censure. Good. Xo knew he'd felt the need his whole life to do as well as Dean on the football field, but had chosen to be a receiver, never in direct competition with his eldest brother. No one had pushed him one way or another. He'd chosen his path and how to walk it. She hoped no pitfalls waited for him. Not her problem.

What was she going to do about Junior who blew out his candles with one mighty gust of air and sliced as big a piece for her as he did for his mother? How could she allow him to live with her?

Chapter Three

Xochi woke in her apartment to the aroma of freshly made coffee and a spicy scent she couldn't quite place. No doubt Junior was up and about. She heard the clatter of pans and the thud of his big feet in the kitchen below. Knowing better than to appear before him in her flimsy hot pink nightgown, she forced herself out of bed and into the bathroom to dress in her Anchi Services purple uniform dress and put on her formal face. As always, she avoided viewing her own aura as much as possible by using a small makeup mirror that sat on the counter surrounded by her tubes of eyeliner, mascara, and lipstick in the brighter colors she favored.

Today, she couldn't help but notice a man's shaving kit neatly zippered and stowed in one corner. Not a facial hair remained in the recently scrubbed sink. A damp bath towel hung on the rack, folded to dry. None of her brothers were this neat despite Mama Nell's constant exhortations for them not to make extra work for Corazon and the maids. Junior Polk had to be the tidiest man alive. Maybe he was gay. No, she knew better and would have to deal with his affection for her. Might as well start now.

Xochi took the stairs down to the living room, kitchen, office floor of the apartment, and breezed into the small dining area to find it completely set for breakfast, a meal she rarely ate. She intended to thank him for making coffee, grab a cup, and be off to work at the World Trade Center. The less contact they had, the better.

Junior turned away from the stove and greeted her with that warm smile of his. He wore pressed khakis, a pale yellow short-sleeved shirt, tucked in and belted. As she drew closer, she caught a whiff of the lime-scented aftershave he'd patted on his round cheeks. "Great, now I can start the eggs. *Huevos rancheros* coming right up. I had to use the salsa from the jar in the refrigerator. It's not too fresh, but I'll make something better later. The tortillas are already warmed. How many eggs do you want?"

"Um, I usually just pop across the street and get a latte and a croissant at the coffee shop on my way to work."

"This is a better breakfast: protein, vegetables, and carbs." Junior cracked eggs into a skillet pooled with butter, one, two, three, four.

"Ah, just one egg for me, I guess."

"Hard or soft yolks?"

"Soft."

"Me, too. I can steam some milk for your coffee if you want, but we need to get a better machine."

"That's the office coffeemaker. I rarely use it anymore since most of our clients prefer to meet at their place of work. I guess we could get one of those pod machines like Tom has. Don't bother about the steamed milk."

"I like to grind my own beans. I'll get a good one today. Here we go." Junior slid a perfectly fried egg onto the warm tortilla and topped it with salsa. He placed it before her on one of Stacy's old grape-patterned plates. "Sit, enjoy."

She did. Xochi broke the yolk and mingled it with the salsa. She took a bite and closed her eyes. "Just like your mother used to make for us."

"Where do you think I learned? Here's your coffee." Junior took a seat next to her. His plate brimmed with the remaining three eggs, a triad of tortillas, and a heap of salsa and beans. He dug in, but blotted his lips on a paper napkin before saying, "I thought we might go out for dinner tonight. I know some great out of the way places. You aren't too well stocked for cooking."

"Oh, I promised Connor Bullock I'd go out with him. It's his first night in town."

"When did this happen?" A storm cloud covered Junior's usually sunny face.

"While you were putting your baggage in the Escalade yesterday. We talked for a while. He's not as familiar with New Orleans as we are."

"Sure, okay. He can come along."

"I think he meant it to be a date."

"Yeah, I guess so. I'm going to the training center today to work out. I'll pick up some groceries after, and hang out at Mariah's Place tonight. Maybe I'll see you there."

"Maybe." Xo bolted her last bite of egg and dribbled salsa down the front of her uniform. The red sauce followed the slope of one full breast. Junior eyed its path and reached out with the napkin. Xochi stood up in a hurry. "See, this is what comes of eating a good breakfast. Now I have to change and rush to work. Later!" She dashed from the kitchen as if the devil, or simply a Sinner, was on her tail.

****

Junior cupped his wide jaw in his hands. Damn! Connor Bullock, brilliant and age-appropriate, had come back to Louisiana. The only team Connor ever played on was the debate team. President of the Beta Club, inductee to the National Honor Society in his junior year, and now a doctor, he represented everything Junior was not.

Junior got up and cleared the table, washed the pans and dishes in the sink, dried them, and put everything back where it belonged. If his career military father had taught him one thing it was to clean up your own mess, leave everything shipshape, and have some consideration for the woman who tired herself out cooking and caring for the twelve Billodeaux children as well as her only child.

His warmest childhood memories were of sitting in the kitchen at the ranch and chattering away in Spanish with his mama and Xochi so rapidly that Tom, Xo's half-brother, who made a good attempt to learn the language, couldn't keep up. Not to say his mother favored these three over the other kids—but she did, just a little. Xochi needed her special care after her trauma, and Junior was her only child. His mother often gave them special treats—miniature sugar candy skulls, *pastelitos*, a kind of Mexican Twinkie, and delicious coconut rolls—that she bought in the bodegas springing up in Chapelle opened by men who had come into the area to do hurricane repairs and stayed to found small businesses.

"You don't tell your mama," Corazon said to Tommy and Xochi. "She say is bad for your teeth. One will not hurt you."

But, Junior often had two or three. Hence his early start in football. The Billodeaux boys weren't allowed to play before age twelve because of Mama Nell's objections. Only soccer for them, not that Daddy Joe didn't toss footballs around to his sons as soon as they could toddle. When his own father enrolled him in Pop Warner, they'd placed Junior a year ahead of his age because of his bulk. He learned quickly how to hold the line—simply push the skinnier kid opposite him over and then do the same to anyone else who tried to pass into his team's territory. Didn't take a lot of brains. He did well and inwardly exalted that he would never be bullied again.

Xo noticed. She came to his games, as did all the Billodeauxs when they had no conflict with soccer. She rewarded him with praise and hugs that that rapidly grew softer as her body matured. Too bad he remained a blob until she left for college when he turned thirteen and finally began to shoot up and harden, worked on his speed, and became a cornerback. By the time he played college ball, Xo had been to Europe to hone her language skills, picking up Portuguese, graduated, and started a business with Stacy. Still, she cheered him on whenever she could, though the Billodeauxs frequently traveled to Tuscaloosa to root for Mack. Why the heck couldn't Mack play for LSU like the rest of his family? Because he wanted to do his own thing, of course.

Now when he finally wheedled himself into Xo's apartment so she could get to know him as a man, along came Connor Bullock! He took his frustration to the training facility, worked on his legs and his abs preparing for the first mini-camp, picked up a coffeemaker to his specifications, and shopped for groceries to prepare his signature dishes for the woman he adored. Meanwhile, Xo had been home, stripped out of her business uniform, leaving it tossed across her bed, and applied makeup for a date night—if the state she left her cosmetics in the bathroom gave a clue. Junior guessed he'd go to Mariah's Place, eat bar food, and hope she'd show up there, even with Connor Bullock.

Chapter Four

Junior nursed his second beer in a dark corner at Mariah's Place and picked at a platter of chicken wings and loaded potato skins. Lots of fiber in the potatoes, protein in the cheese and bacon stuffing them, and the wings came with celery if you could call that a vegetable. It wasn't that he'd never been to Mariah's, the hot spot the tourist guides proclaimed the best for sighting Sinners players. Once he'd come here with a bunch of underage LSU players and been chided by the outrageous Mariah herself in her gold sequin gown and huge white wig for trying to order drinks. She'd had to take a few huffs from her oxygen tank to finish the scolding before the bouncer escorted them out into a night more brilliantly lit by neon than the inside of the always dim nightclub. Of course, they'd managed to get drunk elsewhere in the Quarter, Junior less so than most because Mariah recognized him from her visits to Lorena Ranch and ended her rant with, "I know you, Junior Polk. Don't make me call your daddy."

Now that he was legal, she'd welcomed him with a huge hug to her overinflated breasts and the hindsight prediction, "I always knew you'd be a Sinner. Remember, I look out for my boys."

This being the off-season, the club had more tourists occupying the small four tops than football players at the bar. In fact, he was the only one. A middle-aged man approached him hesitantly. "You play for the Sinners?"

"I will be playing for them this fall."

"Okay. Would you sign this napkin?"

"Sure." A little flattered, Junior scribbled out his name.

"Junior Polk. Never heard of you."

"I play in the secondary defense, cornerback. No one knows who we are."

"Yeah, that's right. But I'll look for you next time the Sinners play." He ended the conversation with a slap to Junior's broad back and a return to his table where a wife, son, and teenage daughter pondered the mysterious unknown name. Obviously from out of state since an LSU fan would have been happy to meet him.

The door to the club opened. Junior looked up from a chicken wing. Not Xochi and Connor, but a pallid pair of celebrities, Tom and Alix Billodeaux, the NFL's first married football players. Tom's red hair and Alix's Nordic blonde looks brightened the mostly black and red room.

The teenage girl rushed toward them with a real autograph book and a tiny pen. She gushed, "I think it is so romantic that you two got married." Both signed and made a little chitchat before joining Junior at the bar.

Tom appropriated a potato skin. The guy could eat anything and still remain slim. Good thing because Alix was quite the cook in a Scandinavian sort of way, lots of heavy food and always a Bundt cake on the counter. "Hey, these skins are cold. Pop them into the microwave for a minute would you, Jackson? And draw two drafts for us," he said to the fat, bald bartender, a fixture at the nightclub since it opened. "You off your feed, Junior?"

"Sure he is." Alix nudged her husband. "He's brooding over Xo because she went out with Connor Bullock tonight."

"Who told you?"

"Girls talk." Alix shrugged shoulders a bit too big for a woman but by no means unfeminine.

Junior noted that the right-footed kicker and the left-footed punter had twined their legs together and sat touching hips. A little burst of envy surged through him. He drowned it out with a slug of beer and another wing. "I thought if I moved in with her it might work out like it did for you two, but she still looks at me like I'm a kid brother."

"Hey, bro, no secret you've always had a crush on Xochi. She knows it, the whole family knows it." Tom thanked Jackson for the piping hot skins. He offered the plate to Alix before setting it in front of Junior again. "Maybe if you dated around some instead of mooning over her, she'd see you as a desirable man."

"Hey, Stacy tried to make Dean jealous, and it did not work out too well," Alix pointed out.

"Maybe it's my looks. I got this round baby face."

"No, I think you are adorable with that little gap in your teeth and big grin," Alix said.

"I don't want to be adorable! I need to be smokin' hot!"

Alix reconsidered. "You got the bod for that."

"Just a second." Tom reached for his phone and called Brian Lightfoot, his former punter and honorary gay uncle. "Busy?" he asked.

"Waiting for Derek to get off work. What can I do

for you?"

"Not for me. Junior needs help with his round baby face." Tom flashed a picture with his phone and sent it. Up front at her private table, Mariah grumbled, "Fricking, blinding nuisances."

"Needs definition. I'd suggest a light mustache and a beard shaved close just around the edge of his face. You could get that going in a week," Brian advised. "Stand up and turn around, Junior. Nicely dressed, impressive body. I'm not needed there and what a pity. You appear to have naturally good taste, unlike some others I could mention." Brian seemed to intuit that Tom wore a wrinkled green plaid cotton shirt.

Alix pecked her husband's cheek. "You don't have to change for me."

"Thanks, Brian. You give me hope." Junior ate a potato skin with a little more gusto. Involved with the conversation, he failed to notice when Xochi and her date made an entrance, a very quiet, low key one. In fact, he jolted when Xo took the seat next to him. Even separated by inches, he felt her warmth envelop him.

"That all you need?" Brian asked.

"Yes, have a good evening." Junior reached over and shut off Tom's phone. "You two hungry? There's plenty. Help yourself."

"Who were you talking to?" Xo picked up a chicken wing and nibbled it so delicately Junior imaged what else she could do with those plump lips.

"Brian Lightfoot. We thought he might like to join us, but he's waiting for Derek. Do you think they will last, Xo?" Tom covered the conversation as smoothly as he kicked field goals.

"They're happy for now."

"What about us" Alix had to ask.

"You and Tom are forever. You know that."

Connor took a celery stick to be sociable, but waved away the cholesterol laden potato skins. "Actually, we just had a great meal at Ralph's. Xo said we could listen to some good music here. Seems we arrived right on time."

Mariah Coy heaved herself from the table nearest the stage and managed the steps in heels far too high and hazardous for a woman her age. Dry ice swirled around her ankles and brilliant red gown. She went into her signature rendition of *Fever* and managed to finish it before running out of lungpower. "COPD, right?" Connor remarked as if the fabulous Mariah were his patient and not an esteemed French quarter fixture that people travelled miles to see.

Mariah bowed, giving a great view of her cleavage, and slipped back stage for a moment to fill her lungs with oxygen. She returned to introduce the band and singer for the night, a recent and very talented castoff from *The Voice*. She began with a Beyoncé song. Tom and Alix got up to dance and began strutting, gyrating, and flapping around the vacant dance floor. The teenage girl jumped out of her bentwood chair nearly upsetting it and began to record the entire show with her phone. "Look, Mom. They're doing their whooping crane dance!"

"Come on, Connor, we'd better help them out." Xo stood and waited for her date so scrupulously attired in suit and tie to join her.

"Mind waiting for a slow one?"

"I got this." Junior rose and led Xochi out to the center of the floor being circumnavigated by Tom and his wife. He started into his moves, ones he'd been practicing for years. Xo soon caught on and matched him. "Smooth, Junior, very smooth."

The girl's camera turned their way. "I don't know who they are but they're really, really good."

Junior gave her a great grin. He wondered if she'd send him the recording if he cleared it with her parents. All too soon the song ended and the next, a slow one, began. Connor wasted no time getting out there to claim his dance. Junior retreated to his stool and devoured another potato skin while he watched the doctor guide Xo rather stiffly around the room. Her wildly patterned floral dress pressed up against his somber suit as if he held large bouquet. Blossom, yes, tonight she was a blossom, an exotic flower too rare to be appreciated by Connor Bullock, Junior thought. That man would subdue her natural exuberance and disregard her special gift, if he had his way.

When the pairs returned to the bar, Junior suggested, "Why don't we go to Paco's next Saturday." Let's see the stuffed shirt compete with him in salsa dancing, Xochi's favorite form of entertainment.

"Oh, I want to go to Paco's. We can really let loose there," Alix exclaimed as if she and Tom hadn't done that already just minutes ago. She called for another cold draft.

"Um, haven't been there in a long time. I guess it's okay to go back," Tom said with a lot less exuberance.

"Are you free, Connor?" Xochi sipped from the glass of red wine Junior had ordered for her. "Oh, this is good!"

"A nice California pinot noir," Junior said. Xo raised her brows at his wine expertise.

"Let me see." Connor consulted his iPad. "The new residents always get the worst rotations. Could we make it Friday?"

"Certainly. I'll invite some of my friends to go along. The more the merrier, right Junior?" Xo claimed.

"Sure." He'd burn up the floor with Xochi while the doc warmed a chair at their table. Maybe Connor would take an interest in one of the other girls.

"Speaking of having to work weekends, I need to get going. Xo, are you coming with me, or do you want to stay here?"

"No, I've had a long day. See you guys later."

Junior lingered a little while after the couple left and danced once with the teenager who had the courage to ask him. He had no desire to walk in on an evening kiss or anything more between Xochi and Connor. Once back at the apartment, he found Xo wearing purple yoga pants, a sweatshirt with an LSU logo, and ballet-style slippers as she flipped through the TV channels. Not exactly dressed for seduction, neither his or Connor's, and that was fifty-percent good.

"Say, you want to turn on the Spanish channel and take in some telenovelas? You know how my mama loves them, and we used to make fun of them behind her back?" He sat beside her on the couch giving her lots of room or at least as much as his large body allowed.

"Why not?"

They settled in to watch television as comfortable as an old married couple. Just what Junior had in mind for the distant future.

Chapter Five

Xo woke to an aroma even better than coffee—bacon sizzling in a pan. A quick splash on her face, a comb through her tangled waves, a jump into Saturday lounging clothes, and she went downstairs to see what Junior had conjured in her kitchen now. As she drew near, the coffee burbled from a machine of such complexity, she doubted if she'd ever learn to use it.

"*Hola*," Junior greeted. "We have stuffed French toast this morning with a side of bacon and freshly brewed coffee. You can start with that papaya half while I finish the toast. Squeeze a little lime on it first." He turned back to a large skillet and flipped over portions as thick as doorstopper sandwiches.

"Stuffed with what?" she inquired as she squeezed a wedge of lime on the fruit and began spooning it from the rind.

"Strawberry cream cheese."

"Exactly what my hips need, that and bacon."

"It's fried crisp." Junior offered her a piece from the pile draining on a paper towel.

He held it in his fingers, and she accepted it with hers, though Xo knew he'd meant to feed it to her. "Coffee is ready. See, the top part of the machine grinds the beans and funnels them into the filter. I press a button, and the hot water runs through. This little side piece warms milk for a latte." He lifted the small stainless steel pitcher and dressed her mug of dark coffee with white. Waiting a moment for the two liquids to mingle to a light brown, he raised the pitcher, poured a circle of milk, and deftly cut through its middle with the stream from the spout. A delicate heart formed on the surface. Junior presented it to her almost as an offering.

"That's lovely. How did you learn to do it?" As often as she'd gotten coffee at the café across the street, they'd never gone to so much trouble.

"My experiences in the last five years have been many and varied." He gave her that full grin, but it only lasted a second before he jumped back to the stove. "Almost burned the French toast." Plating the food—one for her, two for him—Junior used a flour sifter to sprinkle the top with powdered sugar, which he garnished with a fresh strawberry and several strips of bacon. He placed the food so lovingly made before her.

Xochi took a bite of the toast and closed her eyes to savor it. "Delicious."

"I hoped you'd appreciate it."

"Oh, I appreciate good food a little too much, but neither Stacy nor I cooked very often. I didn't even know I had one of those things." Xo gestured to the flour sifter.

"I found a whole bunch of kitchen utensils in a drawer. I suspect my mama brought them when you moved in here."

"Well, we only used the corkscrew and maybe the spatula. Mostly, we ate out and had leftovers for lunch."

"Not good for you."

"Like all this bacon and cream cheese is, but at least I got my fruit for the day." She sucked the strawberry from its stem. "I'm walking over to see how Stacy is doing today. Dean said something about grilling this afternoon."

"It's a long walk to the Garden District. I could get the Escalade out of the parking garage and drive you over there. I had to rent a space since the Koreans downstairs complained that it blocked deliveries to their electronics store."

"Probably did, and I like to keep peace with the neighbors so thanks for moving it. No, I need to walk off this breakfast. I call first dibs on the shower." She pushed away from the table even though the extra bacon called to her. Junior wouldn't let it go to waste.

"You think I could tag along to Dean's place?"

The beseeching puppy dog eyes of his childhood reappeared in the grown man's face, and she couldn't turn him down. "Sure, but you should be looking for condos today."

"Realtors probably don't work on weekends."

"That's when they mostly work since people have time to look then. No off-season for us ordinary folks! Be ready by nine. I want to get there before it really heats up." From the glance Junior shot her, she feared it already had.

****

Junior had to shorten his stride to stay by Xochi's side even though she walked briskly. With his looming escort, no men whistled or called out, "*Chica, chica, chica*" as she strode along. She didn't see any of the dark men either and was grateful for that. With auras flashing by in the crowded city, sometimes she caught a glimpse of those whose souls were so dead they projected a black hole rather than a halo of color. Race had nothing to do with it. The dark men could be white, black, Hispanic, any ethnicity at all. She'd cross a street to move away from the sickening sensation they gave her. But, not today.

Bathed in Junior's deep violet glow, she felt safe as they swung through Downtown where businesses flourished in tall buildings and entered the Garden District lined with stately historic homes sitting behind wrought iron fences. Xo opened the gate to a cheerful yellow mansion, its long windows framed by dark green shutters, the only white on its slim gallery columns and the dentil molding under the eaves. The small front yard possessed two large crepe myrtles not yet in bloom and a welter of ferns grown lush in the hot and humid climate interspersed with the fragrant white blossoms of Peruvian daffodils, the large leaves and incipient spikes of bird-of-paradise blooms, and the deep blue of lilies of the Nile in glazed pots by the steps leading to the entry. From the front, the house looked deceptively small, but two wings swept along its sides enclosing a large courtyard that exited onto the next street. Actually, Stacy and Dean could easily house Junior and a good part of the Sinners team. Maybe he'd decide to stay there after seeing the king-sized beds in the guestrooms. No more need to scrunch up his long legs under Stacy's old duvet.

Xo rang the bell, and Stacy answered. She had a housekeeper who took weekends off and a part-time nanny, but Stace valued family days more than servants, a complete turnaround in attitude from her first days among the Billodeauxs whom she'd treated as her bumpkin cousins. Today, her greeting smile was warm but wan. Makeup didn't quite hide the dark circles under her eyes. Her usual porcelain complexion seemed chalky and her long blonde hair lank.

"Still feeling rotten, Stace?" Xochi commiserated.

"Will until the first trimester is over. I can't imagine why I thought I'd rather have a second child right away rather than waiting, say, another ten years when I forgot this misery. But, I'm hanging in there. I don't want to be hospitalized again, not with Wynn needing me. Dean is in the den already watching baseball. Come in."

"I hope you don't mind that I brought Junior along."

"Not at all. He hasn't seen the house. I'll give him the grand tour."

Junior stepped forward. "No need if you don't feel well. I'll just camp out with Dean and help with the barbecue if I can." As the son of servants, Stacy initially treated him worse than the Billodeaux children, which really showed the depth of her initial snobbery, but she'd come around under Mama Nell's firm hand. Junior graciously bore her no ill will, Xochi noted.

"Actually, that's a relief. Everyone wants to see how we've redecorated, and I'm just not up to it." Stacy led the way down a long central hall with a formal parlor and dining room, all dark wood and crystal chandeliers, sprouting off its sides. She opened a door that gave access to one of the ells, stepped through it and a couple of steps down into a thoroughly modern man cave with a huge wall-mounted television over a gas fireplace, the mantel displaying Dean's Heisman trophy and Super Bowl memorabilia. Enough comfortable black leather furniture filled the area that a whole herd of cattle must have been sacrificed to provide it. Of course, the walls were Sinners' red.

A large bar occupied one corner. Dean Billodeaux, star quarterback of the Sinners, occupied a sofa where he gave his blonde daughter a horsey ride on his famous knees, though his eyes stayed on the TV screen and the opening of an east coast ballgame. Next to him on the floor, his illegitimate son played with Duplo blocks.

"I can't believe Ilsa dumped Beck on you when you aren't feeling well," Xochi murmured so the boy wouldn't hear.

"The custody agreement gives Dean visitation rights every weekend when he isn't playing football. Ilsa takes full advantage of that. I'm just glad she didn't drop off her daughter, too, not that I don't pity the child having her and Prince Dobbs for parents. Besides, only the family knows I'm pregnant. We're keeping it quiet this time. Isla is so competitive she'd have another baby simply to upstage me again."

"I can believe that. You think she and Prince will ever get married?"

"I have my doubts. He said he'd do the deed when his Temple of the Dreadlocked Jesus was finished, but he keeps making changes to the plans. It might never be completed."

"Delay tactics. He's gotten to know Ilsa a lot better."

Stacy raised her voice over the noise of the TV, her daughter's giggles, and Beck's tremendous crash of plastic blocks as he knocked over a tower of them. "Hey, my big lout, we have company."

"Oh, hi, Xo. Good to see you, Junior. Just help yourself to anything from the fridge behind the bar or mix your own drink."

"I think I'll wait until we eat for alcohol."

"Restraint, I like to see that in a rookie. But, we do have soft drinks, orange juice, and chocolate milk in there, too."

"Don't mind if I do. That was a long, hot walk over here."

"Why didn't you take a taxi or the streetcar?"

Junior heaved his big shoulders. "Xo wanted to go on foot."

"I needed to burn off that cream cheese stuffed French toast and bacon breakfast, I told you." She looked at Stacy for support, but Stacy's face had taken on a green cast.

"Excuse me." She rushed from the room.

"Really, you can't even mention food in front of her." Dean shook his head.

"Sorry," Junior said, though he'd just cooked the meal, not bragged about it. He moved to the bar and poured a beer glass full of chocolate milk, chugged it down. "Want something, Xo?"

"A bottle of water would be fine." He delivered it to her, and she pulled out a tissue from a box on the big, blocky coffee table and wiped away the milk mustache on his upper lip. Junior hadn't shaved today and the roughness of his skin reminded her again of how he'd grown. "I used to do that for you when you were Beck's size," she said, reminding both of them of their age difference again.

Dean recited, "This is the way the farmer rides…gallopy, gallopy, gallopy…into the ditch!" as he dangled his daughter between his knees. "Great workout for the legs."

"Again!" shouted Wynn.

Beck stood amid the colorful clutter of plastic bricks. "My turn, Daddy!"

"Hey, I got knees. Who wants to ride the big, brown pony?" Junior took a seat next to Dean and held out his arms. Wynn, fearless and used to seeing him at the ranch, clambered over, and Beck claimed his father's attention.

"You guys seem to have the situation under control. I'm going to check on Stacy."

Xochi heard their hostess retching in a hallway powder room. She knocked. "You okay? Can I help?"

"I'll be fine in a minute." After a flush and a running of water in the sink, Stacy appeared with a wet washcloth held against her throat. "Nurse Shammy said this might help. It does a little. Let's sit outside in the shade for a while and talk. The men can cope with those two little vortexes of energy for now."

They exited through French doors at the end of the hall and onto a verandah overlooking the courtyard. Water burbled into a fountain from the mouths of gargoyles clustered around its edge and mockingbirds squabbled among the pink-blossomed banana trees. Stacy flipped a switch and set the ceiling fans above the porch whirling. She sank onto a chaise longue with dark green cushions and wiped her forehead.

Xo took a wicker chair by her side. "I'd say that reminded me of the aftermath of frat parties, but we never went to any. You always preferred older men because college guys were too immature."

"That's what I said. I had my heart set on Dean. He is three years older than me though."

"And Junior is five years younger than both of us. He's trying to pull off the same ploy that Tom did with

Alix by living with me. When you feel better, could you please show him your guestrooms and offer to put him up?" Xo raised the dark waves of her hair and let the cool breeze from the fans dry the sweat on her neck formed by the trek to the Garden District.

"Is he lots of trouble?"

"Oh, no! Far tidier than I am, and he can really cook."

"I take it that's not a double entendre?"

"Absolutely not! I won't mention what he's been making me for breakfast, but it is all scrumptious."

"So is Junior if you don't mind my pointing that out. Want to borrow my washcloth?" Stacy tossed it her way and watched Xo mop a little dew from the deep cleavage she always had no matter what she wore.

"I need to discourage him. He's right out of college and needs to look around, have some fun, before settling down. Me, I'm getting older by the minute."

"Well, I wouldn't hold up my hair or mop my breasts while he's around for a starter. Every move you make is sexy. You can't help it."

"Did he see?" Xochi flipped the cloth back to Stacy.

Stacy stared at the French doors to the den down on the lower level. "I don't think so. He's chasing Wynn and Beck around the sofa right now."

"See, he's just a big kid."

"Who's had a crush on you forever, same I had with Dean only I covered it up by being mean. Junior wears his heart on his sleeve. Why don't you give him a chance?"

"Well, ah, I'm seeing someone who might be better for me."

Stacy widened her blue eyes. "When did this happen? Why didn't you call me right away? An announcement like that would have taken my mind off my misery."

"It's Connor Bullock. We've only had one date for dinner, really a thanks for showing him around the city—but he paid for the meal. Afterward, we went to Mariah's and danced a little. Friday, we're going to Paco's. You and Dean want to come along? The more people between me and Junior the better."

"One deep back bend, and I'd puke on the dance floor. Dean is free to go he wants."

"You know he won't leave you alone in this condition."

The French doors to the den opened. The blond children tumbled out and raced around the fountain with Junior in pursuit making scary monster arms and growling deep in his chest.

"Stop! Stop! If they slip on the wet tiles someone is going to split a head open," Stacy pleaded just as any mother would.

"Sorry." Junior took one big stride and scooped both kids under his arms. He pretended to nibble on their tender necks as he carried them to the steps and deposited them giggling at Stacy's feet.

Wynn suggested, "Cookie time?"

Beck, older and wiser, held up his fingers. "Two cookies."

"One." Stacy started to rise, but plunked back down. "Brief dizzy spell. Give me a minute."

"Tell me where the kitchen is, and I'll get the cookies. Besides, I want to put butter out to soften. Mixed with some herbs and parm, it makes a great

41

steak topper, I was telling Dean."

"Stay put. I'll show him the kitchen—and the rest of the house." Xochi stood and led the way into the other wing through a large pantry off the dining room, down a couple of steps and into a large kitchen. "The folks who lived here before must have loved to entertain."

"I'll say." Junior rubbed his hand lovingly over the satiny stainless steel of a huge Sub-Zero refrigerator. He stared at the six-burner gas range with its indoor grill and the long prep table overhung with utensils and cooper-bottomed pans. "I think this is my dream kitchen, only I'd want an area for family meals."

"There's a breakfast room on the other side with a staircase down from the bedrooms. Want to see?"

"In a minute." He searched and found a block of butter, checked out an extensive rack of herbs, and bemoaned the lack of real *parmigiano reggiano* to grate. "I guess I'll have to use the stuff in the can. Next time I come over, I'll bring them a wedge of the real thing. Central Grocery probably has a good selection."

"You've been watching too much Rachael Ray."

"Probably, and Iron Chef and Chopped. Don't you know I majored in Food Science with a concentration in Food Business and Marketing at LSU? I'd like to open a restaurant when I'm through with football. See, I think of the future all the time, not just the now."

"That's admirable. Want to see the bedrooms?"

"You bet I do." Junior nodded his approval at the airy breakfast room with all the windows facing the courtyard and a friendly family sized table in light oak surrounded by six chairs and two highchairs as they passed through and took a staircase to the second story.

Four bedrooms and two baths filled the ell above the kitchen and rounded the corner with the last two having access to the front galley. All were austerely decorated, some with antique beds and armoires that opened to give access to a television as well as drawers for storage. The more modern rooms held the king-sized beds Xochi made a point of mentioning.

"Yeah, big enough for two," Junior said as if he were thinking of the future again.

"You'd be so much more comfortable here."

"Naw, don't want to trouble Stacy in her condition. Your place is fine for now. Someday, though, I'd like to have a house like this, only not in the city, back in Chapelle near my parents. They had me late and aren't getting any younger. I need to look out for them."

"That's sweet, but don't ever say that to your mom and dad. I've never met more hard-working, vigorous people."

They peeked into a space overlooking the front garden, obviously Stacy's office and library judging from the computer centered on a spindly gold and white desk, books in a multiple of languages on the higher shelves and kiddie books on the lowest. Peering over a balcony with spindles set close enough together to discourage small children from slipping through, they got the upstairs view of the hall with its oriental runner and marble-topped side tables holding vases of lavish silk flowers.

"Stacy says she got the vases at Pier One. If the children break one, who cares?"

"Wise woman—like you, mature."

"Did you just call me old, Junior?" Why did this sting when Xo kept pushing their age difference in his face? True, she'd passed twenty-five and headed toward thirty, but she wasn't that ancient.

"In culinary terms, mature is the peak of ripeness." His muscular arm went around her, and he gave her forearm a light pinch. "Yes, perfect."

Xochi slipped from his embrace and continued the tour through the second wing where three small child-sized bedrooms and one large suite consumed the space. No doubt the frilly pink one belonged to Wynn. They entered the marital space, scoped out the bathroom with its whirlpool bath and many-nozzled shower, all framed in mottled black marble and hung with gold fixtures.

Junior emitted a low whistle. "I knew Dean wouldn't let me down. This is paradise. I'm surprised they don't have a chandelier in here, too."

"Stacy said no to that. She has better taste than Dean or Daddy Joe."

"But just imagine what a couple could do in here!" Junior caged her in by placing his arms on either side of Xo's body and pressing them against the shower stall. She ducked low and made her escape.

"I'm sure Dean would let you use the Jacuzzi if you stayed here."

"I'm fine where I am right now."

Junior Polk, irrepressible! Another staircase at the end of the wing brought them down to the expansive den where Dean flicked off the television. "Braves are up by seven hits already. Want to see my newly installed outdoor kitchen?"

"Absolutely." Junior followed Dean outside while Xochi rejoined Stacy on the porch.

"Cookie?" Wynn asked, rather crossly.

"Two cookies," Beck reminded her.

"I forgot. I'll get them right away!" Xochi hastened to the kitchen, raided an old-fashioned cookie jar shaped like chubby pig, a good reminder for her not to sample. Suspecting Stacy had Mama Nell's recipe for healthy treats, she returned with four oatmeal raisins in hand for the children.

"So Junior was that distracting, huh?" Stacy teased.

"I had a couple of narrow escapes upstairs. He said I was ripe, and he still isn't moving out."

"Ripe, huh?" Stacy eyed closest friend. "Yes, you are. Ready for the picking. Consider that Stevie Riley is older than her husband, and they get along great."

"Stevie was around thirty when they married, and I think there was only a two or three-year difference there. Both of them were grownups, not right out of college."

Someone buzzed at the rear gate. "It's me, Mrs. Billodeaux, bringing the dog back from his walk."

Stacy stretched out a thin arm and hit the remote on a bamboo table by her side. The gate creaked open and a white puff of an animal raced inside, squeezed in among the gargoyles and lapped from the fountain. Thirst satiated, he bounded up the steps to snuffle for cookie crumbs, licked some off of Beck's face before jumping up next to his mistress and giving her a canine kiss.

"Pathetic that I can't walk my own dog at the moment," Stacy said.

Xo squeezed her hand. "This time next year you'll be doing that again—and pushing a baby carriage."

Exploring the outdoor kitchen, Junior admired the well to boil crawfish and crabs, the vast grill, and finally a wood-fired pizza oven. "Something even my dad doesn't have," Dean boomed. "Let's get those steaks and burgers started." The two men headed for the indoor kitchen to retrieve the meat.

Stacy started to rise. "I should put a salad together."

Junior waved her back into her seat. "I'll do that. Dean, let me show you how to season those steaks."

"That's right, princess, the men are cooking tonight."

In the end, they produced a delicious, simple meal of tossed salad, fresh slices of chewy French bread, plain burgers and carrot sticks for the kids and steaks with Junior's herbed cheese butter dripping down their thick sides. For Stacy, Junior nuked a large baked potato and dressed it with sour cream flecked with green specks. "Mint, not chives, to help your stomach and give you some dairy. Try it."

"Good." Stacy didn't eat much else no matter how often a worried Dean encouraged her to consume some red meat. He had to be content that his wife accepted a small bowl of vanilla ice cream for dessert while the children demanded chocolate sauce, sprinkles, whipped cream, and a cherry on top. Junior made himself a banana split and convinced Xochi to eat part of it.

She leaned away from the teak picnic table where they'd enjoyed an afternoon in the shade before the summer heat set in. "I intended to suggest we take the streetcar back to Canal. Now, we'll have to walk again."

"That's fine with me as soon as we clean up. You and me, let's bus this table. Let the chef and his family rest."

Stacy had retreated to the lounger again and fallen asleep. Dean hushed the kids and whispered, "Unlimited Cartoon Network while Mommy sleeps. Quiet now."

They tiptoed across the courtyard and slipped into the den. Soon he had his children settled in front the huge TV with bright colors flashing by. Closing the door on the noise, their dad returned.

"Stacy lets them do that?" Xochi questioned.

"Nope, but I'm doing the best I can to buy her some rest. Thanks for your help, Junior. You can season my steaks anytime. Wait. That sounds like something Uncle Brian would say. I mean you are welcome here whenever."

"Good to know. Look, we'll clean up and let ourselves out. Be with your family, bro." They exchanged those manly back slaps while Xochi cleared the table.

"Hey, I'm doing all the work here."

"Because you didn't lift a finger up till now." Junior filled his broad arms with plates as if he'd done this chore dozens of times. They finished the cleanup and wended their way back to the apartment.

The heat had ramped up, and they walked as people did on a hot day in the South, a slow and easy stroll trying to keep to the shady side of the street. "Sad to see Stacy so sick," Junior remarked.

"Her idea to get the family completed fast. Two children is the deal, then Dean is getting snipped."

"Brave man—but I'd do it for my wife if she had the same problem. Being an only child I'd sort of like to have a large family though."

"Oh, I don't think Stacy and I have much in

common that way. Lots of babies would be fine by me," Xochi said absently, her mind slowed by rich steaks, banana splits, and a warm afternoon.

"Good," Junior answered with some satisfaction. "We're on the same page."

"I didn't mean us, you and me!" Xochi batted away his arm about to embrace her shoulders and kept her distance the rest of the way home.

Chapter Six

Xochi woke Sunday morning and prepared to go to early Mass at St. Louis Cathedral. She thought about inviting Junior. After all, they'd attended church at Ste. Jeanne d'Arc together most of their lives, Junior in his mother's arms and herself escorted in Sunday best dress by MawMaw Nadine who herded all the boys and her reluctant son, Joe, into a couple of the box pews and kept them quiet with her stern eye and iron will. Xochi recalled Corazon whispering to her son, "Do not disgrace me," even though a crying room sat readily available.

The rest of the Billodeaux girls, Stacy, and Teddy, who'd been raised a Baptist until he joined the family, went to the Episcopal Church with Mama Nell who maintained that the children could make up their own minds about religion when they grew up. In her way, she was as adamant as her mother-in-law. Since Xochi had been baptized in the Holy Catholic Church and attended services with her late mother, Nadine made a good case for carrying on in the same belief system. Xo often thought she'd been traded in exchange for Teddy, but accustomed to the ritual, the incense, and the statues of bloody martyred saints in niches along the walls, she felt at home and nearer to her birth mother than anywhere else.

Xochi paused by Junior's door and heard his

49

rhythmic snores clearly through the frame. Turning the knob gently, she peeked inside to see if he'd awaken, but Junior slept on with his big feet poking out from Stacy's old silver duvet and two pillows covered in pale gray slips propped under his head. The plethora of little purple cushions, some lace edged, that Stacy used to adorn the bed lay scattered all over the floor. Junior's clothes from yesterday draped a girly bedroom chair. She knew if she shook him he'd be appalled at the mess. Every day, he made that bed, replaced each and every cushion, and put his dirty laundry in a bag in the closet well before Xochi appeared at breakfast. Well, no fancy feasts today. She'd let him sleep.

Xochi eased out of her apartment, walked along Canal Street, relatively quiet on a Sunday morning with no work traffic and few tourists yet awake. Turning on Chartres Street, she followed it all the way to Jackson Square, site of the oldest cathedral in the United States. The triple-spired edifice in several resurrections had survived fire, flood, a bombing, and Hurricane Katrina. Xo felt a kinship with the building as she'd survived the murder of her parents, the burning of her home, and later, the arrival of her auras. As far as supernatural powers went, the ancient church was said to be haunted by two benign priests.

She stepped inside its cool, towering space, genuflected, and moved into a pew. Immediately, she fell to her knees and said her usual prayers for all the Billodeauxs, others who had helped raise her—Corazon and her husband, Nurse Shammy and hers, the *traiteur* Rosemarie Leleux—all those who played football and risked injury, and especially for her beautiful mother who had died before reaching the age of twenty-one.

She prayed for Junior and asked what to do about him, too.

Because Jesus preached forgiveness, she also prayed for the soul of her father: gambler, drug-runner, kidnapper, debaucher of girls half his age. She'd learned these facts as she grew older from Corazon who had thwarted Tom's first kidnapping and from Tom's birth mother who had borne him at seventeen after a liaison with Bijou Billodeaux. When she was a small child, he'd showered his Xochi with gifts and hit her with his belt if she gave him any sass. Her mother catered to his every whim, probably for the same reasons. When *Papi* called her mama into the bedroom, she cautioned her child, "Play quietly. Do not cry for me." If Bijou Billodeaux did not already reside in Hell, he certainly served an infinite sentence in purgatory.

Personal prayers done, she lost herself in the ritual of the Mass and left calmed, as always. Answers would come, Rosemarie Leleux said. For the convenience of city dwellers early Mass began at nine, not eight like in Chapelle. By the time Xochi exited into the sunlight and rising humidity off the Mississippi, artists had hung their works on the iron fence of the square. Street performers claimed their corners to catch the eyes of the churchgoers with magic and music, and the mule-drawn carriages lined Decatur Street to begin the first tours of the day. She cut through Jackson Square blooming with lovely but poisonous white oleanders, and crossed to Café du Monde for café au lait and beignets, choosing a small table near the sidewalk where she could people watch. New Orleans never disappointed.

Customers staggered in from a night on the town to

the café that never closed. They took their coffee black with chicory. Whole families devoured mounds of the square donuts blanketed deep in powdered sugar. Xochi finished her order of three and asked for a go-bag of six to take back for Junior. She sipped the last drop from her thick white mug of milky coffee while waiting. Auras, pink and blue, green and orange, drifted by colorful as a circus parade until she saw one of the dark men emerge from the park, a squat, brutal-looking thug with the broken nose of a boxer. He pushed away a panhandler who might have been discouraged with a mere no. Her sack of beignets for Junior arrived, and she lost track of that blot of evil as she paid the waitress.

Still rattled, Xochi bought a Sunday newspaper from a kiosk and headed toward the safety of her apartment with all the locks and gizmos Daddy Joe had installed when his girls moved in, the latest being a camera hidden under the fire escape placed there after the attack on Stacy. She walked briskly to calm her nerves and throw off anyone who might follow. Though dressed modestly for church, without Junior's escort she drew and ignored the usual comments about her fine ass, which seemed to sway no matter how she tried to suppress its actions. Maybe next time she would wake Junior and insist he go to church, get some religion before the football season started, as good an excuse for his escort as any.

When she reached Canal again, she wove in and out of the thickening clumps of tourists and reached her place breathless but safe. Still her hand shook as she dealt with the multiple locks. Glancing up at the fish eye of the camera that recorded her every move, she glimpsed a man across the street and turned her head to stare. Not the same person she'd seen in the square, but black of aura and soul. He quickly passed the gap in the buildings where her apartment entry lay. Her door finally yielded. Xochi locked it behind her and raced up the stairs calling, "Junior, I brought you beignets for breakfast." More than anything, she wanted to hear his deep voice and move into the sphere of his comforting presence.

He stood in the kitchen mixing a bowl of batter. "Shucks, here I am making pecan waffles. I figured you'd gone to church and would come back hungry."

Xo cocked her head. "Did your mom leave us a waffle iron, too?"

"Nope. I bought it when I got the coffeemaker. It has interchangeable plates. We can grill panini too. Doesn't matter. I can freeze these, and we'll eat them tomorrow with warm maple syrup. Let me at those beignets."

He poured the batter into the heavyweight iron and shut the lid before he accepted the white paper bag, got himself a cup of coffee, and delved deep into the powdered sugar to fish out a square donut. "I should have known you'd go to Café du Monde. Mawmaw Nadine always took us over to Pommier's Bakery after Mass if we behaved well in church."

The sugar caught in the scruff of beard around his mouth, and Xo had the greatest impulse to wipe it away with her fingertips. Two days in a row now that Junior hadn't shaved, new for him. "Yes, the carrot and the stick, or rather the beignet versus the tongue lashing if we acted up, especially in front of her friends."

Junior's grin grew around the rim of his coffee

mug. "You never acted up. Made us boys look bad. You were always sort of—pious."

"Pious? Me, no! Wait until you see me dance at Paco's before you say that again."

"I'm really looking forward that."

"But, maybe you'll come to Mass with me next Sunday—like the old days."

Junior didn't answer immediately, which surprised Xo as he sought ways to be near her. Finally, he answered. "I haven't been to confession in a long time, and lately, I've been having impure thoughts on a regular basis." His deep brown eyes left no doubt who figured in those thoughts.

Xochi's face grew warm. She thought she covered it well by saying, "You have all week to give your confession," and tempered that statement with, "Maybe I'll have just half a waffle. They smell so good."

"Yeah, okay, I'll go."

The carrot and the stick still worked.

Chapter Seven

The week dragged for Junior Polk even though he went into the training center every day. When the Sinners scheduled the first mini-camp, he planned to be at the top of his game. At least, he had the satisfaction of making sure Xochi had a good breakfast every morning before she left for work. He suspected she skipped lunch, so he began having dinner ready to serve when he heard her light steps on the staircase—red beans and rice, chicken enchiladas, rich rabbit-sausage gumbo, though he didn't tell her the meat was bunny.

"You're going to make me fat!" she claimed.

He answered with a shrug. "My dad loves my mama no matter how big she gets."

"Does he use the old line about there being more to love?" Xo spooned up gumbo scanty on the rice.

"No, he says a big woman is warm in bed." He'd embarrassed her and rushed to lighten it up. "When I was little, I thought that meant he didn't need as many blankets on the bed in January."

Xochi laughed, a sound that always struck him as rich as deep, dark coffee with a dollop of chocolate added. "Of course, there were those nights *Papi* turned down the air-conditioning way low and didn't explain why. I figured out what went on about the time I turned thirteen."

"None of us ever want to believe our parents have

sex."

"Without it, we wouldn't be here eating gumbo together. You think it's hot in here? Maybe I should turn down the A/C?"

She'd whapped him on the arm with her gumbo spoon. "Cut it out, or you'll have to move."

"Yes, ma'am." Still that little bit of banter was the highlight of his week, and he cherished the small bruise made by the spoon.

Xochi didn't seem to notice or care that he hadn't shaved all week. Thursday morning, he sought out a black barbershop one of the burly linemen who bench-pressed with him recommended. The guy looked pretty sharp, so he took his advice, doubting that Brian Lightfoot would have any better suggestions. No unisex place, this. Call Compton's old-timey. Aged men with grizzled hair and closely trimmed beards flipped though dated Ebony and Jet magazines while guzzling free coffee. "That Beyoncé, she a fine lookin' woman," they all agreed. The gathering appeared to be there for company since the barber took Junior immediately. He shaved away all but a thin rim of beard outlining his face, trimmed the mustache and left two strips on either side of Junior's mouth giving his face more definition and a distinct edge.

"You want me to do something with yo' hair, boy? How about a fade along the sides? Let it grown out a tad on top so you don't look like a casaba melon. I pity the woman who had to give birth to that head." The barber's audience laughed on cue.

Junior went along with the joke. "Got to confess I was a twelve-pound baby, hard on my mama. Sure, do what you can with me."

By the time he left with talcum powder on his neck and his face slapped with a stinging aftershave, a new man stared from the mirror. He picked up the beard trimmer recommended by Compton himself, went home to whip up a crawfish etouffee and astound Xochi. He did a big reveal, keeping his back to her when she bounded into the kitchen and asked, "What's cooking?"

Junior turned and with wooden spoon in hand, posed against the stove, said, "Me."

"I asked what, not who, but you look nice."

Nice? Up until a minute ago, he'd thought great. Compton suggested he might want to leave a small, pointed goatee to seem more devilish. "The ladies love that devil look, uh-huh." His cronies agreed like a call and response choir. "Uh-huh, uh-huh." Junior turned down that idea, but wondered if he'd made a big mistake. Oh well, beards grew back fairly fast.

"Thanks. Salad is on the table, warm bread in the oven." He added the crawfish tails to his roux, last minute, to keep them from getting tough. At least, Xo had begun to look forward to his cooking if nothing else.

****

Finally, Friday night arrived, and so did Connor Bullock in a spotless and sedate silver Honda Accord ready to take them all to Paco's. Xochi inspected his choice of vehicle. "We shouldn't take that to Paco's. The place is deep in the Treme."

Junior jumped to volunteer his SUV again, but Xochi shook her head. "Even worse. I always take a taxi there and back again. I don't want to be responsible for any damage to your vehicles—or for their loss."

They piled into the cab she summoned, he and Connor crammed uncomfortably close in the back, their knees nearly touching because of Junior's size. Xo, not playing favorites, rode with the driver who gallantly handed her out under the neon sign of the tipsy margarita and kissed the back of her fingers.

"*Gracias*, Diego. One of my regular drivers," she explained. "I tip very well."

Tom and Alix stood waiting in front of the blacked-out windows of the dance club like two tall white candles in a dark cathedral. With his usual fashion sense, Tom sported an orange shirt close to the shade of his hair, but much more brilliant. Alix wore a pale blue dress with cap sleeves and a flared skirt that came just to her knees. It might have fit in well at a high school dance, but her endless legs made up for a lack of sophistication. Both seemed relaxed, oblivious to the neighborhood, but Connor peered around as if waiting to be mugged at any minute in his white dress shirt, khakis, and a Rolex watch. Serve the fool right if someone ripped it off his wrist. Junior had considered his wardrobe carefully and gone with a short-sleeved shirt of deep purple, slightly fitted, collar open a few buttons to expose a few tight curls of chest hair and a single gold chain he defied anyone to take, flaunting his new look and a new attitude.

Xochi outshone them all in a sleeveless gown with a deep scooped neck that showed her assets, its dark green bodice hugging her body to just below the waist where it exploded into layers of multicolored ruffles that ended above her knees—Junior's flower, his blossom despite the unsettling snake bracelet that coiled up one arm and winked at him with ruby eyes. She tossed the black waves of her long hair over her shoulders, and the large gold hoops in her ears caught the light from the neon sign. On red Cuban heels meant for serious dancing, Xo led the way into the club.

Ah Paco's, home of the giant margarita, sweet daiquiris churning in drums behind the bar, tequila shots, and six varieties Mexican beer to cool the customers who danced with abandon in the courtyard beyond its dim interior. The Latin music thrummed like jungle insects on a tropical night. Barely inside the door, the puny brown manager pounced on Xo and greeted her with a huge hug. "So good to see you, Senorita Xochi. We been missing you."

"Well, I'm back, and I've brought a few friends."

He peered over her shoulder and retreated. "No, no, not him. You, *pelirrojo*, you and your big shot friend almost start a fight last time you here. Then, he return another night and bust up my place. Go away!" His shaking finger pointed to Tom who held up his hands.

"Hey, Paco, I'm the guy who stopped the fight by ordering drinks for everyone in the house, remember? Dean isn't with us tonight—but he paid for the damages. I see you have all new tables and chairs."

"How many times I got to say there is no Paco. I am Juan. Out, out, but the pretty blonde, she can stay." The manager made up for his bantam size with the attitude of a fighting cock.

Xochi laid a calming hand on Juan's chicken wing of an arm. "I'll be responsible for their behavior."

"Even that one?" The manager's judgmental finger turned on Junior. "He is one of those *futbol* players. I can tell. A giant. He goes loco, who gonna throw him out?"

"Junior is harmless, I swear." Xochi beseeched the manager with her big brown eyes, the dark lashes beneath smoky lids fluttering.

Harmless? Despite all his efforts to banish his little boy face, she still considered him harmless. Junior felt an urge to start a bar fight simply to prove he wasn't, but Juan waved them through the dim barroom. "Okay, but I be watching you and you." The finger forked over his eyes and then moved from Tom to Junior and back again. Evidently, Connor presented no threat—except for coming between Xo and Junior.

Bumping their heads on the festoons of piñatas— some whole, some battered—hanging from the ceiling that appeared to be Paco's only decorations, the four tall friends followed Xo's more compact body toward the courtyard. Junior walked into a black and red piece of papier-mâché with a few straggling streamers on both ends occupying an archway.

As he pushed it aside, Tom leaned in to say, "That Sinners' football piñata started the riot. It's legendary. First, Dean busts it wide open and people start turning over tables to get at the cheap junk. Then, Dean decides to pay for it all by throwing hundred dollar bills in the air."

"Not a good idea."

"He was stinking drunk. That's what happens when he doesn't have his wingman along, only I guess Stacy is his wing woman now."

"Hey, you have your own wing woman. We might as well dance. I don't see a free table anywhere." Alix wedged her way toward the dance floor.

"Good idea. Let's do some salsa, my honey."

In seconds, their long white arms waved above the

crush of shorter, browner dancers, though what style the couple embraced no one could tell. Somehow, they'd lost Xochi in the crowd. Junior loomed next to Connor as if he were the man's bodyguard. Though the doctor had more black blood in his mix than Junior, he stood there as uncomfortable as a white boy on a very dark Treme street corner with his valuable surgeon's hands thrust into the pockets of his khakis and that expensive watch exposed. Dumbass.

Connor smiled with relief when Xochi's firm brown arms waved above the masses to summon them to a table already occupied by a tall, skinny, almost flat-chested woman with magenta streaks highlighting her drab brown hair. She had bold features and wore bolder makeup to hide them. Her lips, also magenta, parted. "About time you got here. I nearly had to lay across the top and spread my legs to save this much space. I've been slapping hands that tried to snitch the chairs for half an hour."

Xochi made the introductions. "This is my friend, Rachelle. I was hoping a few more would join us."

"Ya know, Isabella got that baby now. She doesn't get out much anymore. Donata married a guy who hates dancing, go figure." Rachelle cracked her gum in disgust. "You and me are the last of our group left standing, Xo."

Not if Junior had his way. He started to ask for a dance, but a slithery Hispanic guy, lithe and sole-eyed, came up behind and grasped Xo around the waist. "Ah, *mi chica muy bonita*. Where you been girl?"

"Mostly working."

"Lots of interpreting at the cop shop, huh, probably at night."

"Sometimes. Connor, Junior, meet Angel, one of my best partners."

Angel grasped Connor's slim fingers for a moment and offered Junior a limp handshake. "*Dios mio*, this one is jumbo-sized. All over?" he inquired of Xochi, his eyebrows raised.

"Both are old family friends, so crawl out of the gutter and let's dance." That quickly with Angel's arm still claiming her waist, she merged with the throng.

"Either of you guys want to?" asked Rachelle.

Connor immediately assumed a seat as if he'd gotten into the last lifeboat on the Titanic and had no intention of giving it up for woman or child. "I'll pay for the first round if you can break through to the bar and get it, Junior." A fifty-dollar bill appeared from his pocket. "Get a Corona for me. Anything the ladies want."

"I'll go with the giant margarita. I always do. Get Xo a strawberry daiquiri, and try to be back for the show. Once she and Angel get going, they clear the floor. I'm not so bad myself," Rachelle hinted broadly.

"I'll fetch the drinks." The crowd parted before Junior's greater mass. Though he tried to find a line, a push and shove protocol appeared to be in effect. He envisioned himself slicing through the Falcon's line and arrived before the bar in no time. Remembering Tom and Alix, he added another Corona and daiquiri to the order, and asked for the Negra Modelo for himself. He knew something about Mexican beers and disdained any with a lime stuck in the neck. The bartender approved and offered to have a waitress bring the drinks to their table. Junior declined. He accepted a round tray and balanced it expertly on his blunt fingertips. Again, the crowd parted for him.

Tom and Alix sat sweating at their table. Though the May night was warm, more of the heat came from their exertions and the many bodies that packed Paco's. Alix sipped her sweet drink, but Tom downed his Corona so fast Junior feared he'd swallow the lime. Oh well, that would give Dr. Bullock a chance to do a Heimlich and be a hero. He couldn't let that happen. "Take it easy, Tom. That's not the last Corona on earth. I thought you'd still be dancing."

"Xochi and Angel are out there stealing the show."

Indeed, they were with back bends and magnificent twirls. Their heights were well matched, their rhythm in perfect sync. If only he'd gotten Xo to dance with him first. He should be the one rubbing against her behind not some… His jealousy must have shown on his face because Rachelle gave his hand a sympathetic pat.

"Don't worry, big guy. Angel is gay. Stacy once paid him to make Dean jealous, but Dean figured it out. Think you can keep up with him on the dance floor? Maybe we could make Xochi green with envy?"

Junior stood and offered his hand to this less than attractive lady. Rachelle accepted. "You light on your feet, because there ain't nothing junior-sized about you? I don't want a broken toe. Junior, why do they call you that anyhow? Some kind of joke?"

He replied as they pushed through the ring of folks watching Xo and Angel dance. "Named after my father, Knox Polk."

"Knocks, that fits you better than Junior. I bet you knock men around on the football field."

"No, like Fort Knox."

"You rich?" Rachelle assumed the dance position

63

facing him.

"Not yet, but I will be. Ready?" He started with a fast side step, twirled her out and back at the end of it with such speed she seemed a little dizzy. Junior moved behind her and steadied his partner with his two big hands that spanned her skinny waist. Hips swaying, they moved in time. A back bend, then a reverse putting Rachelle behind him.

"Get set," he cautioned. The music was winding to a stop, and he planned a spectacular ending. Hiking Rachelle up to his waist where she lightly clamped her long legs, he lifted her and somersaulted her over his shoulder. They ended with arms raised in the air. Applause broke out, whether for him and his partner, or for Xochi and Angel, he couldn't tell as he'd been too busy showing his salsa chops to pay attention to the other pair on the floor.

"Ay-yi-yi, has *Dancing with the Stars* come to Paco's?" the bandleader raved. "We take a break now. More music in twenty." He stepped down from the raised stage sheltered by a tin roof and illuminated by two towering palm trees twined in multicolored Christmas lights.

Junior led Rachelle back to the table, held a chair for her, and took one for himself. Connor still sat there as if he were a part of the furnishings, his elbows resting on top of a painting of a Mexican peasant harvesting agave juice to make pulque, and sipping his Corona so slowly it might last all night, his eyes glued to an iPad.

Rachelle took a mighty slurp of her gigantic margarita through a straw and waved her hands in front of Connor's scholarly glasses. "Save me, Doc! I think I got a brain freeze." He rewarded her with a faint smile just as chilly.

"I see you just don't get what we do here. Salsa dancing is great therapy. Let's you go a little wild with no bad consequences. Consider Xochi, a real slut on the dance floor, and she never goes home with a guy. Now me, I do from time to time. Say, let me teach you a few moves when the band comes back. I swear it will loosen you up and take away your cares for a while." She sucked hard into the stem of the margarita glass. "But then, so will alcohol. Who's buying the next round?"

"My pleasure." This time Junior summoned the overworked and overweight waitress with the low-slung blouse and the tight black skirt to the table. "Same all around?"

Connor shook his head. "I'm fine."

Xochi and Angel finally arrived after being waylaid by admirers at the end of their dance. When Angel started to place his slim but tightly clad butt into a chair, Junior said, "Sorry, that's Tom's spot, and the one next to him belongs to Alix."

"No *problema*, man." He snatched a chair from the table behind them and wedged in next to Connor, who attempted to move a few inches, but that brought him in thigh contact with Rachelle, who winked as if he'd done it intentionally.

Angel caught the eye of the waitress. "Angelita, a shot of tequila. Put it on Junior's tab. For a big tip, I can drink it off her belly and so can you, doctor." Connor didn't bother to hide his distaste at the idea.

Tom and Alix returned with a pizza platter sectioned by colorful strips of red and green peppers.

"We got some of everything: tacos, loaded nachos, and quesadillas." The group moved their drinks aside to accommodate the food. "Help yourselves."

Lifting a taco to his mouth, Angel did immediately. Rachelle selected a triangle of chicken quesadilla and nibbled. "I'd better eat something before I get too drunk and easy." Her heavily outlined eyes full of invitation moved from Junior to Connor.

"Ha, you're always easy, Rachelle, not always drunk," Angel taunted.

"Shut up, pantywaist. You're lucky to have someone to take care of you."

"Please, no bickering." Xochi held up a hand. "For your rudeness, you will dance the next set with Rachelle—and Angel, give Connor back his watch."

"Just keeping in practice. I do sleight of hand as well as act and dance." Angel removed Connor's timepiece from an inner pocket in a black silk shirt open almost to his waist. It showed off his smooth, hairless tan chest, and lean muscles.

"Good." Xochi selected a nacho dripping cheese over a lump of hamburger and topped with a jalapeno slice. She ate it in two bites and reached for another.

"I'd like to dance the next set with you, Xo." Junior knew his yearning showed on his face, the one barbered to bring out his manliness.

"Sorry, on our way over here at least eight men asked me to save one for them. I think I need a dance card."

"You always do," sighed Rachelle. "But at least I know who my partner is for the next few. Unless the doc wants those lessons I offered."

"I was hoping you would do that, Xo." Connor

tried to shift his chair again but encountered Angel's leg. Angel gave him a mocking come hither grin.

Xo pretended to miss the byplay. "I'm all tied up for the night. Oh, you should Connor. Really, Rachelle is a great teacher, not that Junior needed instructions. Amazing. When did you learn to dance like that?"

"I asked Dean to teach me a while back. He can't, or won't, do those lifts though. Might injure his shoulder or throwing arm. Maybe the Sinners put that in his contract." He'd learned to dance for her, only for her. Didn't Xochi understand that?

"General clause about engaging in dangerous activities," Tom answered. "We have them, too. We aren't supposed to ski. That really pisses off Alix."

"No problem for me. I can toss any woman here over my shoulder." He shouldn't have spoken so loudly or so arrogantly. The women at the next table lined up to ask him to dance, but not Xo.

"Who needs a dance card now?" Xochi's rich laughter covered him like dark chocolate sauce. And that thought made his mind turn in dangerous directions. He reined in his rampant imagination and pleaded, "Would you save the last dance for me, Xo, please?"

"Please say yes. I hate to see a grown man beg," Tom quipped.

"No need to beg. Of course, I'll save the last dance for Junior." Xochi finished her first daiquiri and let the second sit as the band warmed up again. The first of her long list of partners appeared, and she left the table on his arm.

Drinking little and dancing much, both she and Junior passed the time until the hour neared two a.m.

Connor unbent enough to learn a few steps from Rachelle and apply his lessons to Xochi when she worked him in at the end of one song. Mostly, he appeared tired and bored. He checked his watch frequently, either to tell the time or to see if it was still on his wrist, and fooled around with the iPad he never let leave his hand. Finally, he asked Juan to call a cab. "Next time I have off, I want to take you to a special place I enjoy, Xo. Is that a date?"

"Sure. Sorry you didn't have a good time, Connor."

Angel's caring older lover arrived to take him home well fed and tipsy on tequila shots. "*Muchas gracias* for watching over him, Xochi," he said, pecking her cheek. Giving up on both Junior and Connor, Rachelle had departed around one with a man she met on her way back from the restroom and danced with twice.

"I wish she wouldn't do that. I worry about her," Xochi said.

"What, you can't tell if he's a bad guy with your magical powers," Connor mocked. For lack of anything else to do, he'd consumed four Coronas.

"His aura is brown, the color of deception, but that goes for lots of the men here who will tell a woman anything she wants to hear in order to score. However, as you should know, doctor, there are all sorts of diseases she could pick up, and when drunk, the risk of sloppy, unprotected sex that leads to pregnancy. I didn't notice any sickness on the guy, but I don't see the future."

"Yeah, sloppy unprotected sex, that's how Dean got Beck, but he's a great kid," Tom added. "You ready to go, Legs?" he asked his wife.

"If you are." The couple departed while they still had the energy for safe marital sex.

A man approached the table. To Junior, he looked like most of Xo's many dance partners: brown, lean, slicked-back black hair. This one also sported a pencil thin mustache and three gold chains. "My turn," he claimed.

Xo shook her head. "No, I promised Martin Segura this dance."

"He went home early. We traded."

Xo answered him sharply, so unlike her. "No trades. Last dance, Junior."

He stood at her prompt, mountainous and muscular. Something wrong, but he didn't know what. The band struck up the next number. They pushed past the stranger. Junior took his beloved in his arms and wondered if she felt the same warmth that suffused his body when they pressed together. Onlookers shouted, "*Olé, Olé, Olé*" at every pass they made across the floor as if he conquered his partner instead of cherished her.

The moment came for the lift over his shoulder, sore if he admitted it from doing the same move with so many others that evening, but Xochi soared as she were made of black swan feathers and landed lightly facing the audience. He pressed his lips against her nape where the waves of her dark hair parted and swore he felt an extra surge of heat from her body. Those that remained watching applauded wildly. From the sidelines, the man with the thin mustache glared at them with his dead black eyes.

Xo turned in Junior's arms. "Time to go home."

She insisted on remaining in the barroom while waiting for her favored driver despite the noise and dimness rather than out in the balmy May night where knots of men and women stood smoking and chatting on the broken sidewalk. When the taxi pulled up in front of Paco's, Xo bolted for its door and flung herself into the backseat. Junior joined her and carefully placed one arm around her shoulders, held her tight. She trembled, and he swore he could feel the frantic beat of her heart fast as a frightened dove against his chest.

"Did I do something wrong? Was the lift too much for you? Or was it the kiss?"

"No, no, nothing you did, Junior. The lift, the kiss is part of the dance. That man who wanted to be my partner, he is one of the dark men I've been seeing lately everywhere I go. Soulless men with auras so black they seem to make a hole in the universe. New Orleans is a big city, often a sinful city, and I've seen them before, but never so many or so close to me."

"I'll protect you, Xo. You know I'd give my life for you."

"Don't say that! No one should have to make that choice."

The ride back to their shared apartment wasn't long, especially if the driver knew the ways around the tourist traffic, thick even at this time of the evening. Junior stood guard, watchful, as Xochi worked the locks with shaking hands. He saw no one other than the usual drunks and herds of boisterous college kids pass by on their way to get their cars out of paid lots.

Xo flicked on the lily-shaped staircase lights and turned the deadbolts to secure the door. No longer light-hearted or light-footed, they trudged up the steps to their living room/ kitchen/ office and second bathroom area. Junior headed straight for the stove. "Want me to make you some eggs and toast to settle you down?"

"You know, that might be good."

She took a seat at the table and let Junior work. He never prepared anything ordinary for her, not even eggs. Cream went into the concoction, not milk. He grated cheese over the marbled mixture, no processed product for him—or her. A pinch of herbs and into the warm, buttered pan. Thin slices of bread from a French loaf disappeared into the toaster. The fancy coffeemaker could make herbal tea, as it turned out. Junior set all this before her and watched Xo eat dainty as a sparrow pecking at crumbs.

"None for you?" she asked.

"No. I think I polished off most of those loaded nachos and half the tacos between dances. Tom went back to get more. He and Alix sure can eat."

"They're athletes and work it off like you. Me, I have to watch it. I don't want to know how much sugar is in two strawberry daiquiris or one of those nachos. I try to stay on the dance floor as much as I can. This is so good, protein mostly."

"Sure. Drink the tea. It will help you sleep."

"Having you here really does make me feel more secure." She rose to take the dishes to the sink. "I'll clean up since you did all the work." Xochi turned on the water to start the task, added detergent, put the pan and dishes in to soak.

Junior came up behind her. Couldn't she feel the heat they generated together? He parted her hair and kissed her nape again. When she turned, brown arms upheld and lacy with soap bubbles to ward him off, he took the kiss he really wanted. His lips were broad and hers soft and plush, yet they fit together so well. He outlined hers with the tip of his tongue, asking for entrance, not demanding it, surprised when she granted his wish. A soft, wet tangle of tongues and more pressure on the lips ensued as they imitated the act of love. When both needed air, Xochi pulled away leaving behind the imprint of her wet fingers on both shoulders of his purple shirt.

"That was no amateur kiss, Junior. You've had some practice."

"I thought you'd want a man with experience because you had some years on me to learn." Damn, he'd brought up the age issue without meaning to at all. He sensed her withdrawal. "I practiced some other things, too, and got pretty good at it." Might as well confess and let it all out. He studied his big knuckles.

"I guess you had to suffer through that like you do at a mini-camp."

"Nope, sex is pretty wonderful, right? But, I think it would be even better with someone you love."

"Sure, I guess."

"If you have to guess, I'd say you haven't done it with the right man. He's standing right here." Junior held his arms out and offered to enfold her again.

Xochi turned and scrubbed eggs from the dish and pan. "We shouldn't kiss again no matter how great you are at it. I changed your diapers when you were a baby."

"Did not! You always used to say that when you didn't want me tagging along somewhere. I finally asked my mama if that was true. She said no, what kind of nursemaid or mother would she be if she let a five-year-old take care of me, all of that in indignant Spanish. You could barely lift me. So there!"

And she laughed. "You aren't the boss of me, Junior. Sounds like we're having a childhood argument."

"I don't want to be your boss. You know I have something better in mind." He kissed her nape again and let his tongue run down her spine to the top of her gown.

She shivered and faced him. "There are things you don't know about me, things I haven't told anyone, not Mama Nell, not Stacy."

"If you mean that your birth mother had you at fourteen and was probably a child prostitute, it makes no difference to me. Your father might have been Daddy Joe's cousin, but he was scum in so many ways. That doesn't matter. The whole family figured that out years ago. The auras—who cares? Maybe they are a medical problem like Connor Bullock says, but if you believe in them and they protect you, then great. Nothing can change my love for you."

Xochi laid two fingers on his lips to quiet him, and he wanted nothing more than to suck on the tips and kiss her palm. "I need to make a major decision in my life soon. Right now, I have no time for your love, for anyone's love."

"Love chooses its own time, Xo. When you feel it might surprise you."

"That's the most mature statement I've ever heard from a man."

"See, age doesn't really matter."

"Maybe you will convince me of that one day, but not tonight. See you in the morning." Xochi left the dishes to air dry and pulled the plug. Suds and water swirled down the drain and disappeared.

Chapter Eight

Xochi's phone rang at ten a.m., way too early for a woman who'd been out past two in the morning. She fumbled it from its place on her nightstand. "Hello," she said in a voice a little dry from last night's daiquiris.

"Hey, it's me, Rachelle. How'd it go after I left with restroom guy? Did you take home the I'm a serious doctor man or big, brown, and bodacious?"

"The last because he's my temporary roommate and childhood friend—but is way too young for both of us. Nothing happened." She intentionally tried to blot out that kiss, the memory of his tongue sliding along her lips, the slightly rough feel of the new mustache he'd grown, and did not succeed.

"Maybe his age bothers *you*, but I don't consider myself too young to be a cougar. If his flavor is not to your liking, can I have a taste?"

"No! I mean what about the fellow you went home with last night."

"We did the deed fairly decently, but after he seemed more interested in you. Why hadn't you been to Paco's lately? Who were the men at our table?"

"And you told him!"

"Didn't seem like a big deal. He crept out before dawn like they always do. Can't even remember his name. Some Hispanic dude. I just keep thinking of him as *restroom guy*. Those giant margaritas really mess with your brain."

"You should lay off of them. Look, I'm sorry I snapped about Junior. I guess I feel protective since I remember when he was born. Of course, you can go out with him if he asks." Feeling as if she'd just given away something very precious, Xo pressed her pillow tight against her chest to calm her hard-thumping heart.

"The way his eyes follow you, I'll have to do the asking, but what the hell. Say, you want to go shopping at the Riverwalk this morning? We can catch lunch there and shop some more after."

"Sure, I haven't done that in a while. Give me an hour. I'm still in bed and not dressed."

"Is Junior?"

Sometimes Rachelle and her innuendos really got on her nerves. Besides salsa dancing, they had little in common. "I wouldn't know as he uses the other bedroom."

"Don't get your panties in a wad. I'll meet you at the entry in sixty."

Glad when Rachelle disconnected, Xochi rose from her bed and headed for the shower. Clearly, Junior had made use of it already, not because of any mess he left behind, but by a damp towel neatly folded on the rack and the steamy mist of his lime aftershave in the air. Xo inhaled deeply, then prompted herself to stop that at once. Before she turned on the water, she detected his bustle in the kitchen and hoped he hadn't prepared another big breakfast.

After bathing, she put on daytime makeup, no smoky eyes or lipstick red as her dancing shoes. Dressing in a loose lemon yellow summer dress and white sandals because summer had already cranked up the heat in New Orleans, she went downstairs to face Junior après the major kiss.

He beamed at her. "*Muy bonita.*"

"*Gracias.* I don't have time for breakfast." She tried to shut him down. Didn't work.

"It's so close to lunchtime, I only made my Bananas Foster toast and coffee. See, I put thinly sliced bananas on the buttered bread and sprinkle it with Foster mix. A minute under the broiler, and it's ready." He shoved a cookie sheet she didn't know she owned holding six slices into the oven and poured her coffee with exactly the right amount of steamed milk.

Xochi found herself sitting to accept the beverage and a couple of pieces of his invention, way better than ordinary cinnamon toast. "Thanks, but I really can't linger. I'm meeting Rachelle at the Riverwalk to do some shopping. We're having lunch there."

"Can I…"

Xo waved her slightly sticky fingers in his face. "No, you cannot go along. I-I babysat for you."

A wide grin exposing that charming gap in his front teeth spread across his broad face. "No, you didn't. If my mother was busy or needed a break, Mama Nell just folded me into the pack of Billodeauxs. With all those kids, it was no big deal she always said."

"Okay, fine, you still can't go along. We might want to buy sexy lingerie."

"That would be entirely great with me, especially if you modeled it, but that's not what I wanted to ask. Can I take you out to dinner tonight?"

Xochi sorted through her defenses. "Only if Rachelle is invited, too."

His smile dropped, but otherwise he hid his disappointment well. "Sure, if she wants to tag along. Meet me at Coop's Place around six. It's on Decatur not far from the French Market."

"I don't think I know it."

"One of New Orleans' best kept secrets."

Xochi licked her fingers clean and instantly regretted it. Junior eyes trailed them to her mouth as if he'd gladly do that service for her. "I'm running late. Gotta go!"

"Have a good time shopping. Pick up a pound of chocolate fudge for me." He cleared the table without further comment.

She raced upstairs to get her straw handbag, but found Junior waiting at the bottom when she returned. Damn, he looked good in anything—worn jeans, a plain white V-necked T-shirt that showed a little curly chest hair, and huge athletic shoes. She'd rein him in immediately. "You can't go with us."

No smile this time. "I got that. Honestly, I really don't like shopping with women. But, I was thinking you might want an escort to the Riverwalk because of those dark men you're seeing around."

Remembering the man with the slim mustache, Xochi sucked in a breath. "Probably just my imagination. You shouldn't take my auras seriously. Connor doesn't."

"I do. Let me walk with you. As soon as you meet Rachelle, I'm gone."

Xochi considered his offer, weighing encouragement of Junior with his major crush against her genuine fear of being followed. "Okay, I appreciate the offer. Let's go."

"I should put on something better than this." Junior gestured to the rather thin, clingy T-shirt that made love to his pecs and six-pack.

"Don't bother."

"Just give me a minute." He took the steps two at a time and returned in seconds with a yellow tropical shirt patterned with large banana leaves and left unbuttoned. Lots of men would have looked ridiculous in it, especially her brother Tom, but not Junior. He came across as one big kahuna.

"This okay? Adam Malala gave it to me. The Sinners hired him to work with me and the rest of the secondary. It's an honor to learn from him."

Modest, too. Xochi simply nodded. "That will be fine. I won't lose you in the crowd." As if you could lose anyone that big and fine in a crowd.

They started down Canal Street, already working up a sweat by the time they reached the wide plaza in front of the newly proclaimed Outlet Collection at Riverwalk. Fanning her gloomy face with her hand, Rachelle waited in a spot of shade.

"You're half an hour late. I swear you could fry chicken on these slates. I'll bet it goes past ninety today." She paused in her tirade. Her angular face brightened. "Say, you shopping with us, Junior? I love having a man along to carry my bags. I'll bet you could carry a lot of luggage." Rachelle's eyes travelled from his feet to his face. "Nice shirt."

"Ah, thanks. I don't think Xo wants me along."

"Why not? The more the merrier."

"He probably has other plans. Don't you, Junior?"

Junior heaved his heavy shoulders. "Just what I usually do, go to the training center and work out."

Rachelle placed her sweaty palm on his rock-hard bicep. "I think missing one day won't turn you to mush. Let's get into the air conditioning." She slid her fingers down his arm and tugged his big hand. Junior shot Xochi a "what can I do?" glance and followed the woman into the wonderfully cool interior of the mall.

Fuming at both of them, Xochi brought up the rear. "Where do you want to start?"

"Oh, oh, the free wine tasting place," Rachelle suggested with enthusiasm.

"The sexy lingerie shop," Junior piped up with a grin.

"Too early for both. Let's just stroll and window shop for a while." Xo took the lead.

They made a short foray into the expensive purse store. Taken with a display in bright soft leather, lime greens, orange, and hot pinks, Xochi checked a few price tags. "They call this a discount? I'd hate to see their normal prices. You could feed a village for a day with this much money."

Junior cupped a hand to his ear. "Do I hear Mama Nell speaking? She never got used to being rich."

"Probably, but that doesn't mean she isn't right."

"If Daddy Joe were here, he'd buy it for you. Let me get one and for you, too, Rachelle."

"Absolutely not!"

"Hey, speak for yourself, kiddo. I clerk part-time in a phony voodoo shop by day and help with the occasional graveyard tour by night. Got one this evening in fact. The tips and the employee discount don't cover designer handbags. Let the man be generous. I like this one." Rachelle picked up a lime green clutch. "Believe it or not, I got a dress this will match."

Junior studied her questionable attire, skinny jeans that showed off a bony rear and a tight scarlet top emphasizing a heavily padded bra. "I believe you. Xo?" Junior waited with patience ruined only by the gotcha smile on his face. He eyed the straw purse she'd brought along—about the size of a beach bag. "I see you like big ones."

"They do come in handy," she admitted.

"We'll take this one." He selected a hot pink tote for her.

Xo cocked her head. "I shouldn't let you do this, but it would enliven my Anchi Services outfits quite a bit."

"Buy it, buy it!" Rachelle chanted loud enough to draw the attention of a roving clerk as stylish as the merchandise.

"You'll take these?" she questioned. Junior nodded. "I'll check you out."

As if she weren't already doing that, Xo thought. He presented a platinum credit card, and the clerk's blue-eyed interest increased as she studied his name. "You played for LSU, right? Got drafted by the Sinners. I'm a big fan of both teams. I might work in a swanky shop, but I can't afford the home game tickets."

Junior, innocent Junior, walked right into her trap. "I'll see you get some passes when the season starts. I won't forget."

They left the store with a large shopping bag stuffed with purses and tissue paper as well as the business card of the blonde with the tight chignon, her home number written on the back. Junior stowed it in a pocket. He'd keep his word, darn it. A bell clanged loudly somewhere in the concourse. Xochi swore Junior's ears pricked.

"The Fudgery show is about to start. Let's go!" Junior broke through the mass of shoppers as if he needed to intercept a wide receiver, but had the consideration to stand in back of women and children whose view he might block. He placed Xochi and Rachelle in front of him as a hefty black woman tipped the contents of a brass kettle onto a marble slab and began working the fudge with a wide paddle. She sang, she swung, she shook her booty, and blended that chocolate fudge with handfuls of pecans until it shaped up into a nice loaf. Buyers began to line up, Junior among them. "Ladies, what's your pleasure?" he asked.

"Creamy vanilla," Rachelle shouted.

"None for me," Xochi said.

"That's okay, you can share mine." He claimed the freshly made loaf of chocolate pecan as well as Rachelle's choice before he backed away from the counter. "One of my favorite stops when my parents brought me here long before it became a discount mall. I wasn't sure they still had a Fudgery."

"And a branch of Café du Monde along with a food court," Rachelle informed him. "We'd better get a real lunch before we snack on fudge."

They settled on MOOYAH Burgers with cups of thick cut fries, shakes for Junior and Rachelle, unsweetened iced tea for Xochi. She asked for her turkey burger in a lettuce wrap while Junior piled the extras on his double along with the free mushrooms and grilled onions. Rachelle went for the classic cheeseburger. As the other two sucked their mint chip shakes, Xochi watched Junior eating with his childhood glee, the juices from the messy burger cascading down his chin. Xo reached out with a napkin, but Rachelle sopped up the mess before it reached the thin line of his beard. Maybe she never had changed his diaper, but she'd sure wiped his face more than once when it was still baby smooth. Her fingertips tingled as she recalled running them along that scrim of beard the other night. Damn Rachelle for usurping her job!

"Let's hit some of the dress stores before this lunch goes to our hips," she said.

"Puleeze! You had an Iceburger and tea. Good thing I don't have to worry. I could use a little more padding, but I just burn the fat off with my boundless energy. That's how I got into salsa dancing. Needed an outlet," Rachelle informed them. She finished the very last fry in the cup she'd shared with Xo and wiped her fingers with a napkin. "Good to go shop for dresses."

Xochi suspected adult ADHD in her friend's case, but refrained from saying so. Rachelle had no education, no boyfriend, and two crappy jobs. She could afford to be kind to the woman who wanted Junior. Except Rachelle wasn't his type. But, who was? He'd admitted to having experience somewhere along the way. With whom? Anyone she knew? Probably not considering the age difference. And why did she care? "Yes, dress shopping. Maybe you want to leave, Junior."

They moved out of the food court and back to the region of high-end shops. Junior paused by the mall's version of Café du Monde. "I'll wait here, get some coffee and beignets, watch the ships go by on the river. Come get me when you're finished."

Before they were out of sight, he'd gotten in line

for his dessert and beverage and remained in the area for all two hours of their excursion into woman world. Most men would have bailed, so add steady and reliable to Junior's résumé. Sharing his fudge with two small children while a tolerant star-struck mother watched, he sat on the deck just beyond the glass door and pointed out a cruise ship moving ponderously past. "Bet it's on its way to Mexico with two-thousand people on board," he told the kids who stared, awed and chocolate smeared. "I've been there. Cool place."

Add *good with children.* Xochi shook her head. She needed coffee to clear her head, but Rachelle had other ideas.

Her dancing buddy dashed over to Junior. "We should hit that wine bar now. I need to refuel."

Junior carefully wrapped his fudge, high-fived his new friends, and accepted the shopping bags Rachelle thrust at him. He went along willingly to sample Louisiana wines. Xo figured with his size and bulk, he could probably down an entire bottle without feeling the effects. She recognized that warm, relaxed feeling spreading through her body after three small samples and cut herself off. Rachelle held out her glass for numbers four, five, and six. Junior purchased a stone fruit wine and bottles of traditional red and a white to go as if to make up for her mooching. "Hey, they got wine smoothies, too," Rachelle hinted.

"It's getting on five o'clock, and I want to treat y'all to dinner at Coop's. Save room for the best jambalaya in the city. We'll eat early since you have a cemetery tour at eight." Deftly, he steered her into the concourse again and toward the exit.

When had Junior become so diplomatic, so grown

up? Xochi recalled his gentle handling of Stacy and her illness as they stepped into the heat that pressed down on them like a panini grill. "Do we gotta walk?" Rachelle complained. "Let's take the trolley, huh."

"Oh, I think a little walking right now might be a good idea. We don't want to arrive too early. We'll stay in the shade." Junior set out bedecked with Loft outlet, Forever 21, and high-end purse bags, not to mention a sack of fudge and a clinking carrier of wine bottles. No one mocked him, unwise to laugh at a guy that big who could carry so much in his two hands.

Xochi hung onto her own modest purchases, a scarf streaked in purple, hot pink, and silver that would match the handbag so well, and an inexpensive lace halter dress in coral with a plunging neckline from Charlotte Russe that would make Junior's eyes bug out when he saw her in it. Not her thought, but Rachelle's when she'd modeled it in front of her. Maybe that idea had been way back in some secret chamber of her mind and better stay there. Xo planned to hang it with her dancing dresses, would never wear it anywhere else despite Rachelle's opinion that if she had boobs that big she'd flaunt them, too.

Rachelle draped an arm around Junior's shoulders as if to say *I'm with this guy*. Didn't he have enough to carry? Perhaps, she needed the stability he offered as they dodged crowds of tourists, kids tap dancing for coins, and stretches of uneven pavement. They neared Jackson Square lightly perfumed with the odor of mule dung from bags hanging beneath the haunches of the carriage animals this late in the day. "Carriage ride?" Rachelle swerved toward the first in the line.

"No, dinner." Junior steered her away and past the

84

park. Not much farther on, they entered Coop's Place with its unpretentious exterior façade and blinking video poker machines illuminating the dim interior. The air smelled slightly of smoke, not from cigarettes but rather from the meat used in their specialties': duck and tasso ham. Being early, their group had little trouble getting a table, but what amazed Xochi was the greeting extended to Junior by the hostess, bartenders, wait staff, and manager, all of whom appeared to know him. He introduced his companions and asked the ladies if he could order for them. Both nodded.

"Rabbit and sausage jambalaya for my friends. Make that the Supreme. I know it's not breakfast, but could you whip up a Hangtown Fry omelet for me?"

"For you, Junior, anything. This young man right here bussed tables and worked in the kitchen free in exchange for learning how to cook our recipes. Never wanted to take his share of the tips. Everybody in the place loved him." The manager gave Junior a friendly slap on the back. "You got their order?" he asked a waitress hovering at his elbow.

"Sure. Great to see you again, Junior." Petite and pretty with a black China doll haircut, her face made edgy with piercings through her eyebrows and nose, the oriental girl gave off a vibe that told Xo there might have been more than tips shared between them. Or maybe she imagined that. "Drinks, ladies?" their waitress asked. "I know Junior wants a Turbo Dog."

"Unsweetened iced tea," Xochi said, primly.

"You have margaritas?" Rachelle asked.

"The bartender can make one."

Junior squeezed Rachelle's hand. "She'll have iced tea." When Rachelle pouted with her thin, red-coated lips, not attractive with magenta hair, he said, "You have to work tonight. Kiki, you finished with art school yet?"

The waitress shook her head. "Another year and I hope I won't be serving food anymore for a living. But, with art you never know."

"You have talent. You'll make it. Say, if you still have that oriental screen you painted, I can afford it now."

Her almond-shaped eyes lit. "There's no one I'd like to have it more. Where are you staying—in that spectacular retro condo? I'll deliver it personally tomorrow afternoon."

"Um, no, with my friend, Xochi here."

Xo narrowed her eyes at him. So, he had stayed at Daddy Joe's place and worked in the city when she assumed he'd been carousing with his football buddies in Cancun or Cozumel like Mack did. He needed someone to show him around New Orleans, did he?

"If that would be awkward…" Kiki said.

Xochi denied it. "Not at all. Junior is a childhood friend I'm putting up until he gets his own place. Besides, I'm going out Sunday afternoon. You'll have time to visit."

"You are?" Junior took a turn at being surprised.

"Connor has a few hours off. We're taking a picnic to City Park to see the sculpture garden."

Their waitress endorsed the date. "That's a great idea! Be sure to go inside NOMA and see the art if you have the time. I hope you like the screen since I guess you'll have it for a while."

"Oh, I think Junior will be getting his own place real soon." Xochi gave him a hard stare.

"Well, better put your order in before we get too busy. Nice meeting you." Kiki knew when to make a quick exit.

An awkward silence fell over the table like a checkered cloth. The clink of billiard balls and a wailing song on the jukebox filled the void. Rachelle did her best to combat it. "Man, I already love this place. No kids allowed because of the poker machines."

Junior tried to keep up his end. "You don't like children?"

Rachelle possessed a rather hawk-like nose that didn't lend itself to wrinkling but the rest of her expression said no. "I'm the oldest of eight. Guess who had to take care of that brood when Ma went to work. Me, me, me. I've wiped enough snotty noses and dirty faces to last a lifetime."

"I noticed you were quick with a napkin back at the food court. Thanks."

"Yeah, I got the skills, but I don't want any of my own. Moved out as soon as I could. How about you?"

"Only child of older parents."

"I used to dream about being an only child." The beer and iced teas arrived. Rachelle gulped half her glass after adding several packets of sugar. "Thirsty from that trek over here."

That and all the wine she'd swilled, but Xochi kept her self-imposed silence until Kiki set down an overflowing bread basket. "Extra for you, Junior." Then, she mumbled ungraciously, "Just what I need, extra bread," as the other two helped themselves and slathered on the butter.

"So, you want a family?" Rachelle asked just prior to stuffing her face with French bread.

"Well, I wasn't lonely with all the Billodeauxs around, but I think I'd like to have more than two but way less than twelve."

Xochi forgot she wasn't speaking to him. "*You* won't have any children! Your wife will do all the work of squeezing out those huge, big-headed babies you want. Twelve pounds, you were a twelve-pound baby. Your mother had to have a section done to get you out."

Rachelle gulped and not on her iced tea. Under her garish makeup, she turned a little pale, covered all that with a laugh, a comment, and a change of subject. "Xo is way more fun at Paco's. Anyhow, you ever been on a cemetery tour, Junior?"

"No, never had time for it when I was in the city."

"Because I could get you in free tonight. I'm just learning the tour right now. Mostly I bring up the rear and make sure we don't lose anybody. You could help me wrangle the tourists. I'll bet there won't be any purse snatching with you around."

"I don't have any other plans, do I, Xo?"

"I wouldn't know. Your plans are your own same as mine."

"Okay, I'll go."

The food arrived with Kiki deftly setting the healthy portions in front of them. Junior's omelet burst with fried oysters, bacon, and cheddar cheese next to a pile of fries. Large bowls held the rice mixture displaying cubes of ham, chunks of rabbit, curls of crawfish, and a rim decorated with sizeable shrimp. A nice topping of chopped green onions gave color to the dish. Xochi was forced to agree with the best jambalaya in the city designation.

"I know how to make it, but it's getting the right

ingredients like that tasso," Junior said, not bragging, just saying.

"You can make it for me anytime. Let me have one of your oysters." Rachelle opened her mouth, and he popped one in with his fingertips. Evidently, he had no problem sharing food or a fear of germs. She closed her lips and left behind a suggestive red ring around one digit. Who knew where that mouth of Rachelle's had been in the last twenty-four hours? What Xo didn't like was her friend's usually lovely pink aura indicating her eternal optimism that she'd finally pick up a good guy at Paco's or in a bar and live happily ever after rather than using her round heels to rebound again and again. That aura had picked up little tinges of Junior's deep violet. Xochi couldn't deny Junior's good guy status, but really, could he be falling for Rachelle?

When Kiki returned to ask if everything was okay, she noticed the girl's sunny yellow aura had also acquired a corona of indigo. Did everyone love Junior or did that strength of his simply rub off on them? "Box, please." Xo said. "I can't eat all this." Meanwhile Rachelle mopped her bowl with another slice of bread.

Junior finished the last of his fries and asked for the check. Maybe the waitress got that extra glow from the thirty percent tip he left. "We'd better get going if we want to walk Xochi home and arrive at the voodoo shop in time for the seven o'clock tour."

"No need to go out of your way. I can get home by myself." Xochi picked up her box of jambalaya and gathered her shopping bags.

Junior loaded Rachelle's baggage and the wine. "Not going to happen. We'll walk with you in case any of the dark guys are lurking."

"Dark guys are all over this city," Rachelle said, puzzled.

"No arguments. Let's roll."

They delivered Xochi to her door. Junior turned over his fudge, the wine, and the hot pink handbag before marching off with Rachelle still loaded with her purchases. Settling in for a quiet evening, Xo put away her leftovers and purchases. She got comfortable and found a movie on TV to pass the time. Her apartment seemed empty without Junior filling the space. He'd soon be back, and they'd have a talk about living arrangements. The tour started at seven, well before dark this time of year. When the movie ended, she checked her watch. Nine p.m., he'd be home fairly soon. At ten-thirty, she ate more fudge than she should have and watched some of the late shows. By midnight, she still sat up waiting for her boy to come home like some over anxious mother. At twelve-thirty, she heard his heavy tread on the stairs.

"Exactly how long was this cemetery tour?" she offered in greeting as he entered the living room.

"Two hours, Mom. Gee, did I break my curfew?" He enjoyed making fun of her concern a little too much judging by the smirk on his face. "Rachelle had to help wait on customers at the voodoo shop where the tour started and ended. Afterward, we stopped in at Pat O'Brien's for a few drinks, then I saw her home. She lives in a kind of dicey area. I couldn't let her go alone."

"She invited you in, right?"

"Yep. I feel sorry for the girl. She tries too hard to get attention, but I didn't pity her enough to go inside."

Xo realized she had no idea where Rachelle lived,

or in what conditions. They met at Paco's or the mall or wherever. In fact, her dancing friend had only been to the Canal Street apartment a couple of times, once to sleep off a really bad drunk that made Xochi afraid to put her in a cab and another when a short-lived boyfriend blacked her eye. All this made Xo feel pretty small for being jealous. Yes, call it what it is, jealous of the time Rachelle spent alone with Junior.

"You should have come along, real interesting in St. Louis Number One. All sorts of people buried there besides Marie Laveau: Etienne de Bore who discovered how to granulate sugar, Homer Plessy of the Civil Rights case, Delphine LeLaurie, the sadistic slave owner, and Nicolas Cage who is going to be. He bought a pyramid-shaped tomb in there." Junior moved to the kitchen and returned with a large glass of milk and a handful of the peanut butter cookies he'd baked earlier in the week wrapped in a napkin. "Want one?"

"No, I overdid on the fudge."

"Glad you enjoyed it so much. You got a little right here on your chin." He erased it with his thumb and licked its pad. Was he trying to tempt her?

"Did you make a wish at Marie Laveau's tomb?" She knew what he wanted.

"Heck, no! Rachelle knocked a marker out of the hand of one our group who tried to put an X on it, do the knock, turn around three times, and shout out what you want to Marie. There's big fine for that now, and the tour company will lose its forty-five hundred dollar license to show the place if they let any vandalism happen. You can still see some of the crosses others made even though the Diocese pressure-washed it a few years back after someone dumped pink paint all over the tomb. There are some dumb shits in this town."

"Agreed. We need to get some sleep if we're getting up for early Mass."

"Yeah, forgot about that." He gulped the last of the milk and wiped the cookie crumbs from that bit of a mustache before she could do it for him. A tinge of regret passed through Xochi. "About your date with Connor, could I…"

She stood up in her robe and would have stomped her slippers if they'd made any noise. "No! You absolutely cannot go along. And don't show up *accidently* at the art museum like Tom did when he followed Alix around."

Junior's face mimed hurt. "I was going to say I'd make a heart healthy lunch for you and the doc to take to the park. Besides, Kiki is coming over, remember?"

"Oh, right. No need. We agreed to pick a Central Grocery muffaletta and get some drinks." The heat rose up in her face.

"You think he's going to approve of all that ham and salami and cheese?"

"Connor is an orthopedic surgeon, not a heart doctor. Half a muffaletta won't kill him."

"I guess not," Junior said almost as if he hoped it might.

"Well, if you and Kiki get busy, put a sock on the door. I don't want to walk in on anything."

Junior rose up to his full and imposing height. "I believe we are also going to be discussing art." Having taken the high road, he brought his milk glass to the sink to be washed and left Xochi standing there without another word to say.

Chapter Nine

Xo used the shower first before waking Junior for Mass on Sunday morning. Only took two minutes of pounding on his door to do that. If he hoped for a more personal wakeup call like a gentle shake of his enormous shoulders as she bent over the bed, he would not get it. She shouted that the bathroom was his and not to eat before leaving. They made the early service at nine a.m. easily. He took communion to her surprise.

"You've been to confession?" Xochi whispered as they lined up for a space at the communion rail to receive the host.

"I worked it into my busy schedule. Nothing much to confess but impure thoughts. I was hoping for more by now." She elbowed him in the ribs, not that he felt it.

By ten-fifteen, they'd squeezed through the maze of tables at Café du Monde and secured seats near the sidewalk. "You see any of those dark guys today?" Junior asked after they'd placed their orders for the usual, beignets and café au lait.

"No, never in church. Last time they were lingering outside and in the park. Not today. Eat slowly. Connor is going to meet me here and parking is always a problem. In the meantime, we should have a discussion about your getting your own place. I'm setting a two-week deadline for you since you lied about knowing New Orleans. I'll bet you've been on a cemetery tour before and didn't tell Rachelle."

"Nope, when I spent time in the city, I worked on my culinary skills. No time for tourist stuff. Only two weeks, that's harsh." He gave her the puppy dog eyes again, and she closed hers, blotting out their effect.

"You just wanted to get into my—apartment."

"Hey, I buy groceries, I cook, I clean up, asking nothing in return but the sunshine of your presence."

Xo had seriously dark eyes, large and lustrous, which she knew how to roll at cheesy compliments. "How much time did you actually spend in Mexico because that sounds like a Latino pickup line if I ever heard one?"

In the process of lifting another powered sugar heaped beignet to his lips, Junior snorted and blew a cloud across the deep green dress shirt, sleeves rolled up now, he'd worn with black slacks and a gold tie now stuffed in a pocket for church. Xochi refrained from dusting off that massive chest, and let him do it himself. He seemed disappointed.

"I spent enough time there to polish up my Spanish, *querida*. Stayed with my mother's relatives. No lying about that."

"Good, but you still get two weeks and out." Why did her firmness pinch a little in her heart? When would Connor get here and rescue her from rescinding her demand?

Junior called for a second order and worked through it just before the doctor showed up hoofing it from the Jax Brewery lot, a sheen already on his lean, intellectual face, his wire-rimmed glasses foggy from the humidity. Connor wiped them with a pink pocket square taken from his pale gray jacket pocket. "Sorry,

I'm a little late. I'd forgotten about the New Orleans traffic and the parking problems."

"Better take that coat off. You're gonna stroke out from the heat. You ain't in Baltimore anymore," Junior advised.

"I'm sure I can find something to hydrate with at the grocery and the amount of salt in those sandwiches will surely restore the balance of my bodily fluids. Thanks for your concern."

"Any time," Junior replied as if he regretted the warning and wished the guy would pass out on the sidewalk, maybe right now. Xo dug in her purse, the hot pink one he'd bought for her, searching for her wallet. "I got it. Go have a nice art walk."

"I'm sure we will. You have a great visit with Kiki."

"Kiki?" Connor raised critical eyebrows. "Sounds like a stripper name."

"An artist's name," Junior corrected. "Because I know real artists."

"Good for you. I know medical specialists who can put you back together again, way more useful."

Xochi made her way fast around the iron railing to join Connor who had been leaning in from the sidewalk. "Let's go get our sandwich order in before Central Grocery has a line." She dragged him off before another pissing contest could take place.

They entered the battered old door with the red surround and inhaled all manner of things Italian, strong cheeses in the deli case and hard salamis hanging from hooks, briny olives and sweet basil, a hint of garlic. Early, they still had to take a number, but gathered other items for their picnic while they waited, water and soft drinks and a bag of Stella D'Oro cookies for dessert. The huge wheel of the sandwich dripping with the olive salad over the cold cuts came severed into quarters and wrapped heavily in butcher paper. Xo, worried about her new purse, asked for an additional plastic bag and stowed all within. Confident in his masculinity, Connor offered to carry the hot pink bag, but Xo said she could manage. They weren't that far from his car—which had already heated up enough to melt the cheese in the muffaletta.

The air-conditioning barely kicked in by the time they drove to City Park and found a space not too far from the art museum. Still full of beignets, Xochi suggested they walk a while before eating. Thanks to the benefactors, Sydney and Walda Besthoff, the sculpture garden boasting over sixty pieces of art remained free to the public. They found the site for the audio walking tour on their phones and entered the perimeter to stroll through the pine and magnolia grove and around the lagoon studded with art in the water. Reaching the deeper shade of the two-hundred-year-old live oaks, she and Connor laid out their lunch on a bench between them.

Xochi noted he ate as meticulously as he dressed, no olive oil shiny lips for Connor Bullock or cookie crumbs on his chest to be whisked away by her fingers. He had conceded to the climate, shed his jacket, rolled up his sleeves, and opened his collar, but he still seemed very buttoned down.

Of course, they discussed the art. Connor was not impressed by the glass baubles bedecking one of the oaks or the giant safety pin. He referred to *Venus Victorious* as chubby and *Big Mama* as obese.

"When the Venus was created, being fleshy was in style. I hate to think how you'd describe me if I were a sculpture." She'd dribbled some of the juice from the sandwich down the front of the patterned cotton dress she'd worn to church. At least the small flowers of the print helped disguise the stain, but Connor hadn't tried to wipe it off.

A man who thought before he spoke, Connor paused a moment before answering. "I'd say you are voluptuous and in the prime of womanhood—but you'll have to be careful of your diet after thirty and especially after menopause when women really pack it on. You could wind up looking like Junior's mother."

"One of the best people I know. Who cares if she's fat? What did you think of *Heroic Man*?" Junior's pledge that he would love her fat or thin, young or old, flashed through Xochi's mind as she removed her hand from the cookie bag, closed it, and shoved the sack back into her purse.

"Reminded me of Junior all bulked up, but the head is too small to make the resemblance complete."

"Are you saying Junior is conceited—because he is truly modest about his talents. I believe he still thinks of himself as a fat kid."

"I was speaking physiologically. He does have a big head, and I do recall him as an overfed blob of a child until the dads got him into football. Even then, it took years to convert all that mass into muscle. Right now, he's working out hard, but when he retires, he'll have to be careful, too."

"But I suspect he'll always be sweet and kind like your father."

"My dad is a minister. That goes without saying. It

must be hard to maintain in the face of all the evil in the world. I hate to say it, but the Rev is a heart attack waiting to happen despite my mom's best efforts to control his diet. He can't say no to anything at those church dinners, and ladies keep bringing fried chicken and cakes by the house."

"Because they love him and want to show thanks."

"Yeah, they're loving him to death."

That dampened the mood like the humidity did her dress. "Let's walk some more." Xochi rolled up the sandwich wrapper to be disposed of later with the drink cans and bottles, her purse weighing a lot less now. Maybe toting it through the garden had worked off the muffaletta calories. She hoped so.

"I think my favorite pieces are *Monkeys* and that ladder leading up to the window, just hanging there in space. They're clever and whimsical."

"Here's one we can both agree upon." Connor took her arm and pulled her behind a sculpture that spelled out LOVE. His lips were thin and dry, not matching hers very well. He didn't try to gain entrance to her mouth, but cupped her cheeks with those long, slim fingers, soft and expert with none of the hardness Junior's had developed from the thwack of the footballs. Pleasant and experienced without becoming too intimate, the kiss wasn't bad for a first try, but where did Connor hide his passion, his zing? Not there, not yet.

Two teens separating themselves from a group of parents ran ahead and photographed them through the opening in the big O of the letters. "Do it again," they insisted. Connor moved in, but Xochi shook her head and went back to the path.

"Awesome bag," one of the girls proclaimed.

"Thanks, a friend bought it for me." She walked swiftly away.

Connor slowed her down by taking her hand. "Not into PDAs, huh?"

"Not into showing up on Pinterest or Instagram."

Then, she saw him, the man with the thin mustache and black aura. He smoked a slim cigarillo and sullied the ground of the sculpture garden with his flicked ashes. "*Buenos dias*," he said cordially as he passed, but Xochi thought he might have been following them for some time.

"We should go. The heat is getting to me."

Connor checked his expensive watch. "Right. I need to get back, too."

They lost no time returning to the car and leaving the park. Connor dropped Xo by her door and waited for her to go inside before leaving. Not knowing what she would find, she tread upstairs putting some oomph into her steps to give Junior and Kiki fair warning. Upon entering the living room, a traditional tri-fold oriental screen blocked her view of the plum-colored sofa. Beyond it, a series of grunts and groans originated. What was she supposed to do—assume the lotus position, contemplate the exquisite screen, and pretend she did not hear?

The artwork did deserve her minute contemplation. It portrayed a garden, very traditional in Japanese art, but departed from there with poufs of gold and silver flowers on lavender stems. Fantastical insects and butterflies flitted among the leaves and small, charming imaginary beasts peered from the foliage. Kiki truly was an artist, not a stripper. Another deep groan obviously belonging to Junior sounded beyond the screen. Perhaps, she should back up and retreat quietly downstairs, go to the coffee shop across the street, and give them some time. The leftover cookies in her bag would go well with a black brew.

Acting hastily on her thoughts, Xochi tripped over her own feet and very nearly punched a hole in the screen as she windmilled to regain her balance. It wobbled dangerously and would have crashed to the floor if Junior hadn't been there, huge and barefooted but otherwise dressed, to steady it. "Xo? Why don't you join us instead of abusing the art?"

"A threesome on the sofa? No, thanks."

Junior laughed, big like he was. "No, in a foot rub. Kiki gives the best, another of her many talents. She's teaching me exactly where to press."

The top of Kiki's head appeared beside him, the girl not as tall as her screen. She must have used a footstool while painting it. "Yeah, shiatsu is another of my part time jobs, massaging the feet of weary tourists. Sometimes, they tip better than the restaurant clientele."

"Because they are really grateful. Few people want to rub feet. By the way, this screen is simply magnificent. I, um, tripped and nearly damaged it. Very sorry. Anyhow, it is worth whatever you asked for it."

"Junior to the rescue. He's always there if you need him. Come on, since you've been walking in the park you could probably use a massage. Isn't the sculpture garden abso mag? Let me do you. Junior, watch and learn." Kiki moved around the screen and took Xochi's hand to move her to the purple sofa and take off her shoes. "Lean back, relax. You have strong feet. Junior tells me you love to dance."

"Ah, yes. I hope you meant muscles and not stink."

Kiki laughed musically like tiny wind chimes stirred by a soft breeze. "I've smelled worse. Junior, observe." She began pressing her fingers and palms on various parts of Xo's sole, sometimes pausing to stretch the foot. Xochi tried hard to suppress a low moan very similar to the ones she'd heard when she entered the room, but it escaped against her will.

"Now Junior, you try on the other foot."

He knelt on the floor, and Kiki delivered Xo's heel into his wide palm. His long, thick thumbs covered more area than the girl's delicate hands. Powerful, too. Xochi groaned. As he continued, she experienced something akin to sexual arousal, a definite dampening, a desire to stretch out full length on the divan and offer herself to her masseur. She yanked her foot from Junior's grip. "Thanks, I enjoyed that."

"Ask me anytime." Junior stared at his hands as if her very relaxed toes still rested there right above his crotch. She thought he might be hiding something as well.

Kiki glanced at her My Little Kitty watch. "I need to get over to Coop's for the dinner setup. Those ketchup bottles don't fill themselves." The petite artist tugged Junior's earlobes. "Also an erogenous zone, the earlobe. I appreciate everything you did for me. That sale is rent and tuition all wrapped up in green."

She kissed Junior smack on the lips and gave his lobe a tiny tweak. Observing from her place on the sofa, Xochi thought their lips didn't fit well together, hers much too tiny, lost on his, but it ended quickly. Kiki rounded her screen and pattered down the stairs.

Alone with Junior and still slightly aroused, Xochi

repeated, "Two weeks. Having you here is messing with my decision-making process. I need space to think." She stood to give more authority to her words.

So did he. "About what?"

"Not ready to discuss it yet."

"You can tell me anything." Dammit, he leaned down and kissed her, their lips so attuned they almost vibrated—like the rest of her. Her bare feet curled, and she stood on his to better meet his height. Her hands came up, holding him in place. His roved across the sensitive sides of her breasts, down her back, and cupped her bottom. She had to push back, had to, because she felt his arousal matching her own.

"Stop! You need to go. Two weeks." Leaving her shoes behind, she scampered away up the stairs to her bedroom, locked the door though she knew he wouldn't follow, and threw herself on the duvet. Feeling cowardly and weak, Xochi pounded the covers with her fists. She needed to make up her mind, and soon.

Chapter Ten

Junior cupped his hands around the big white coffee mug and took a swallow of the coffee made in Tom's pod machine. He brewed a much better beverage, but wasn't about to alienate sympathetic ears by saying so. Alix sat on one side and Tom on the other at their dining room table. He'd already consoled himself with several slices of her almond-flavored Bundt cake gently drizzled with frosting, topped with slivered nuts, and far better than the drink.

"So, Xo wants me to move out in two weeks. Says she needs space to think."

Tom bobbed his curly red head. "Her place is a lot smaller, and you do take up a lot of room."

Alix shook hers, straight white-blonde hair flying. "That's not what she means, Tom. Junior's large presence is distracting her, probably sexually."

"See, that's why I wanted Alix to stay. Get a woman's perspective. Any ideas how I can keep from getting kicked out? I mean I want her to be aware of me—sexually."

"Watch it. Xo is my sister." Tom stuffed a piece of cake into his mouth before he said too much, chewed, considered, swallowed. "I mean I think you are a great guy and would treat her right, but that's up to her. You should back off."

"But, you and Alix lived here together until you

worked things out between you."

"Doesn't work for everyone. There might be an apartment in Daddy Joe's building."

"Yeah, Brian Lightfoot and Howdy McCoy still live there. That would be like having two meddling uncles checking up on me."

"Didn't you stay there last summer?"

"Sure, but Howdy, your mom, and half-sibs were at the Oklahoma ranch most of the time, and Uncle Brian was distracted by Derek Steele. I mean mostly I worked at Coop's day and night and hardly had any girls over."

"Then you didn't do Daddy Joe's old bachelor pad justice. If those walls could talk. I guess you didn't remove Mama Nell's plants from the bidet." Tom stood to make himself another cup of coffee.

"No, I promised to keep them watered. The location made that easy. Kiki called it whimsical. I'd say practical."

"Oooh, Kiki, the artist, waitress, foot massager, not a stripper, and former lover," Alix reeled off.

"Who told you all that?"

"Xo when she called late last night because she couldn't sleep. With Stacy sick, she didn't want to wake her, but needed another woman to listen. I'm proud to be that woman. She says Rachelle gossips too much." Alix took a second slice of cake. They'd worked out hard that morning at the training center and a bunch of carbs refueled all three of them.

"Yeah, we aren't sick so she didn't mind bothering us," Tom grumped. Obviously, Xo's call interrupted something.

"I am getting to her then," Junior said with a hopeful note in his voice. He gazed out the window across broad Canal Street to Xochi's apartment knowing she'd be at work. This morning, she'd turned down his offer to escort her to the trade center, but had eaten the blueberry pancakes he made. "Any chance there is an opening here?"

"I think the second floor is on the market," Alix offered before Tom could put a hand over her mouth.

"Look, I promise I wouldn't be up here all the time, and I'd be near if Xochi needed me."

"Not another guy pining for his lady love across the street like Dean did over Stacy," Alix just had to mention. She followed that with a girly sigh.

Tom rushed in to defend his brother's manhood. "Dean didn't pine when he broke up with Stacy. He took up with another woman because that's what guys do when someone rejects them."

"Good thing I didn't move out when we were fighting," Alix said. "We all know how Dean's fling with Ilsa turned out."

"Beck is a great kid, illegitimate or not. I wouldn't mind having a son like that."

"Later," Alix said. "I have a football career going on. Junior, you and Kiki are over, right? You wouldn't go back to her because Xochi is a little confused right now."

"No, right from the start we both knew it was just recreational, but I have to say Daddy Joe is right. Those tiny women can surprise you. Kiki said she loved to climb big trees and suck on lollipops as child. She proved it."

"TMI. I might be a football player, but I'm still a girl. I don't need to hear any more about your exploits with Kiki. If you move into this building, I want you to promise me no other women until Xo makes up her mind about you."

"Honey, we can't stop him from leasing here."

"The management will want references, and they'll ask us because he's a Sinner."

Junior's large hands abandoned the coffee mug and slammed against the heavy wooden table as if he'd splinter it to pieces. "I don't want anyone but Xochi, but I'm not so sure about her." He dug in his jeans pocket for his phone. "See here all over Facebook, shared and reshared. 'On our vacay to NOLA, we spotted Xochi Billodeaux making out behind the LOVE statue with this sexy guy. How cool is that?' Xo forgets your entire family is famous. She should be more careful about her PDAs. Alix, do you think Connor Bullock is sexier than me?"

Alix cocked her head to the side and studied Junior. "Connor isn't my type, but he's very serious and smooth and yes, good looking. The kiss isn't very hot though. You aren't really my type either. I go for tall, skinny redheads."

"I guarantee I kiss better than that. Xo's toes curled right on top of my feet yesterday when I kissed her after the massage."

Tom's freckled face reddened. "You gave my sister a massage? Better have been one with all her clothes on like at the airport."

"A foot massage. Kiki told me they can be very arousing. She was right. I could feel the vibes between Xo and me and this rush of heat. Then, she pushed me away."

"Okay, I don't need any more details. Might be a good idea if you moved in downstairs right away. I'll endorse you."

"If you teach Tom how to do that foot massage, you have my vote," Alix said, grinning at her husband.

"You two are like rabbits, big white rabbits doing it all the time."

"Yeah," Tom said almost boasting.

"I have a purer reason for wanting to stay near Xochi. Did she tell you about the black men she sees? I'm afraid for her."

"Black men? Xochi is interested in multiple black men?" Alix's fair complexion pinked up a little. "I guess I don't know her that well after all."

"No, no, no! She sees these guys with black auras and thinks they are following her."

"If Xo says they are, then they are. She can read people the way we read play books." Tom wrinkled his freckled forehead.

"I know she's frightened because she wants me to continue going to church with her even if I don't live at her place anymore. She always sees them lurking around Jackson Square after Mass."

"You still go to Mass, do confession, all that rigmarole? I quit after I got out from under Mawmaw Nadine's thumb. We're going to raise our kids Lutheran, right, babe?"

"When we get around to having them. We aren't exactly good church attenders now, but I can volunteer to go with her regardless of not knowing what happens at a Catholic Mass. That would have to stop when football season begins because of Sunday games, but I could escort her the rest of the summer."

Junior observed Tom's usually jovial face droop. There went his leisurely off-season Sundays with morning sex, Alix's Swedish pancakes with lingonberry jelly, and more sex after they'd read the *Times-Picayune*, diminished though it was. He'd mentioned it often enough. Tom reached across Junior to take his wife's pale hand. "I'd have to go with you because you'd be in danger, too, a beautiful blonde like you." He leaned forward to gaze into Alix's wide blue eyes.

Talk about feeling in the way. Junior pushed back his chair to retreat from the love fest. To him, Alix appeared to be a very tall, somewhat broad-shouldered woman in peak physical condition, who could most likely kick the shit out of any man who accosted her. She'd make a great bodyguard, but Tom treated his wife as if she were as delicate as the mystical flowers on Kiki's screen. Junior stood without commenting on this.

"Thanks, Alix, but I really want to look after Xochi and don't mind going to church. My mama still makes me attend whenever I'm home at the ranch. Doesn't matter how much bigger or taller I am than Mom, she always guilts me into it."

Another thought suddenly entered Junior's mind. "Xo is fairly devout, not like the rest of us. Do you think she is considering becoming a nun? She keeps saying she needs to make an important decision in her life, and I'm interfering with that."

"She never mentioned anything to me," Alix said, eyes wide. "Lutherans don't have that problem. I mean I can see how giving up salsa dancing and sex would be a really big deal to her."

"Sure, my sister goes to Mass every week, but a nun? I don't think so." Tom gave an emphatic shake of his head. "She'd tell me first before Stacy or Alix. We share a bloodline."

"Good. I'm relieved. Wonderful cake, Alix," Junior said eyeing the quarter that remained. "You've both been a great help. I'm going downstairs right now and see if I can get a lease on the second floor. You'll give that reference, right?"

"He's a young man of good character. He attends church regularly," Alix replied, while Tom guffawed. "Take the rest of the cake. I'm going to make another one today, chocolate maybe." She wrapped the hunk in foil, handed it over to Junior, and waved him out the door.

He went directly to the office and applied. Acceptance did not come immediately, but few could afford such prime real estate. With an endorsement from his upstairs neighbors and Reverend Bullock as a reference, he would be sure to get the place. Might as well do a little furniture shopping in the meantime. With mini-camp coming up, he'd be short on time in the near future. Number one on the list: a king-sized bed. He wouldn't admit it to Xo, not ever, but Stacy's old queen-sized mattress really didn't fit his far bigger body. Maybe he'd get memory foam, great for aching bodies and no springs to squeak during the sex act. With that happy thought in mind, he crossed the street to spend his final days as Xochi's roommate. Next time, he wanted to be more.

Chapter Eleven

After leaving the cake at the apartment, time weighed heavily on Junior's hands. He went out to do mattress shopping and found himself with an entire set of bedroom furnishings on order by the time he left the store that had memory foam on sale. An attractive young black woman with a wonderful smile encouraged him to lay on any mattress he chose. Did he want the bed adjustable, firm or soft or medium? Maybe adjustable would be good in case he broke anything playing football and probably medium, the way he liked his steaks. Glorius—because that was her name—laughed at his joke.

She laid a hand with beautiful gold nails striped in purple for LSU, all but the thumbnail, which possessed a small tiger decal, on his arm. No doubt she recognized him. Glorious led him to a bedroom set she felt certain suited his masculinity. Dark wood, but contemporary, substantial with clean lines, not fussy. Before he knew it, he'd purchased a massive dresser with handsome gold drawer pulls and a huge mirror, two matching end tables, a set of tall brass lamps with modern parchment shades, and a vast padded headboard that exactly matched his skin tone, or so Glorious claimed as she held his hand against its soft, suede texture. "Just stroke that and imagine how good it will feel against your back."

"I'll take it all, the whole room, but I need to hold off on delivery until I sign the lease on my place."

"We can do that." Glorious gave him her truly glorious smile. He figured she worked on commission until she offered to help him with any other interior decorating needs on her own time. Tempting, very tempting as she had full breasts and a bodacious booty shoved into a dress that showed both off to advantage.

Junior began to see how staying true to Xochi as a pro football player might be a struggle, but he was a man up to the task. He turned down the offer. "I'm using a friend's decorator." As he recalled, Dean and Tom described the woman who did their place as motherly, middle-aged, and handpicked by Mama Nell. He'd go with her.

Stopping for groceries for the evening meal made him late. Junior planned on crispy fried catfish rolled in cornmeal, a large salad, and biscuits with honey-butter. Making sure all the ingredients were fresh slowed him down. When he arrived at the apartment, he found Xochi, a go-cup of coffee at her side, cramming Bundt cake into her mouth at the kitchen table.

"Hey, you'll ruin your dinner as both our mamas used to say. I planned on that for dessert."

"So, I had my dessert first. There's still a piece for you. I didn't eat it all, if that's what you're worried about."

"Nope. I had plenty when I visited Tom and Alix. She sure can bake."

"I can't," Xo replied, as if this were a major flaw and a reason they could never be together. "Your mother did all the baking while we were running around at soccer games, playing in the pool, and riding the ponies."

"She didn't mind. Mamacita loves to cook for people. That's why I got so big. I'll show you how to make her biscuits tonight, the recipe she got from Mawmaw Nadine so you know how good."

"I remember them. Melt in your mouth."

"Up, and we'll get started. Pop them in the oven while I fry the fish. You can make the salad."

Xochi eyed the sacks of fresh produce. "You can't just buy it in a bag? Only the best for you?"

"That's right. I only want the best." He let her know with his warm eyes, the way he leaned in as she rose that included her, at least he hoped so. She ducked under his arm and frantically began washing field greens, dicing heirloom tomatoes, and slicing the red orbs of radishes, dumping all into a large wooden bowl.

"Okay, I'll whip up those biscuits." He did, cutting the elastic floured dough into circles with the top of a glass for lack of a better tool and putting them in the oven. Meanwhile, the oil heated in the frying pan on the stove. Junior dredged the catfish filets, once in flour, then in an egg wash, and finally in the seasoned cornmeal. The grease splattered as he lowered them into the pan. Xochi, making herself useful, set the table, and with Junior's directions whisked a simple vinaigrette dressing together. He softened butter in the microwave and blended it with honey about the time the biscuits came from the oven nicely browned and the fish curled crispy at the edges. Xochi poured iced tea with lemon. They sat at the kitchen table to eat.

"Heaven," Xo said as she slathered the honey-butter on her second hot biscuit. "The catfish is as good as any I've had in a restaurant. You really are exceptional, Junior."

He paused with a forkful of salad halfway to his mouth. "You finally noticed."

"An exceptional cook, I meant, and you'll be a great football player, too." She backed away from her previous words, stumbling verbally as she had physically against the exquisite oriental screen. "I'll-I'll miss having meals with you when you move out."

"I found a place right across the street in Tom's building, second floor. I'll be out of your hair as soon as they approve the paperwork." Her long, flowing black hair that he wanted to tangle with his fingers. He forced the thought aside and put his hand in the biscuit basket instead.

"So soon. I thought you'd wait until the last minute."

Did he detect regret in her voice? "If you'll be happier with me gone, I'm gone. In fact, I bought a bedroom set today with a king-sized mattress from a very helpful young lady at the furniture store."

"I'll just bet she was."

Junior hoped that remark indicated jealousy. "She offered to help me decorate."

"Is that so?"

"Yep. But, I'd rather have your opinion."

"Maybe I could make some suggestions."

"I still plan to walk you to church on Sunday. I want you to be safe." Junior covered her hand with his. He felt the warmth surge up his arm. Didn't she feel the same? Her eyes said she did, but she swiftly lowered her lashes.

"No need this week. I'm going to Chapelle to take care of some business and visit with the folks."

"I could drive you."

"No, I need to go alone. Stacy is loaning me her car. We'll have a long talk when I get back. Maybe clear some things up, I promise."

"Like you and Connor all over the internet? Him, not me?" If that statement didn't show jealousy, none did. Junior knew he should have held that in, but it sat on his tongue like the bitterness of the field greens.

"Let me see!" She seized the phone he waggled in front of her outraged face. "Oh, no, I warned Connor. He isn't used to being a celebrity."

"Seems he isn't used to kissing either. This is how you should be kissed." Junior raised her from her chair by both elbows, not rough but assertive. Tossing the phone aside, he smoothed her round cheeks with his thumbs and went for the sweet taste of her mouth. He claimed the right to run his fingers into her dark hair and down her back, pressing her closer to his body every moment. The heat between them mounted.

They melted against each other like honey-butter on biscuits, one so much better with the other. She still wore her Anchi Services dress with the fuller skirt she'd campaigned for with Stacy. Knee-length and professional, it still hiked up easily when Junior ran his hands down her thighs to the hem and up again to discover Xochi wore silky bikini pants beneath it, and the crotch of those panties had dampened in the little time he'd extended the kiss. He rubbed a finger against them lightly, then harder. She hadn't pushed him away yet. When she moaned, he worked his way past the silk and applied more pressure. She came against his hand so suddenly he drew back just as her nails raked down his shirt. Xochi murmured, "Stop, we have to stop

114

now."

"Why?" he muttered into her hair, redolent of tropical blossoms as he knew it would be.

"Because there is so much you don't know about me. Wait only a little while longer. Please."

She'd asked him to wait, and he would. He lowered her skirt, straightened her dress, even finger-combed her mussed hair as if they had to face a set of angry parents after breaking curfew. "I'm going to clean up the dinner dishes now."

"Yes, that's what we should do."

Good as he was going to get for now, he figured. Junior Polk knew when to hold the line and when to rush.

Chapter Twelve

To her immense surprise, Dean suggested Xochi take his black Mustang convertible instead of Stacy's silver Lexus sedan. "Too much trouble to take the baby seats out of the back," he said like an experienced family man and a generous brother. He tossed her the keys. "Don't wreck it."

Now, she tooled along the road to Chapelle with the top down, her eyes shaded by large sunglasses, and her hair held in place somewhat by a hot pink visor that matched the handbag on the seat next to her. She wore a dress as bright yellow as the hot, sunny day. For these three hours on the road, she let go of all her troubles and enjoyed the breeze whipping her hair out behind, keeping the sweat off her neck and shoulders.

Too bad she'd attracted a pickup truck around Morgan City crammed with brown young men who decided to play highway tag with her, first passing at a high rate of speed as they hooted, honked and waved, then slowing until she had to pass them. They'd tailgate for a few miles, pass, and begin the game again. The exit for Chapelle lay ahead. She veered off without using her turn signal, causing the pickup to overshoot the back road into town. Xo doubted they'd bother to seek the next annoying J-turn recently installed on the highway allowing cars to safely reverse directions. Didn't those boys realized she was much too old to be impressed by this type of juvenile courtship?

Her hometown surrounded by sugarcane fields lay on a flat ridge along the bayou, but this particular approach featured several rolling hills before reaching the plateau. She accelerated creating a fun rollercoaster ride as the big engine surged. At the top of one hill, she glanced in her rearview mirror and spotted the same pickup truck cresting another and coming on fast, but she knew Chapelle and they most likely did not. Nearing the city limits, she slowed to forty-five, then braked to thirty-five sedately entering town. Xo gave a friendly wave to the cops running a speed trap with their squad car hidden by a tall ligustrum hedge that also provided a little shade. They knew all the Billodeauxs and waved back. She turned onto Main and then again into the old neighborhood of small white cottages, some well kept, some not. In the distance, she heard the siren of the squad car activate and smiled. So long, boys.

Xochi sought out the house with the shrine to the Virgin Mary in a bathtub shell on the front lawn. Marigolds bedecked the statue's feet, and one whitewashed rock stood out amongst their brilliant yellow color. Xo parked and made her way up the walk that crumbled more each year. She entered a screened porch, its rockers rarely used since the advent of air-conditioning, and rapped on the door. Feet shuffled and approached.

The Cajun healer, Rosemarie Leleux, opened the door and embraced Xochi. She'd inherited the house from her grandmother, the redoubtable Madame Leleux who had the sight and could tell the future as well as conjure up good luck and love potions that always worked. Mostly the locals called the younger *traiteur* Miss Rosemarie, but they still left their cash offerings to the Virgin under the white rock after a consultation.

"Xochi, girl, so glad to see you. Come in, come in out the heat. I got cold lemonade."

The living room no longer smelled of the freshly baked cookies Madame Leleux gave away so generously to all callers. It now had a faint taint of turpentine from Rosemarie's workroom where she painted pottery to be sold in Chapelle's gift shops and galleries. Some believed her jam and honey pots, her magnolia-strewn teapots, and figurines of happy flying pigs brought luck, but Rosemarie never claimed they did.

She freely admitted the sight had skipped over her. She couldn't crochet afghans exactly right for the sex and personality of the child to come like her granny. Xo had one of these in the colors of Mexico placed in a chest long before she arrived in Chapelle. The thought gave Xochi a small frisson instantly noticed by the plain, stocky woman with a broad face marred by ancient chicken pox scars and a gray bun piled messily on top of her head.

"You cold, baby? I keep the air-conditioning down low to help circulate the air and dry my paints. Let me turn it up." The *traiteur* fiddled with the thermostat, and the blasting cold air ceased. She unbuttoned a paint speckled blue smock the color of her eyes and hug it on an old coatrack, revealing a housedress not much more attractive. "There, you more comfortable now?"

"Yes, ma'am, but you didn't have to do that."

"I have coffee on. You want some, not the lemonade?"

"I think I would, thanks."

As Miss Rosemarie hustled to the kitchen in her flapping slippers, Xochi roved the room instead of taking a seat on the sofa that still boasted several layers of Madame's afghans. She approached a mirror, an antique cheval glass on a heavy stand that took up far too much room in the small space, and forced herself to look at her reflection after stripping off the visor and sunglasses. Its broad width and height showed her entire body, but mostly it revealed her aura, a lovely, light peridot green, the sign of a natural healer. Yet, she felt no calling to be a doctor or a nurse. She asked Stacy to do the jobs for translators at the hospitals because the signs of disease she saw distressed her and instead lent her talents to the police department. Many of the culprits possessed the dirty brown auras of deceit, the black holes of evil, but she dealt with that better than innocent children terminally ill or beloved elders riddled with cancer.

Rosemarie returned with the coffee tray. "That old mirror, granny found it at an estate sale, and the trouble we had getting it back here! She did alterations until her knees gave out and liked to have a full-length glass for her customers. I know it bothers you. Sit. You been thinking about our talk?"

"Yes, for a while." Xochi huddled into the comforting nest of afghans on the sagging sofa and prepared her coffee with milk. "I thought I was ready to apprentice myself to your Uncle Nestor, but things have gotten more complicated. I'd feel better if I could work with you."

Rosemarie shook her head as she liberally added sugar to her cup, one of her creations with dogwood blossoms on a pale green background. "No, the knowledge must be passed from man to woman to man and so on. My daddy taught me the prayers, the treatments, and the potions, but he died long before Granny who taught him. Uncle Nestor learned beside him, but none of his kids want to carry on the tradition. Superstitions, they say. Maybe some are, but the charms and such, they provide a focus for healing energy, and the prayers give all that a boost. At least, I think so. But, Xochi, you have a true God-given gift not to be denied. Cookie?"

The *traiteur* offered a plate of Oreos. Xochi shook her head.

"Not as good as Granny's homemade, I know, but I still like to dunk 'em." Rosemarie did just that. "Now don't you worry about Uncle Nestor. He's way up in years and got a bad prostrate. He won't bother you any no matter how pretty you are. He wants bad to pass on what he knows before he dies. When you touch his hand, he'll know you are the one. I felt that healing warmth when I helped you deal with the onset of the auras. It's best you live by him to pick up the ways. You never know what will pop into that old man's head out of the blue, things I didn't learn or have forgotten."

"I know I can't cure cancer or mend a bad heart, and people will expect that of me."

"Xochi, there are many kinds of healing, not all of it physical like a doctor gives. You radiate wellbeing, confidence, and love. You can still the troubled mind, help the hopelessly ill pass over peacefully."

"Is that enough?"

"For some it will be. They might need a charm or potion to reinforce that. Nestor will teach you those."

Xochi nodded. "I thought I'd made up my mind to give this a try, to see if I could help people, but recently two men have come into my life."

Miss Rosemarie's face radiated with a good-natured smile. "My granny would have seen that coming and described each to a tee—but I don't need to know all that, only if you want to go on with your training as a *traiteur* or give it up to be a wife and mother."

"Is that mutually exclusive? You mean I can't be both?"

"Sure, you can, sugar. I never could catch a man with this face, but you are so *belle*, I am surprised you only got two beaux."

"Maybe a few more," Xochi admitted. "But, I love your face. It's so open and generous." She squeezed the woman's hand.

The *traiteur* chuckled. "See, I feel better about myself already. Still, the generosity you mention is probably fat." She helped herself to another cookie and dunked. "Lost my figure years ago and don't much care anymore. You can be a wife and a *traiteur* if you find a man who will allow it."

Xochi scowled. "I'd like to see any man stop me once I make up my mind."

"True enough, men seem to be getting better, but there are still drunks and abusers and those who would take the money given to the Virgin Mary and spend it on themselves. Then, the prayers and the charms won't work. Though if you short on groceries or can't pay your light bill, the Virgin, she won't mind if you use a bit for that, but you can't set out to get rich doing this. Still, I think your special talent will help you weed out the bad ones."

Xochi squared her soft, rounded shoulders. "I can support myself with my translating and interpreting services, but if I do move here and stay with Uncle Nestor, I'll have to give up the more lucrative contracts I have and rely on doing work on the internet. Does he have wi-fi?"

That question set off a round of boundless mirth. When Rosemarie finished laughing and wiping her eyes on a paper napkin, she said, "*Cher*, he barely got electricity, and wouldn't have that if he didn't like to watch a ballgame now and then. Big Sinners fan. Won't he be *s'exciter* to have a Billodeaux in his home, a sister of a Sinner, and more than one those."

"I don't know about Uncle Nestor, but my brothers and beaux aren't likely to be thrilled when I tell them I'm going to move in with a codger and learn about healing herbs and prayers."

"A man who loves you accepts you as you are."

"I guess he'll have to. I'm going to give this a try. Even if I have no true healing powers, it is important that the lore isn't lost. Give me a few weeks to settle my affairs in New Orleans, then I'm coming home to learn the skills of a *traiteur*."

"You like my own daughter, baby." Rosemarie cupped Xochi's face and gave her the benediction of a kiss on the forehead. "It's good to know the old ways won't die with me."

"Before I go, have you got any fresh honey? I don't want to return home empty-handed, and it might sweeten the news."

"*Mais*, yeah, from Nestor's own hives."

Xochi followed the slap of Rosemarie's slippers to

the small side room where Madame Leleux once told fortunes and sold her potions. The walls were still papered with holy cards growing yellow. The small table with the varnish worn away where so many had rested their hands for a reading sat covered with paint stains now, the *traiteur's* current project of a pretty pin dish with a rose design centered in the middle on a plastic placemat. Behind the tables, shelves held a row of brown bottles marked with different colored ribbons, paints, brushes thrust into Mason jars to soak, quarts of honey, and a selection of jams and jellies—strawberry, fig, mayhaw, and dewberry.

"Here you go, *cher*, some of Uncle Nestor's best wildflower honey. A gift for your family."

"No, no, I intended to pay." Xochi delved into the depths of the hot pink tote and unearthed her wallet.

"If you refuse a gift, you hurt the giver." Rosemarie bagged the honey jar in a plastic grocery bag from Walmart.

"Okay, but give me one fig preserve and a mayhaw jelly." Xo held out a ten-dollar bill, which the *traiteur* accepted. Her purchases joined the honey, and she settled them all carefully in her big purse. "I'll let myself out. I can see I interrupted your work."

She leaned over the table to hug the woman who had created the gris-gris bag that chased away the nightmares of her parents' deaths. "You stop by any time you want more jam or just to visit. I don't think you'll be needing any of the love potions with all those men in your life," Rosemarie joked.

"Only your prayers."

"You got those, my honey."

Decision made, Xochi left more lighthearted by the

always-unlocked front door. She made two more stops, the first to Pommier's Bakery for two-dozen Mexican wedding cookies and a sack of *orielles de cochon*, pieces of fried dough shaped like pig's ears sticky with Steen's cane syrup and sprinkled with chopped pecans, plus two cups of coffee to go. She dropped the coffee and two of the pig's ears off at the squad car lurking for its next victim.

"Nice to see you on the job, Officer Chauvin. I thought it might be time for a coffee break. Did you stop that pickup truck full of guys looking for trouble I brought your way? They tailgated me on the highway."

"Sure did, Miss Xochi. Doing seventy-five in a thirty-five mile an hour zone, *and* busted them for not wearing seatbelts."

"Do you know where they are now?"

His partner accepted a coffee and a pig's ear. "If they know what's good for them, they went straight to the courthouse to pay their fine. If not, they probably left town on the other road and headed back to New Orleans where they come from."

"I didn't notice them tailing me until Morgan City."

That prompted Officer Chauvin to offer some fatherly advice. "I got daughters, me. Don't drive a fast car like that with the top down alone. You attract all kinds of trash. They asked where the Billodeaux ranch was located, lots of tourists do. These guys, we give 'em directions that will take them to the next parish speed trap if they don't go home. Friends of yours always know to ask for Lorena Ranch if they get lost on the backroads."

"Thanks, nice to know I'm be looked out for,

officers."

Xochi lost no time getting into the Mustang and driving slowly out of town in a direction opposite the one given to her followers. Once free of the city limits, she gunned the engine and made record time arriving at Lorena Ranch wrapped all around by gnarly live oak trees veiled with Spanish moss. All the grown children had remotes to open the wrought iron gates, though she knew an alert went directly to Knox Polk, Sr. in his capacity ranch manager and guard. Before she traversed the long lane, he would be in the security hut checking the cameras to identify the new arrival. By the time she came to a stop at the kitchen door, he'd be waiting for her or anyone else who showed up without warning.

Yes, there he was, standing straight, tall, and lean, his close-cropped hair silver, his green eyes startling as ever in his tan face. Except for the height, Xochi saw little of Junior in him. Knox rarely smiled. A girl just had to know he was glad to see her. In a minute, his wife Corazon joined him and wrapped Xo in her warm embrace, proof positive that opposites attract.

"So nice a surprise! No one know you coming." Corazon glanced hopefully at the car as if it might hold another person, maybe in the trunk. "But not Junior."

"I suspect he might be moving into his new condo this weekend. He's leasing the place below Tom and Alix."

"He don't do nothing wrong that you kick him out?" The grooves of age and worry deepened in her brown face.

"Absolutely not! Junior is a perfect gentleman and an excellent houseguest." Add a damn good kisser, but don't say it. "Just time for him to have his own place."

Knox Polk exhaled slowly as if relieved to hear he'd raised his son right. When Xochi popped the trunk, he went immediately to retrieve her small overnight bag while Xo offered the baked goods to Corazon. "I have honey and preserves I got from Rosemarie Leleux. Let's get out of the heat and enjoy them before the Billodeaux horde shows up. Where are they anyhow?

"First day of Camp Love Letter. Most of the guests arrived last night. Big weenie roast, lots of trash to burn this morning." Knox filled her in on the activities of the charity for seriously ill children. "Lorena is on lifeguard duty. Trinity and T-Rex are giving pony rides. Edie is organizing games for the little ones. Mack, he's lying around somewhere resting for his mini-camp next week." The last sentence implied unvoiced criticism. Everyone pitched in for Camp Love Letter, no excuses.

How could she have forgotten? Now that she took a moment to listen, the distant shouts and laughter of children filled the air like the songs of the mockingbirds. "I can pick up Mack's slack while I'm here," Xo offered as they moved inside to the commodious kitchen where thirteen children once ate their breakfast. Home.

Tonight, she'd sleep in her deep yellow childhood bedroom bordered with red roses and full of colorful accents like a green glazed pottery vase filled with huge paper flowers in gaudy colors, a fiesta of a room Stacy called it. This evening she wouldn't have to compete with Stace for the use of their shared bathroom that linked her space with Stacy's gold and white princess bedroom. She'd sleep well knowing how safe Daddy Joe and Knox made the ranch, but she'd still place the gris-gris bag beneath her pillow to banish bad dreams.

No dark men here.

Xochi coaxed the very busy Knox and Corazon to sit and have coffee and cookies with her. The housekeeper insisted she eat some lunch, too, and served up a heaping helping of the jambalaya leftover from the campers' meal and a small salad. "Nobody takes as good care of me than you, except maybe Junior," she sighed in contentment.

Junior's parents exchanged a concerned glance. "What I meant is Junior has been doing all the cooking. Not to insult you, but his jambalaya is fantastic."

Unoffended, Corazon shrugged those comfortable shoulders that Xochi had often cried upon. "Catered and good enough for so many. Finally, Mawmaw Nadine, she don't insist we do all the cooking."

Shocked, Xochi said, "Is she dying?"

"No, no, just slowing down a little."

Her brother Mack slouched into the kitchen. His wrinkled pajama bottoms hung low on his narrow hips, and his long black hair straggled loose around his shoulders. He needed a shave rather badly. His facial hair had gone beyond scruff but not quite reached a beard. Scratching his patch of chest hair, he slumped into a chair. "Got any of that for me?"

"Sure, Mr. Mack." Corazon left her coffee and a half-eaten wedding cookie to fetch another meal.

No Mr. Mack for Knox Polk. "Lorena is waiting for you to spell her at the pool, boy." Talk about steely gazes that could bore right through a person. He hadn't been an Army ranger for nothing and took no crap from lazy goof-offs.

"Soon as I eat. I only have to put on a pair of trunks."

Xochi had to admit her brother could pack away a plate of food in less time than it took to reheat it. He also finished off what Xo didn't want and grabbed a handful of cookies to go. Minutes later, he passed through the kitchen again, dressed for lifeguard duty in flip-flops, a Cowboys ball cap, aviator sunglasses, and a Speedo he certainly had the body to wear.

Lorena replaced him at the table. She tossed her long, black braid over her sun-glazed shoulders and attacked her meal much as Mack did. She'd covered the bikini she also had the tall, lean body to wear with a terry cloth wrap, but otherwise resembled her brother with flip-flops on her narrow feet and sunglasses pushed up into her thick hair, almost his female duplicate with her large, dark eyes and high cheekbones. The tang of chlorine and suntan lotion surrounded her.

When she paused between bites, Lorena said, "Honestly, if Mack weren't my triplet, I'd punch him right in the nose for leaving me out there with no lunch until one-thirty. He thinks he's a big deal because he's going to play for Dallas, and I'm only traveling to Australia to play women's volleyball."

Xo nodded with sympathy. She'd done her time at the pool. "I'll be here tomorrow if you want a break."

"Since I can't depend on my brother, that would be great, but the pool doesn't open until one on Sundays. First church services in the theater for those who want to attend, then lunch and the one-hour rule, though I've never believed that to be true. Remember, you have to keep a good watch on the kids. Some are so afraid of the water. Others will jump in no matter what their handicap."

"I recall."

Lorena's rather bold nose sniffed as if something other than her own aroma were in the air. "What are you doing here anyhow? Those who have a real life are exempt from helping at camp."

"You know Dean and the honeymooners will give the camp some hours along with numerous former Sinners, but I came to discuss something with Mom and Dad." Xochi set her determined chin on top of her steepled hands.

"What, no team meeting in the den with all of us swarming around to get on your case? Don't tell me you and Connor Bullock are getting engaged! I saw the way he looked at you at the graduation party." Lorena released the famous Billodeaux smile, the one inherited from her daddy and just as effective on a woman.

Cleaning up Mack's dishes at the sink, Corazon sucked hard against her teeth and placed a soapy hand over her heart. "My Junior will be so, so de-vast-stated. He loves you, Xochi."

Knox Polk sidled toward the doorway. "If things are getting girly, I'll go back to work. Those ponies need a break and a good rubdown." Xochi had never seen their guardian flee from anything before, but evidently mushy emotions were his weakness. He left as fast as a cottonmouth could strike.

"I'm not engaged to anyone, and I've only seen Connor twice, though he does text me now and then. No, I'm planning to move back to Chapelle, but I want to discuss arrangements with the parents."

Corazon exhaled. "Your room is always ready here from the first day you arrived as a scared child with bad dreams."

"I know. There's more I need to tell them."

"Junior, he don't get you pregnant, no? 'Cause he marry you right away."

Only if people got pregnant from kissing. Xochi waved her hands to erase both thoughts. "No, no, no. He's a perfect gentleman, remember?"

A deep voice sounded from the doorway. "Good, because I'd have to shoot him if he did." Daddy Joe to the rescue.

Petite Mama Nell was there, too, obscured by his size. She ducked under his arm to enter the kitchen and took charge as usual. "Now is as good a time as any as any to talk. It's free time for the campers and a lot of them rest. I need to do the same, but first, come into the den and tell us what you have to say." Nell grabbed a bottle of water from the fridge and broke off a piece of pig's ear in passing. Joe scooped up the rest of it in a napkin and led the way.

The couple settled side-by-side on the long, brown leather sofa and waited. Like good parents everywhere, they excelled at listening. Add in that Nell had a degree in psychology and could wait endlessly for the words to come out. Xochi chose hers carefully. "Both of you know how I've benefited from Rosemarie Leleux's aid over the years. She helped me understand my auras, that they could be a gift and not a curse. Her gris-gris bag still lets me sleep at night. I want to follow in her footsteps and study to be a *traiteur*."

Mama Nell's doe brown eyes grew even larger. Usually she perceived what bothered her children, but obviously hadn't seen this one coming. While she sat stunned like a deer in the headlights, Daddy Joe questioned first. "Are you sure you don't want to be a nurse like the twins, or a doctor like Connor Bullock? We are good for the tuition if you do."

Xochi shook her head hard enough to set her curls flying. "I was afraid that's what you'd say. Please don't tell Jude and Annie yet. They'd both think I'm crazy. This won't cost you anything. I'll still be continuing my translating service, probably online because I need to work with Nestor Leleux here in Chapelle."

"We'd love to have you home again doing whatever you feel you must." Mama Nell bounced back fast.

Well, that's the thing. Miss Rosemarie says I need to stay with Nestor to learn all he knows."

Daddy Joe exploded. "Live with Nestor Leleux! I mean he's a great hunting and fishing guide, but a real curmudgeon. I been to his house, me. Nuttin' but a shack on the edge of da swamp. Why not in town with Rosemarie?"

Nell patted her husband's hand. "Now, now, settle down. Your Cajun comes out when you get excited. Yes, why not Rosemarie?"

"Because the lore must be handed down by someone of the opposite sex she tells me."

"Now that is crazy. You stay here and commute to his place. We'll get you a car. No daughter of mine is going to…" Joe's hands flailed in the air, another sign of agitation.

Xochi reached out and stilled them. "I love you both so much, but this is something I need to do. So, no team meeting and no objections. I am way over twenty-one, and have lived in a city far more dangerous than the edge of the swamp. I will be fine." Rosemarie claimed she had the power to soothe troubled minds.

Her hands did feel warm against his though the house was well cooled. With one thumb on his wrist, she felt the pulse of the man who had promised her a home and kept that promise go steady.

"Please don't tell the rest of the family yet. Give me a little time to get things set up and break it to them in the right way." Xochi got their nods if not a verbal promise.

"You'll still need a car, but something safer than Dean's Mustang. We expect you to come home often so we know you are all right. We'll start working on getting one for you."

"I will be fine." Xo kissed them both on the cheek.

A rattle of glasses on a tray disrupted the moment. "I bring you iced tea and the rest of the cookies." Corazon set the tray down carefully on the coffee table. Tears ran down her cheeks and followed the furrows to drip off her chin. "My Xochitl is going to be a *curandera*, and that is a wonderful thing."

At least one person beside Miss Rosemarie was happy for her. But what about Junior—and Connor Bullock?

Chapter Thirteen

Xochi returned to the city content with her decision and relieved that on the edge of a swamp the chances of seeing dark men would be as rare as a snowfall. Hands full, she ran up the stairs to the apartment to tell Junior before the news leaked from the family grapevine. Hoping they could talk over a cup of his excellent coffee and the sack of fresh pig ear pastries she'd brought along, she also toted his mother's cheese enchilada casserole.

"Junior, I'm home." Xo entered the living room. Silence weighty as a medicine ball dropped on her. Of course, he had mini-camp this week. Mack had taken off for his in the white Porsche he'd bought with his bonus money yesterday afternoon while she'd stayed to help Lorena at the pool.

Xo carried the casserole into the kitchen and considered trying to finesse a cup of coffee out of Junior's complicated machine. Her old office coffeemaker sat in its place, the first hint that he'd gone. A note in his big, loopy handwriting sat anchored by a saltshaker shaped like a cluster of grapes on the table.

Dearest Xochi,

My lease was approved, and I had my bedroom furniture delivered Saturday. I kept the coffee machine since I can't survive without a good cup in the morning, and I didn't think you'd use it anyhow. Kiki's screen is yours, my gift to another beautiful blossom. I'll be staying out at the training camp all week with the other rookies. The Sinners want us to bond as well as sweat. If you need anything, Tom and Alix are right across the street. They only tag in at camp when the return team practices. I told them about the dark men. Keep safe, my lovely, while I am gone.

Junior

P.S. Feel free to visit whenever you want real coffee

As If she needed to confirm the note, she dragged her overnight bag upstairs and opened the door to his room. Another note on the pillows read:

I stripped the linens and put on fresh. The ones I washed are in the closet.

Jr.

Xochi put her cosmetics away in the bathroom and missed the sight of his shaving kit sitting on the counter tucked away from the mess she usually left. She sniffed. Gone, the scent of his lime aftershave that hung in the moist air when he'd showered. Ridiculous to miss him so much when they'd only lived together for a few weeks and shared just two kisses. Especially, when she was about to leave him behind in New Orleans.

Oh well, that enchilada casserole would serve her for four meals without Junior around, and she could have pig's ears for breakfast the next few days. In fact, lunchtime approached, and she could eat one now. Xochi returned to the kitchen, scooped out some of the casserole and poured iced tea from the container in the refrigerator. Her phone rang as she settled in to eat. Rachelle checking in. If she'd been working, she would have let it go to voice mail, but right now a little company might be good.

"Hey, girl, I'm between graveyard tours and my shift at the voodoo shop. Where you been? I missed you at Paco's Friday night. Everyone did. Juan was so happy to have you back, and this suave guy with a little mustache wanted to know where you'd gone. I said how the hell did I know, probably home to help out with that Love Letter camp business. I'm not your babysitter. Still, it would have been nice to get a heads up if you weren't coming."

"Sorry, I did go home to take care of some business. I have so much on my mind right now."

"Like which gorgeous guy to take up with next? I'm thinking Junior has the edge since he's right under your nose, and the doc probably has to work a lot. Under your nose." Rachelle voiced a salacious little laugh into the phone. "With a guy as big as Junior, you most likely have to be on top to avoid getting crushed. Tell me, is he that big all over if you know what I mean?"

Xochi shook her head against the phone even though Rachelle couldn't see her. "I'm not going to discuss it. He's moved out."

"If you broke up, tell him I'm still available. We had a great time that evening we spent together, really hit it off. Basically, I think I'm more fun than you are."

"Maybe." She didn't possess the cattiness to tell Rachelle that Junior felt sorry for her.

"So, we on for Paco's sometime this weekend?"

"I'm tired of Paco's. Let's go to Tipitina's for a change."

"They having Free Fridays yet, because you know it costs? Paco's has no cover charge."

"My treat."

"Great! Madame Laveau—as if—is giving me the evil eye. Good thing she's a fake. Got to go. Let me know day and time and if the two hunks are coming along as soon as you can. Yeah, yeah, I see the customers waiting to buy black candles. Bye."

Xochi finished her lunch. She should go out and walk it off even though the afternoon sun turned the sidewalks into frying pans, but couldn't make herself do it without Junior's company. It seemed silly to disturb Tom and Alix who would tell her she was crazy to walk in this heat even though they worked out in high temps fairly often.

She'd strolled to Dean's house early the day she left for Chapelle and not noticed anyone following her. But if Rachelle had suggested she might go home, the man with the thin mustache could have had the two most likely routes watched for her passing. Damn him for taking the pleasure out of driving the Mustang and making her feel hunted.

Glad Dean had driven her back to the apartment when she returned the car in perfect condition, no thanks to her tailgaters, Xo made the decision to stay in the rest of the day with all the bolts Daddy Joe installed locked into place. Tomorrow, she'd resume her normal routine and break the news to her customers about leaving town. Let the dark men try to find her in the Atchafalaya Basin.

****

Right, the usual routine. Xochi donned her Anchi Services dress accented with the pink, purple and silver scarf from the Riverwalk shopping spree, stocked the hot pink handbag for the day's activities, and tried to step outside with confidence before the temperature ramped up. She decided against day-old pig's ears and fell into her old habit of getting a latte and croissant at the coffeehouse across the street. Business slowed down in the summer with people taking vacations to the beach or mountains to escape the traffic and the heat, but she still had plenty of company crossing broad Canal Street, getting stuck halfway at the streetcar stop when the light turned red. She stayed in the middle of the pack when the pedestrians surged to the other side on a green light and got in line at the coffee shop, always busy at this hour.

The handsome enough barista who played bass guitar in a yet to be discovered band on weekends greeted her like a long-lost love. "Xochi, my only customer with that name, where have you been?" he asked as he inked her name on a cup and mixed a latte forming a foam heart on top, first time ever, without asking for her order. "We thought you'd sold us out for Starbucks." He bagged her usual almond croissant.

Was she so predictable? She'd gone to hear him play a few times and knew he had the attitude and the tats to succeed, but she'd turned down his advances. As he threw in an extra chocolate chunk cookie without charging her, he evidently still had hope—about to be dashed. No sense in giving him the whole story. She kept it short. "No Starbucks for me. I'll be moving home in a few weeks. I went back there to make arrangements."

"Aw, babe, you break my heart. You're my favorite customer."

"I thought I was," said an elderly lady next in line.

"In your age group, you are, Miss Lily."

"Bye, Edward," never Ed but sometimes Eddie, he'd told her. Xochi slipped a couple of dollars in the tip jar to cover the cost of the cookie and turned to leave. She saw them immediately outside the window partly steamed with morning humidity. One, a husky thug robed in a black aura she'd seen before in Jackson Square, blocked the doorway as if he considered entering. The man with the thin mustache leaned against the wall next to him and smoked his cigarillo in a gold holder. The glint of it in the morning sun caused a frisson of fear to run down her spine like perspiration. The cup in her hand shook so fiercely the lovely heart of foam broke into pieces.

The last time she'd seen a holder like that it rested in the mouth of Esteban Miro, the drug lord her natural father had cheated. Again, she was that five-year-old child hiding among the giant clay pots and chimineas their neighbor sold to tourists as Miro's minions executed her *Papi* and shot her beautiful, young mama in the chest. Miro passed that golden holder with a burning cigarette as if it were an Olympic torch to another of his men who entered her small home. Smoke came out the windows opened to encourage the flames. Then, her half-brother, red-haired Tommy, jerked her away to hide in a pickup truck headed for the border. Tom saved her life, simple as that, but he wasn't here now.

Xochi backed up the two steps leading to the street. "Edward, would you mind walking me to the corner? There are two unsavory men blocking the doorway."

"Escorting beautiful women is another of my talents. Be glad to."

"Hey, what about my order, lover boy?" Miss Lily

protested.

"Amy, get Miss Lily a chai tea and two vanilla scones. Be back in a minute."

The door opened outward and forced the thug to back up. Edward took her arm and gallantly walked Xochi the short distance to the corner. Behind them, Miss Lily's grumpy voice said, "Hey, get out of my way you loiterers unless you want a cup of hot tea in the face."

Xochi glanced over her shoulder to see the dark men step back and give the old lady some room. She looked down the street and saw another pair coming her way at a fast pace. Thank God, not like those who followed her. Tom and Alix jogged side by side, his yellow and her blue aura overlapping to create the lovely turquoise color that always made Xochi joyful. She hailed them before they could turn off on the side street to enter their brownstone condominium. They waited, running in place, on the corner until the traffic passed.

"Thanks, Edward, I see my brother and his wife. I'll be fine now. Just nervous, I guess. You are a true gentleman."

"Does this mean you'll go out with me?"

"I'll consider it."

Xo dashed across before the light turned again. "I am so glad to see you two. I thought some guys were following me." She turned to look around. Both men were gone, whether hidden in another doorway or whisked away in a car, she didn't know.

"Dark men?" asked Tom.

"How did you…"

"Junior told us. He asked us to watch out for you.

Just call, Xochi." Alix took her arm and sandwiched her in beside Tom. "World Trade Center, right?"

"You must think I'm crazy because they aren't back there anymore."

"Nope, I know you see things other people don't." Her dear brother, Tom, always on her side. If Alix thought her sister-in-law was paranoid, she didn't voice it. In fact, they promised to meet her at five for the journey back to the apartment.

Her escorts did their cool down walk, still moving so fast she had no time to dig out a dollar for her favorite bag lady who always had a cheery good morning for everyone and a little dog to feed. They left her at the entrance to the imposing building. Xochi burrowed deep into the lobby and sat drinking her coffee and forcing down the croissant hoping both would steady her nerves. Then, she went about her business, taking care of scheduled appointments and leaving letters drawn from her bright pink bag explaining her relocation and giving out an e-mail address that clients could still use to have contracts or other documents transcribed.

She stayed in the building all day, having that single cookie for lunch, not a good idea as she felt a trifle faint by five. Tom and Alix arrived, and they emerged into the heat that seemed to be pushing on her shoulders hard enough to make her knees buckle. Alix caught her arm. "You need a good meal, Sis. Tom made early reservations at Besh Steak in the casino, private curtained booth. Our treat."

The area around the Trade Center abounded with great steak houses and grills to serve the businessmen. No need to enter Harrah's casino since Besh's lay right inside the door. George Rodrigue's friendly Blue Dog paintings goggled at them as they passed the amber lit bar and the open kitchen before sinking into the comfortable brown leather of their secluded booth. The waiter took their drink order and closed the curtain for privacy.

"Let those dudes try to find us now," Tom said.

Xochi mustered a wan smile for her brother. "I really appreciate this."

The waiter returned with wine for the women and a beer for Tom. He and Alix went for the aged New York strip steaks. Xochi ordered the Lobster Crispy Rice. Salads all around. As they waited for the meal, Alix offered, "We're glad to help and will meet you at your place the next couple of days and the Trade Center after work. If you'd feel better, you can stay with us."

"No, I'm fine inside my locked apartment. These dark men seem to pop up at various places on the street. Maybe I'm paranoid, and they just live in the area. That could be why I keep running into them. The squatty thug outside the coffee shop I've seen in Jackson Square. It's the guy with the thin mustache I see most often."

"Creepy," said Alix as the bleu cheese salads arrived. "We do have a problem with Thursday. Tom and I need to be at the mini-camp all day to do kicks and punts for the newbies. Dean will be there, too, throwing passes to the rookie receivers. Could you take a cab?"

"Of course. I'll call a driver I know." Xochi toyed with her greens. "Did Junior make the move all right? I haven't heard from him since I've been back."

Both Tom and Alix gave a hearty laugh. He said,

"And you won't. Coach Buck lines all those rookies up first day of camp and tells them he doesn't want any crybabies calling home to complain to their mamas and girlfriends about how tough it is."

Alix lowered her voice to a gruff level roughly resembling Coach. "You think your opponents are going to be nice to you? Man up. I see any phones out during practice, I'll knock them from your hands."

"That bad?"

"Oh, yes."

The main course was served with flair. Xochi picked at her delicious food while Tom and Alix devoured theirs. "So, Junior is settled in all right?"

Tom paused in forking up chunks of tender steak. "Sure, he showed us his bedroom set. Dual controls on the mattress to move it up and down, and the furniture jumbo size to suit him. Other than that, all he has is his clothes and a really complicated coffeemaker. Said something about your helping him decorate the rest of the place."

"Yes, I said I would." Take that pretty salesgirl. Tom and Alix exchanged a glance, which she ignored. A little friendly furniture shopping meant nothing.

They cajoled her into getting bread pudding for dessert before they left. She and Alix shared a portion while the ever-slim Tom gobbled his down. Afterward, they played the slots for fun and finally exited at the blue hour when the air turned balmy. Her escorts left her at her door and waited until she shot the blots.

Funny, she'd never felt alone in the apartment before, but missed Junior's company now. Maybe five years wasn't such a vast difference in age. She'd known the cubby boy Junior since childhood and now knew him as a man of unexpected talents. While his big, warm smile dwelled in her mind, the phone rang, hopefully the man she thought about, but no. Connor Bullock wondered if they were on for a date Friday night, but please not Paco's.

"We're going to try Tipitina's for change."

"By we, you mean…"

"Rachelle and Junior if he isn't too worn out from mini-camp."

Connor's voice held a dry tone. "I'm sure he won't be. Probably does the two-step as well as that salsa stuff."

"We'll see. Do you want to meet us there?"

"No, it would be my pleasure pick you up."

"See you then."

But, she did not.

Chapter Fourteen

Tuesday, Alex prepared a Wisconsin hot dish supper, and Tom supplied an evening of popcorn, DVDs, and yes, a brown sugar Bundt cake. Xochi invited them along to Tipitina's on Friday, her treat. They somehow passed the word to Junior who said he wouldn't be tired and would be there, especially if the doctor planned to attend. He'd be free to escort her to church on Sunday.

Wednesday, a phone call interrupted their seafood takeout dinner at Xochi's place. NOPD officer Tony Ancona needed her help in interpreting for a female witness who spoke only Spanish. "I know you have people in the department who can do that for you," she told him.

"Yeah," he said. "But, they don't have your insight on who's lying. This lady is real nervous. One calming touch of your hand, and she'll open up and spill about the drive-by shooting she saw. I've seen you do it before. How about I promise to take you out for dinner besides your regular pay, that great Italian restaurant on the other side of the bridge?"

"You've already paid for my lunch plenty of times."

"Not the same at all. What do you say, Xo? Give a cop a chance."

"You are welcome to join me and my friends at

Tipitina's on Friday night."

"Are these friends Sinners who will make me look short and puny?"

She rewarded that with her steaming hot chocolate laugh. "Oh, Tony, as they say, size doesn't matter. You're still taller than me. You already know Tom and Alix. My friend, Rachelle is coming along."

"Is she as gorgeous as you?"

No way near even if Xochi didn't regard herself as gorgeous and stayed away from mirrors. "She's taller and a great dancer." Not telling lies here. "Also some childhood friends, Dr. Connor Bullock, and Junior Polk, the Sinners new cornerback."

"Wonderful, the competition has both brains and brawn. I know who Junior Polk is. I catch some college ball. You'd better get a big table, a really big table if he's going to be there. I'll see if I can get a night off, find my elevator shoes, and the zoot suit with big, padded shoulders simply to be in your company."

Xochi sprinkled her laughter over him again. "I'll look forward to seeing that. Okay, send a squad car to pick me up.

"Be there in ten."

"Finish your dinner," she told Tom and Alix. "I'm needed at police headquarters."

Despite getting a similar escort home after the witness, holding both of Xo's hands and gazing into her deep brown eyes, did indeed spill the details of the crime, she found her brother and his wife adorably and probably uncomfortably curled up on her couch asleep. They woke after a gentle shaking of shoulders, stretched like giraffes reaching for the choicest leaves on the top of a tall tree, and headed to their condo.

Maybe she should break the news about leaving New Orleans and learning to be a *traiteur* at the gathering on Friday night. She'd buy a round of drinks and ask them to toast her future. How could they object in a crowded, music-filled room? Yes, that sounded like a good plan. Almost like breaking up with a boyfriend or three.

****

After days of being escorted and almost smothered with care by Tom and Alix, Xochi summoned her favorite cabbie to take her to work on Thursday. She waited just inside her door for his arrival, opening it only a crack to make sure the right taxi pulled into the access-way to her apartment. Diego did not get out to open the door in his usual courtly gesture, but she dashed across the space so quickly that perhaps he had no chance. Smelling the usual pineapple air freshener that filled the cab, Xochi slid into the back seat and slammed the door. "World Trade Center, *por favor*," she said before realizing she was not alone.

A sweet medicinal scent overwhelmed the pineapple aroma. Chloroform, the favorite of kidnappers, serial killers and rapists, at least on TV— the thought shot through her mind as the gauze pad descended and pressed against her nose and mouth. Holding her breath, she groped in her favorite hot pink purse, Junior's gift, for her pepper spray, and did not find it among the lipsticks in the bottom of the bag. Should have kept it handier. Regardless, another hand knocked the purse to the floor. Xochi struck out with her feet, clawed with her fingers, wishing now she wore icepick heels instead of practical business shoes so she could go for the groin, and had inch long acrylic nails instead of natural nails, short and lacquered pink.

"Breathe, bitch, breathe!" A fist punched her midsection, and she did, sucking in that sickly sweetness, feeling almost high and definitely disoriented. She continued to flail her limbs but sensed they weakened, did not hit home.

The driver, not Diego, but a Hispanic man with a very thin mustache, peered into the back seat. "Maybe a little more on the cloth, Indio."

"Yeah, she's kicking the crap out of me. One knock on the head and this would have been over."

Her wild eyes discerned the thug from the coffee shop kneeling on the seat, pressing on the cloth, Mexican but American born by his use of the idiom. Not that it mattered at the moment. If only the Korean couple who ran the electronics store beneath her apartment would decide to empty their trash right now since the cab had pulled far into the cul-de-sac near the dumpster. No luck. They never did that until the store closed. She shoulda known, shoulda suspected when the cab parked so far back and not at her door. Shoulda, woulda, coulda. Too late.

"She must be free of damage, perfect, intact for the goddess," the man designated as Indio replied. "I know what I am doing. Soon she will sleep. You will not touch her. El Jefe's orders." Large aquiline nose, burnt almond eyes, light brown skin, and a head shaved to make his sloping brow even more prominent, his heavy neck bore a necklace dangling charms and totems. He strove to appear Mayan and had earned his nickname.

Defiant, the driver, not her driver, reached out to grasp her weakly kicking ankle. He ran a hand up her leg to her thigh, naked because the heat and humidity of the city made stockings unbearable. "Ah, yes, silky and rounded, not like her bony friend."

The Indian slapped his hand away, something to be grateful for. Vaguely, she wished she'd stuck to the straight Xochi Services skirts Stacey favored. Giddy, beneath the cloth she laughed and took in more of the drug. Another regret, not giving into Junior's love. He would have been gentle. Sleepy, so sleepy.

****

Xochi woke with no sense of time or place. Sunlight streamed through a porthole. The long Mississippi channel that led the Gulf of Mexico carried her away. Goodbye New Orleans, though she hadn't planned to leave by sea. Farewell Chalmette Battlefield that passed by the porthole. No more sightseeing. The light made her headache worse. Her pathetic breakfast of stale pig's ears and mediocre coffee tried to come up. Just the thought of Junior's pecan waffles made her want to hurl. She twisted aside and spewed over the edge of the bed into a conveniently placed plastic bucket. They'd thought of everything. No one would miss her until evening.

Xo wanted to fall back on the bed, a fairly large and comfortable one for a ship, but forced herself to stay seated, head between her legs, breathing deep and shoving her long hair out of the way behind her shoulders. Steadied, she stood up and did the obvious, tried the door, locked of course, not that she could escape from a moving boat into the Mississippi without killing herself. Maybe later she'd think that preferable to what the kidnappers planned to do with her. Extort money from Daddy Joe most likely, but would they let her live after he paid up? Even if they didn't kill her, she might be sold into sexual slavery, not that she would be any different from easily obtained Mexican girls.

She needed water. Letting the wall support her, she found a mini-fridge well-stocked with both bottled and mineral water, a carton of milk, soft drinks, even a few cans of beer and small bottles of wine. Beyond the beverages lay a good assortment of sandwiches, salads, and foods that could be heated in the small microwave. Her stomach roiled at the thought of eating. Cracking open a water, Xochi sipped slowly knowing her stomach would revolt if she did anything more. She opened a door to the bathroom, again larger and more luxurious than provided by most cruise ships. She'd been on plenty of those for family vacations, but always buddied up in cabins with bunks and a small bathroom to share. How Stacy hated that! How glad *she* was to have been taken into a family that could afford cruises for twelve children. She used the facilities and felt better.

Back to the locked door again. She pounded on it with her fists.

"*Que*?" answered someone on the outside. "What the hell do you want, bitch?" said another voice, the one she'd identified as Mexican-American in the cab and, as he'd said himself, kicked the crap out of.

"*Por que*?" she asked. Why, why, why?

"They don't tell us nothing. We get to be on guard duty day and night. No one goes in or out like you're something special. Any other time, me and Diaz would be by the pool or fucking women who want to be fucked. You got a bed, a nice place to take a shit, and enough food and water for the trip. We'll be in

Cozumel in a couple of days. So shut up and enjoy."

"Pardon, Senorita Xochi. They do not call my companion El Animal for no reason. He does not understand your importance."

The man who drove the cab, who had followed her in the sculpture park and elsewhere, spoke. Not a native speaker of English, heavily accented, he pronounced the sobriquet Ani-mal. What good these conclusions did her, she did not know. Just a habit of analyzing speech patterns. That he had a black aura said all no matter how soothing his words.

"I have no importance except being the adopted daughter of a rich man."

"Much more than that. We will be well rewarded for our service to El Jefe."

"With a piece of her after the chief is finished?"

"*No se.*" He did not know.

Xochi thought she understood. El Jefe did not hold her for a ransom. He intended to complete his revenge against the family of Bijou Billodeaux. She and Tom were the only survivors. Tom would find her. Then, El Jefe would kill them both.

Chapter Fifteen

The doc seemed miffed, checking his expensive watch every few minutes as they stood sweating outside the yellow, two-story frame building on the corner of Napoleon and Tchoupitoulas waiting for Xochi to show. That merely increased Junior's good mood. He wished he could have arm wrestled Connor Bullock for the privilege of escorting Xochi to the music hall, a bout he certainly would have won because an arm that played tennis and golf could not compare to one that pressed weights. But, cranky Coach Buck had kept his new recruits secluded at the Metairie training field until the very last second. The best Junior could do was take a thorough shower, trim his face-defining beard close, and lave himself with the lime aftershave Xo mentioned she liked, before racing to Tipitina's to meet the group.

Evidently, Xochi had stood up Dr. Bullock with his sharp features, light skin, green eyes, and big brain, not like her at all to do so. Alix suggested Xo might have been delayed by last minute business at the Trade Center or called upon by the police.

The unexpected addition introduced all around by Tom to their group, Tony Ancona shook his head. "No, I would have heard."

"I waited a half hour past the time I was supposed to pick her up. She should have called me if delayed." Irritation showed in every word Bullock spoke.

151

"Finally, I thought she might have forgotten I was going to pick her up and come here directly by cab."

"Cab! That's it." Tom's worried face brightened. "Rachelle, do you have the numbers for the drivers Xochi prefers?"

The angular woman took her phone from the lime green clutch purse Junior bought her. She really did have a dress that matched, unflattering enough to make her resemble an unripe banana. "I got a couple of numbers she gave me, always hounding me to be safe, but I usually find a guy to take me home."

"I believe she also wanted me to give you a lecture on safe sex," the doctor said in a voice so prudish all of them stared.

"Live and let live, doc. Who wants the phone?"

Despite his shorter reach, Tony Ancona's hand shot out first. "Let me do this. Which numbers?"

"Diego and Javier."

He punched the speed dial with one short, strong finger. "Hey, this Diego? I don't care if you have a fare. This is Officer Ancona of the NOPD speaking. You pick up Xochi Billodeaux this morning or tonight?"

A blast of rapid Spanish spewed from the phone. Ancona shook his head. "Any of you guys speak the language?"

"Not as well as Xochi, but I'll try." Tom accepted the phone. "*Diego, hermano de Xochi aqui.* Yeah, *hermano pelirrojo.*" Tom rolled his eyes. "They always have to mention the red hair."

"Well, you are Xo's only redheaded brother. I love it." Alix tousled his curls.

"Cut it out. Not you, Diego. *Despacio, por favor. Si, Si. Momento.*" Tom, gone pale beneath his freckles, held the phone against his chest to block their conversation. "He's pretty upset. Says his cab was stolen early this morning, but the police found it by the docks this afternoon. Xo's purse was inside. The officers took it. He knows nothing about that. He did not steal. He did not see Senorita Xochi today. He had to clean all the fingerprint dust from his cab before he could use it, a whole day of work lost."

"Jesus, Mary and Joseph, I take one day off to spruce up and get a haircut, have an evening out, and something like this happens. Gimme the phone." Tony ripped it away from Tom's grasp. "Look, you spick, I know you speak English. Listen to me. You're not in trouble yet, but you will be because I know you're holding back important information. Drive that taxi over to Headquarters. Ask for Officer Ancona. Be there, or I'll have you picked up."

Tom raised his russet eyebrows at the cop. "You'd better learn to omit spick from your vocabulary if you want to make any headway with Xo."

"Yeah, yeah, I got carried away." Tony tossed the phone back to Rachelle.

"Gee, nothing this exciting ever happens to me."

"Be grateful. Any of you guys got a ride?" All three men held up a hand. "You, her brother, give me a lift to Central. The rest of you enjoy the show."

"No way. I'm following you over there," Junior said, no give in his deep voice.

"I'll go as well." Connor fished his keys from a pocket.

"Waddabout me?" wailed Rachelle. "I'm promised an evening out and got no way to get home after dark."

Junior opened his wallet and drew out a large bill.

"This should cover admission, a few drinks, and a cab ride home. Call Javier."

"You staying, blondie?" Rachelle said, looking for company.

"No, I'm family to Xochi now. I'll remain with Tom," Alix answered, pallid but unrattled.

"Suit yourself. I already missed some of the music." Working that lime green dress like a pro, Rachelle moved inside the club.

"I doubt they'll talk to anyone not family if the rest of you want to go home," Tom said.

"We're sticking." Junior answered for both him and Connor who gave a precise nod.

"Let's roll, then."

****

No kidding about only talking to the family. Junior figured he'd checked his watch more often than Connor. They drank bad coffee, ate vending machine snacks to keep going, and sat in uncomfortable chairs that smelled like they'd been peed on by homeless people. At last, Tom and Alix appeared from some inner sanctum to bring them up to date. Alix decided to remain standing and leaned against the wall. Tom plopped down in one of the chairs despite the reek and raked his fingers through those wild, red curls.

"Okay, the officers who found the purse tried to contact Xo in the afternoon. Her phone, IDs, and credit cards, are all in her purse. They couldn't track her down. She had some pepper spray unused, and form letters announcing that she would no longer be available for interpreting because she intended to leave New Orleans. Either of you know anything about that?" Two heads shook.

"That letter made them wonder if she planned to disappear without telling her family. We told them about the men she thought followed her. They said maybe she'd spooked and wanted to leave the city. Alix and I never saw these guys."

"I told them to talk to Edward at the coffee shop since Xo was nervous enough to ask him to walk her to the corner on Monday," Alix added.

Connor raised his bowed head. "I might have. When we were at the sculpture garden, a Latino man, well-dressed, thin mustache, passed us and greeted her pleasantly enough, but she seemed upset and eager to leave after that."

"Maybe you can help ID him," Alix said.

"Why didn't I see him? I mean, I walked her to church, and she said they lurked in Jackson Square." Junior cracked his large knuckles.

"I think you just answered your own question, badass football player," Connor needled. "I doubt they wanted to take on anyone your size in a public place and laid low."

"They probably thought they could take you! Anyhow, I'm glad if I did her some good, but now I feel sort of helpless."

"We all do. The taxi was wiped clean, no prints, same with the handbag. Since she doesn't have her phone, they can't trace her. I guess whoever took her hoped someone would steal the bag from the unlocked cab and use the credit cards here in the city to confuse the police. No blood found. That's something to be thankful for," Alix said as she placed her hand on Junior's shoulder and gave it squeeze.

Tony Ancona trudged into the waiting room like a

surgeon bearing bad news. From habit, he tried to push black curls he'd recently had shorn off his swarthy forehead. "We sweated Diego, and he finally broke. Wednesday, three Mexican men broke into his house and threatened his family. They wanted to know the next time Xochi called him for a ride, and stayed at his place until that happened. He was allowed to go to work, but they kept his wife and children hostage until she phoned, then they stole his taxi and left saying they'd come back and kill them all if he notified the police about the cab before noon. I doubt that will happen, but we're assigning a man to watch the house."

"Not good," Tom said, his voice shaking.

"Some good did come of it. They finally bumped the case up from missing person with a twenty-four-hour wait—because ya know sometimes young women go off with bad guys and show up again when the thrill is gone—to abduction. Your parents are being contacted to see if any ransom demands have been made. Usually, families are warned not to tell the police. Considering the Billodeaux fame and fortune, the FBI is being notified right now." Tony slammed his fist into his hand. "Dammit, we already wasted over twelve hours!"

Alix spoke in a soothing female voice. "Her kidnappers were clever. We all know not to call Xo when she's working. The soonest any of us noticed her absence was when she didn't show at Tipitina's and we started to call her. Went right to voice mail."

"Yes, we checked those messages and your alibis. You three Sinners were at camp until past five, and the doctor, here, got off from Ochsner about the same time."

"Alibis!" Tom's face flamed. "As if any of us would hurt Xochi. We all love her."

Ancona gave them a jaded shrug of his shoulders. "Sometimes, it's a case of if I can't have her no one can." He tried to stare down Junior and Connor, but neither blinked nor looked away. "Like I said, you're all clear. A few of the guys still think she had the resources to disappear if she wanted, get a false passport and go somewhere she feels safe. With her language skills, that could cover a lot of ground."

"No. She'd tell us or get in contact when she got there," Tom swore.

"None of you seemed to know she was shutting down her business and supposedly going back to Chapelle. Maybe you ain't as close as you think."

Alix hung on Tom's right arm as his flush grew deeper. "No."

A welcome interruption came in a summons for Officer Ancona. He took the message. "We reached your parents. No ransom demand, but they do know why Xochi planned to leave town. Come on, they want to talk to you. You, too, Doc. We have some pictures you can look at."

Not about to be left behind, Junior stood. "Maybe I did see one of these dark guys, but Xochi didn't point them out." Frankly, he'd been too busy being jealous of Connor to make any clear observations, but had no intention of being left behind.

"Sure, sure. The whole circus can come to town, and I'll be the ringmaster that leads the way." Ancona stalked off, the rest trailing behind him, Junior at the rear of the procession like the only elephant in the parade.

They crammed into a rather small but private office. Another officer handed over the phone and left. Before taking a look at several glossy photos splayed out over the desk, Connor nodded at the telephone. "Are you recording the conversation?"

Tony nodded. "Consider yourself notified. Doc, take a gander at the photos while they talk."

Junior planted himself in one corner of the room, the outsider without a task. Though he couldn't hear the words, the worried tone of the conversation came across loud and clear. Tom listened intently to his folks. Alix pressed as close as she could to hear. "She's going back to Chapelle to become a *traiteur*. That's just nuts!" Tom exclaimed.

"Actually, it's not. My mother believes in them. We have a couple of Mexican ones, *curanderos*, in Chapelle since the Spanish speaking population increased after Hurricane Katrina with the workers staying behind after the cleanup. She gets herbs for her hot flashes from them."

Junior drew Dr. Bullock's scorn. He glanced up from the photos. "I could prescribe something more effective than a handful of leaves. These people mean well, but what they do is mostly psychological, a prayer here, a calming chant there."

"You, the son of a minister, don't believe God can heal?" Junior challenged him right back.

"I didn't say that. Medical miracles do happen. No one knows why, but my father would give the credit to God."

"You two shut up," Tom ordered. "I can hardly hear. Okay, we'll see you tomorrow." He concluded his phone call. "Team meeting at the ranch around eleven for all who can attend. That includes you, Junior."

"I would have come without an invitation. Want me to drive?"

Before that question received an answer, Connor drilled his finger into a photo. "This is the guy from the park."

Ancona picked it up. "That's bad news, one of Esteban Miro's right hand men, possibly an illegitimate son being brought into the drug business. Same guy Diego identified as leading the men at his house."

Tom sucked in a breath. "Miro had Xochi's parents executed, and we shared the same natural father before Joe Billodeaux adopted us. Miro burned her home in Laredo. I was there, supposedly on a 'vacation' with my father. He failed to tell me he'd asked for a ransom for my return. Joe and his friends came after us. We escaped, but at least one of El Jefe's men died in the confrontation. Dad only went to get me back from Bijou but walked into a shit storm. Self-defense if he killed anyone down there. He never said."

Junior kept his mouth shut. He knew who'd taken out most of Miro's men with nothing more than a high-powered hunting rifle, his own father, the former Army ranger. Told as a cautionary tale about the cost of poor decisions and the danger of old enemies, tight-lipped Knox Polk, Sr. opened up one day when his chubby son rebelled against his demanding sports training and threatened to run away to his mother's family in Mexico. The moral: Don't endanger your friends or make enemies unless you absolutely cannot do anything else.

He noticed Connor Bullock stayed silent as well. His reverend father went on that expedition into Mexico along with Connor Riley, his godfather. Joe made both of them go back to report the crime and wait at the border station. As for the rest of the rescue party— Tom's feisty birth mother, Cassie, and his future stepfather, Howdy McCoy—he did not know what their part had been.

Ancona smirked. "The FBI probably knows more about that than any of you do. They'll be tugging those lines as soon as we notify them Diaz was in town."

"These aren't mug shots?" Connor sorted through them again searching for others he might have seen.

"No, surveillance photos. Miro rewards his men with trips to New Orleans aboard his super yacht, *Los Siete Pecados*."

"The Seven Sins," Tom muttered.

"Shouldn't that be The Seven Seas?" Alix asked, Spanish not being that popular in her home state of Wisconsin.

"The Seven Deadly Sins: Pride, Greed, Lust, Envy, Gluttony, Anger, and Sloth. My dad is a preacher." Connor shrugged in a self-deprecating way, but Junior found him guilty of pride in his knowledge. Hell, he could reel those off in Spanish if he wanted.

"We know about your father, Dr. Bullock," said Officer Ancona in a way that implied he'd run their backgrounds, perhaps even Xochi's. "Those sins are practiced in full when *Los Siete Pecados* comes to town. Miro is never aboard. We've raided the ship twice. Once on a tip that women were being forced aboard. We get there, and all we find are more than willing working girls. Another time, we try for drug possession. The most illegal thing we find are Cuban cigars. The ship either has some very sophisticated hidey-holes, or Miro's thugs called in the tips to make us run our asses off and find nothing. Ha-Ha. Part of their fun. She left port this morning."

"Xochi?" Junior asked.

"The ship. By the time we made the connection, she'd sailed into international waters."

"Xo is aboard. I feel it in my heart." Tom slammed a fist against chest. "Miro sent for her to take his final revenge."

"She's due to dock in Cozumel in a couple of day. The Feebs will have eyes there."

"Miro's men could dump her overboard or—or do other things to her." Alix embraced her husband and buried her face in his shoulder.

Ancona shook head. "Miro is a possessive son of a bitch. No one touches what he wants. That's the best news I can give you. She's got a few days, and I want to find her as much as you do. Honestly, I told you more than I should. Go home and console your parents. Out, let me and the professionals work this case."

"You're lead on this case?" Tom said, doubt in his voice. Junior didn't like the idea either. Wasn't Tony just Officer Ancona, not Detective Ancona?

"I'm this far from taking the detective exam." Tony pinched two of his short, thick fingers together. "The powers that be are letting me in on it for now because I know Xochi and some of you guys. I care about her. Satisfied?"

"I guess we have to be. Yeah, Junior, you drive my SUV. I don't want to travel with Dean if Stacy is going to be puking along the way, not to mention hauling Wynn along with her happy music playing on a three-hour drive. I need to be able to think. We'll talk along the way." Tom stood hunched over as if in pain.

"Do you have a seat for me? I'm calling in for personal emergency leave," Connor said.

How Junior wanted to tell him to drive by himself, but he could not claim the Escalade lacked room. He couldn't shut out the Rev's son. That good man had coached and encouraged him so much over the years. In fact, he'd gotten along fine with Connor despite the occasional condescending remark—until he became a rival for Xochi.

"Sure. The more heads we put together about this the better."

He wouldn't sleep tonight. None of them would.

Chapter Sixteen

Junior drove Tom's SUV past the swampy lowlands and small towns, his eyes on the road, his ears open to every word Tom Billodeaux spoke. Tom, the jester of the Sinners team, the man with the rapid-fire imagination, sat next to him making rescue plans.

"I say we go after her the way Daddy Joe came for me in Mexico. We can fly to Cozumel this afternoon. Everyone brought a travel bag, right? Passports like I told you." They had.

The voice of reason spoke from the backseat. "If you count on carrying weapons, flying is not the way to go," Connor Bullock said. "A private charter, perhaps."

"We can go by sea, Connor Riley's cabin cruiser. Alix loves to fish. I've learned how to use the GPS, the radio, the charts, get fuel, everything. We've spent nights out on the water. He leaves the key at the Intracoastal City marina, said we could take it out any time we want. Besides, the Rileys are following their son around on some kind of junior golf tour, so they won't miss it. No need to spend hours getting to the Gulf from New Orleans. It's docked right on the coast. We might even pick up some time on the super yacht being smaller and faster."

"Tom, don't you think we need to tell Dean about this plan before we act?" Alix interjected from her seat beside Connor. Dean, the natural leader, Dean, the white knight, Junior knew the whole team would follow the man anywhere.

"Hell, no! He has a sick wife, a child, and another on the way. If anything happens to him, the Sinners fall apart. I'm sort of dispensable—and Xochi's blood brother."

"You're the best kicker in the league and not dispensable to me, but I guess I can watch your back well enough."

"You're not going, Legs."

Alix slammed the back of Tom's seat. "Why, because I'm a girl? I'm just as strong as you are and can shoot a rifle better from all the hunting I did with my dad."

"Not because you're a girl. I know you can handle yourself and kick the shit out of any one man. More because you're my wife, and I'd worry about you when I have to concentrate on rescuing Xo. Not to mention if more than one of Miro's thugs came after you, I don't want to imagine what they'd do to a beautiful blonde Amazon. After they had their fun, I wouldn't put it past Miro to sell you to some Middle Eastern sultan for his private harem."

"He does have a point, Alix," the ever-cool Dr. Bullock said.

Alix punched him in the arm and crossed hers over her chest as she sank back into her seat.

Junior tried not to intervene. Recalling Dean tiptoeing around his ailing wife, and now this argument between the honeymooners, marriage appeared a whole lot more complicated than I love you, you love me, let's start a happy family. He thought he could do it though, being so attuned to Xo.

"However, you'll need someone with good reasoning skills, not to mention medical training in case there is violence," Connor replied to Alix's frowning displeasure reflected in the rearview mirror.

"Good point. You're in, Connor," Tom pronounced.

That riled Junior. "What am I? Just the chauffeur? When my dad taught all the children to use handguns, who always got the highest scores, the nice cluster in the heart? He wanted me to join the military and gave me extra training none of you got once I hardened up."

"You're the guy who can knock down an opponent, run faster, and carry more than any of us. Not to mention how you feel about Xo. I thought you realized you were in from the beginning."

"Good, because I am."

Tom became thoughtful again. "Dad has his hunting rifles in that locked cabinet in the den. Wish it didn't have a glass front because he'll notice if they're gone, not to mention he'll hold the team meeting there. The house is probably crawling with Feds. Difficult to get anything out of the house."

"I can get weapons. I know the code to the security building." Junior said that matter-of-factly, but he noticed Tom's eyes go wide.

"Dad never gave that code to any of us. Said we didn't belong in there."

"Mine trusts me—and he's ready to defend Lorena Ranch from the Zombie Apocalypse if necessary." After this, would Knox Polk, Sr. ever trust his son again? Hard to say. His dad didn't think the way most men did, which made him good at his security job and prepared for anything.

"Good then. Junior gets the weapons. Connor, can you put together a medical kit in case we need it?"

"We'll stop at my mother's clinic on our way out of town. I can get what I need there."

"And I do nothing," Alix grumbled.

"You can provision the boat, make up a hot dish, bake us a cake to take along."

This time, Alix slapped the back of Tom's head. "Sometimes, I think you will never understand me! I can cook *and* kick ass."

Tom rubbed the stinging spot on his scalp. "Hey, an army travels on its stomach. It's an important job. If I should die, I hope it's with a piece of your Bundt cake melting in my mouth—because that is heaven."

Junior had to credit Tom with quick thinking after his blunder. Alix's soft, "Oh" signaled an end to the debate. She seemed to absorb the fact that Tom might not survive the rescue of his sister this time even though it had been disguised by a joke. Junior stepped on the gas. The sooner they got to Lorena Ranch, the better.

Their group found the parking area by the house already crowded and spilling over into the open area by the barn. Junior could name the attendees by their vehicles: Dean and Stacy in her car with the safety seats in the back, the twins with the red Prius that belonged to one of them, Teddy's van with the hand controls and wheelchair lift, the Rev's black SUV with the gold cross on the back, and two anonymous black sedans. No sign of either of Mack's SUV or his sports car. Lorena was in far off Australia. Had she gotten word yet? She'd be angry if left out. The rest of the Billodeaux offspring still lived at home, though Trinity would probably head out on his own at the end of the summer.

Camp Love Letter kids moved around the property, some staring at the mass of cars gathered by the house, others oblivious, while being herded to activities by the high school and college students the Billodeauxs hired to help out since their own family members had thinned. Inside the big house, Junior witnessed the Billodeaux equivalent of going to the mattresses Godfather style.

The giant coffee urns used for parties stood on the kitchen counter. A glimpse into the formal dining room revealed the large table covered by platters of cold cuts, fixings, and baskets of bread and rolls. A few bagels and Danish leftover from breakfast remained on a tray. His mother bent over the stove to place a huge casserole of Mexican lasagna into the oven. Her hands wobbled. Strangers in dark suits sat at her kitchen table along with one man he knew, Tony Ancona, the dark circles of fatigue showing under his eyes despite his Italian complexion. He'd added a dark jacket to his rumpled clothing of the night before and cradled a big mug of coffee in his hands. For the moment, Junior ignored him.

"Mama," Junior said. "Let me help you." He took the casserole from her grasp and placed it into the oven, got the door shut before his mother engulfed him with her soft form and warm hug.

"My son! Xochi, like my daughter. How does this happen to her?"

"I don't know, Ma. Everyone loves her."

"I know!" Tom snapped. "Esteban Miro's men took her to him. What are you doing here, Ancona? I thought the FBI is running the show now."

"I rode up here with some agents from New Orleans. The quick skivvy—Rachelle and the guy from the coffee shop both identified Ramon Diaz, and the barista fingered another of Miro's men known at El Animal. No ransom calls yet."

"El Animal," Corazon wailed as she cried on Junior's chest. "My beautiful Xochi with El Animal." He patted her back, small comfort.

In contrast the family butler, Brinsley, entered the kitchen with perfect solemnity and announced, "Team meeting in five minutes. Feel free to bring your beverages. Luncheon will be served directly after." If his skin hadn't taken on a gray cast, no one would have known him to be sick at heart.

The kitchen emptied. Most of the family sat assembled already, youngest members on the floor to give room to their elders, Teddy in his wheelchair as usual. Connor slid in beside his massive father and slim mother. He immediately glued his eyes to the iPad he'd been fiddling with on the drive. Knox Polk, Sr. placed a comforting arm around Corazon and gave his son a nod. That trio remained standing. Tom and Alix flopped down among the siblings.

Daddy Joe, still handsome and always imposing, took the floor to quiet the crowd. Mama Nell stood beside him holding his hand. "Thank y'all for coming home at such short notice. We told you what we knew when we called. Not much has changed. No ransom demands have been issued. I'll turn the meeting over to Agent Maguire now."

"Just a second," Mama Nell said. "I can only say we worry about each of you, but short of locking you in your rooms here on the ranch, we know you have lives to live. Please live them with caution because you are dear to us." Blinking tears away, she went to take her place next to Stacy on the long sofa. Her agitated husband, spring-loaded, only stepped out of the circle and sank his fingers into the back of a leather recliner holding his white-haired mother, Mawmaw Nadine.

The agent took the floor. "We believe Xochi Billodeaux was not taken for the purpose of ransom. We obtained information from the security camera mounted under the fire escape stairs at her residence."

"Damn, I should have thought of that!" Tom exclaimed.

Agent Maguire, a man so plain of face and receding of hairline he would have made a nicely anonymous spy, held up a hand. No doubt his dark suit, white shirt, and black tie covered a body more fit that it appeared and possibly a weapon. "No interruptions, please. I will answer questions after I finish. Although the stolen cab passed rapidly by the camera, we have been able to enhance the brief view of the driver, one Ramon Diaz, also known as *Hijo de Diablo* and believed to be an illegitimate son of Esteban Miro."

Tom sucked in a breath at the mention of the name. "Last time I saw Miro, he sent a man to kill me and Xochi."

"Yes, given the Billodeauxs' last encounter with Miro, we believe this to be a revenge kidnapping. We are not as sure of the role of the second man known as Indio. He seems to provide some sort of medical hocus-pocus for Miro. El Jefe as his men call him is known to be terminally ill. His henchmen abandoned the cab close to the dock, and we believe these men took Xochi aboard Miro's yacht. Perhaps, this is El Jefe's last attempt to tie up loose ends."

Tom's hand shot up despite a tightening of the agent's lips. "Is my sister being taken to Cozumel or not?"

"Miro is currently in residence there at one of the hotels so that is most likely the destination of his yacht. Whether he will board it or have your sister brought to him, we do not know. The last would be better for extraction."

"You'll try to save her."

"Of course. Leave the logistics to us. Do not interfere in any way." Maguire eyed Joe Billodeaux and the very out of shape Reverend Bullock, then flicked his glance to the fit and stony-eyed Knox Polk, Sr. "We are asking you not to notify the other members of your former ill-advised rescue party."

"Hey, I went to bring my son home from Mexico. It was a family matter involving my cousin Bijou. We didn't know we'd find the scene of an execution, no." Joe crushed his famous hands together to stop them from waving in the air. "Can't you bring in da SEALS and board dat boat?"

"Dear," Nell cautioned.

"Y'all should do it," Mawmaw Nadine said, giving more solid support for instant action.

"It's a large ship. Xochi might be killed before we found her. We don't want to force a quick execution. Let us handle this when the ship gets to port within the next day or so. We can't divulge any more of our plans for the moment. I suggest everyone have something to eat and then go about your business as normally as possible."

No one appeared to agree with this pronouncement.

Face flaming, red curls flying, Tom jumped to his feet. "I can't eat! How can any of us eat and go about our business. You are doing nothing, nothing at all."

"Tom, take it to the barn," Mama Nell said quietly. Taking it to the barn in Billodeaux parlance meant kicking hay bales or cleaning stalls until their temper subsided.

"Yeah, I'll take it to the barn. Then, I'm going back to New Orleans to go about my business as if that is possible. Junior, Connor, Alix, you coming with me or finding other rides?" His friends rose along with Reverend Bullock.

"Just a moment, young men and young lady. If I might offer a prayer for Xochi's safety." People bowed their heads whether they were AME, Episcopalian, or Catholic. The Rev did a worthy and lengthy job of it, extolling Xochi's virtues almost as if delivering a eulogy. He commended her safety into the hands of God.

All the while, Junior's feet itched to move, to get the rescue underway. He could sense Tom's tension and Connor's concern as the prayer dragged on. The instant the Rev finished, their group left for the barn with Mawmaw Nadine shouting after them in her still surprisingly strong voice, "You come back here and eat. I brought my bread pudding," as if food solved everything.

Tom ditched Alix as he stormed through the kitchen. "Honey, make some sandwiches to go."

"You'd better not leave without me, Tom Billodeaux!"

"We save time if we eat on the road. Please, Alix. Meet us in the barn." Grumbling, she veered into the dining room and started slapping ham and cheese onto rye bread.

Once outside the kitchen door, Tom gave Junior a command. "Junior, do your thing."

Junior nodded and peeled off toward the security building where his father kept an arsenal handy for any occasion. He punched in the code to the stout, windowless structure and moved quickly inside. A flick of the light switch revealed the bank of screens showing various parts of the ranch from the front gate to the swimming pool to the palm grove where some of the more able of the Camp Love Letter kids played an innocent game of hide-and-seek. Taking a canvas bag from a hook, he surveyed the selection of weapons all neatly racked along the wall. He skipped the rifles and went right to the handguns, selecting three that packed a punch and took the same ammo. Doubting Connor had any shooting experience, Junior added three assault weapons, easy to use, and possible to send out a swath of rounds without much targeting. He dumped extra clips into the bottom of the sack.

Done in under five minutes—except when he exited the building, his father stood before the door. "Just coming to check the screens. You?" he asked with perfect calm. "No lies, Junior."

"We're going after Xochi."

"I figured." Stepping inside, Knox Polk, Sr. held out his hand for the canvas sack. Feeling that he'd failed Tom, Junior relinquished it. Knox took a look. "Good choices. Do you remember what I taught you?"

"Everything. Moving targets are hard to hit. Don't get your friends killed. Come back alive. I think those are the most important points, sir."

"They are. I wish I could come with you. As your mother would say, *Vaya con Dios*." His hug came quick and unexpected. Father and son were about the same height. Knox's trim body pressed against Junior's muscle and bulk for only a moment. "Now, let me leave first and patrol around the grounds. I'm being watched. I'll draw my shadow off toward the pool. You slip out in a few minutes and stow those weapons right away before you do anything else."

That fast, his father acted as he said he would. Junior waited five minutes that seemed like an hour before striding directly to Tom's vehicle and putting the sack in its rear. From there, he moved to the barn to find Tom kicking hay bales, Connor seated on one, and Tony Ancona leaning against an empty stall. Uh-oh. More trouble. At least, he wouldn't be caught with the weapons, though all were legally registered to Knox Polk, Sr.

"Have a seat," Ancona said as Alix burst into the barn with her well-toned arms draped in plastic bags. Her hands carried a mountain of plastic containers, and her fingers were threaded with plastic forks.

"Ah, hi Tony. We thought we'd have a picnic in the barn since the house is so crowded." Her rosy cheeks and guilty blue eyes gave her away.

"Right. You're up to something, all of you guys. Me, I've been booted off the case since the Feebs are here. Got nothing to do with my time the next few days as I decided to take off to study for that detective exam. I thought maybe I could study better on the beach at Cozumel. How about you? Going on a trip?"

Tom stopped abusing the animal feed and answered bluntly. "We're going after Xochi."

"Sure, you are. Ever considered that a man in law enforcement might have some contacts south of the border and easier access than a bunch of amateurs? I could be a huge help."

Tom's eyes shifted around the group. "Any objections?" None. "Then let's get going. I'll drive since I know the way. It will take us two hours or less. Alix, sit by me." For the first time in hours, she seemed happy.

"I couldn't carry the drinks, too," she said, though it looked like she'd emptied an entire fruit bowl into one of the sacks as a bunch of grapes hung over the edge.

"No problem. There's a convenience store near the clinic. Pick up some cases of water and soft drinks while I get the emergency bag from my mother's closet," Connor suggested.

Even Junior couldn't fault that idea. They piled into the SUV and carried out the first phase of their plan. Connor placed a large medical bag in the rear with the weapons and beverages. "My mom always has this handy for local emergencies."

"Any problems with the staff?"

"No, I said my mother wanted it out at the ranch. Dr. Arminta Green Bullock rules that place, and they all know me. No questions asked. Worst part was having to chitchat about my residency in order to seem normal. That took some time."

Tom put the pedal to the metal the second Connor snapped his seatbelt. He did remember to cool it until they'd passed the speed trap and put Chapelle in the rearview mirror. Onto the four-lane, off on good road leading to Abbeville, then a long thirteen miles through nowhere to the small port with its helicopter base and dry docks. Riley's sleek, white cabin cruiser appeared out of place among the shrimp boats, but he paid a local to keep an eye on his watercraft. The old dude with the grizzled beard turned over the keys pleasantly enough to Tom with a friendly, "Me, I never forget that red hair or your pretty lady. You going after redfish?"

"No, just using *Wideout* for cruising. The little woman wants to take a tan," Tom answered casually.

Alix at nearly six feet was no little woman and looked bigger when angry sort of like a cat. Junior watched her bristle at her husband's remark. The caretaker didn't seem to notice. "You two of the whitest people I ever did see. Be sure to put on your lotion now."

"We'll do that. Alix, grab the food. The rest of you get the supplies."

No one argued, but Junior could see Alix wanted to start another round. He slung the canvas bag of weapons over a shoulder, hefted twos cases of bottled water under his arms, and started down the dock. Connor followed with the medical bag. Doing his part, Tony Ancona carried the rest of the drinks, twelve packs stacked two deep to his armpits. They boarded and stowed the gear amid the gasoline cans with extra fuel.

Still miffed, Alix shoved the plastic containers at Tom. "Corazon insisted I take part of the Mexican lasagna so Junior won't starve. Mawmaw Nadine wouldn't let me leave without enough bread pudding for four, and Mama Nell bagged enough raw vegetables to keep us all healthy."

"That's dinner. I'm going to miss you so much,

babe." Tom moved in for a kiss.

Alix stepped back. "Exactly how am I going to explain that you are leaving the little woman who needs a tan behind? Tell me that. Because I should be going along with you."

Yes, Tom's mouth had tripped him up again. Junior waited to watch and learn.

"Say we had an argument and you don't want to go along with four guys who will spend all their time drinking and talking sports."

"Ah, you don't think he knows I play football?"

"With all your gear on, no one can tell you're a girl."

"Tom, I'm as famous as you and Dean!" Alix's face grew as red as if she had a sunburn.

"Guys, could we have a minute? Wait on the dock." He offered Alix a hand aboard, led her to the cabin, closed the door behind them.

From their position, Junior could hear raised voices, then silence followed by thumping, and at last sobs as Alix emerged and climbed up to join them.

"Quickest quickie ever, but I bet it was a good one," Ancona murmured to Junior. The lesson learned: Sex could not solve everything, but it sure helped to smooth things out.

"Okay, just leave, but I'm going to find a place to stay nearby and be here when you get back with Xochi. And all of you better come back." She strode away from *Wideout* and passed the perplexed caretaker.

"I thought you was gonna take a tan, no?"

"No. Because men are assholes," Alix answered loud enough for them to hear and gave no other explanation. She sat behind the wheel of the SUV staring at the boat until Tom took *Wideout* down the channel, into the bay, and out to sea.

Chapter Seventeen

No sense in being weak with hunger if she had a chance to escape, Xochi reasoned. As soon as her stomach settled, she rummaged in the small refrigerator. If this were her last meal, she might as well forget about fat and cholesterol. She selected a rich lobster salad, an individual bottle of white wine, and some grapes from what appeared to be a standard bon voyage basket that sat atop it. The chocolates interspersed with the fruit she marked for her dessert.

Settling on the roomy bed, she flicked on the remote for the small television mounted on the wall. No news. No weather. Only a selection of movies both new and classic as well as some porn. She chose a romantic comedy, but found she couldn't laugh, and switched to an action/adventure where brave and built shirtless heroes fought the forces of evil and won. Satisfying if fantastic. Afterward, she napped longer than she would have thought possible.

The sunset gleamed yellow and orange in the waters of the Gulf. The ship headed directly into its glory moving west. If only she could tell someone. Xochi tried the door again and roused the same response, a curt *Que*. Locked and still guarded. "*Nada*," she answered and continued her survey of the room. Also nothing she could use as a weapon. The bathroom held a nice array of scented soaps and shampoos, citrusy rinses, and thick hand creams. A cheap plastic toothbrush with a tube of paste and a comb that appeared too flimsy to tame her thick waves made up the rest of the amenities. The towels were thick and the one on top of the stack had been twisted into the shape of a seal. Cute, but unhelpful.

Xo wondered how long it took to make a shiv from a toothbrush handle and what she could sharpen it against. Every surface appeared slick and shiny. No hair spray and no lighter to make an impromptu flame-thrower. All her basic needs had been considered and all possible weapons removed.

Giving up for the moment, she dined on a cheese and cracker plate augmented with more fruit and a handful of chocolates from the basket. She nuked a paper cup of chamomile tea to sooth her nerves and ran another movie in which Bruce Willis saved the world. Dozing off in the middle of it, Xochi dreamed of a quartet of men coming to her rescue, Junior Polk bare-chested and wearing a bandoleer of bullets, Tom blazing with a halo of yellow light and firing pistols from both hands. Off to either side, Tony Ancona, shirt half-unbuttoned over a hairy chest, wielded an automatic weapon, and Connor Bullock carried a medical bag in one hand and a similar weapon in the other. She woke with a start when the final explosions of the film blasted on the screen. Turning off the set, Xochi fell to her knees beside the bed and prayed.

"Mama Pilar in heaven, your daughter Xochi needs help. Please whisper in the ear of Mother Mary and send me rescue." She recited the rosary from memory and calmed.

Next, a hot shower, erasing all her makeup. Why

try to appear more attractive for kidnappers? She washed out her underwear and carefully hung her purple Anchi Services uniform in the tiny closet, draping the pink, purple and silver scarf over the hanger attached to the pole. Fortunately, the towels were lavish enough to cover her body, though she wondered if spy cameras infested her room like cockroaches. Xochi slid beneath her covers before stripping the towel and allowed the sound of the ship cutting through the water to lull her to sleep.

In the morning, the pale pink sunrise woke her because she'd forgotten to cover the portholes. With the sun to the rear, they still headed west. Too awake to drowse anymore, Xochi wrapped the towel around her again, rummaged in the fridge, and found a breakfast burrito to heat, added a banana to her meal, and made instant coffee so bad she immediately recalled Junior's perfect brew. Would she ever see him again or Tom or even Edward from the coffee shop? She wanted her life back. She'd be more open to new ideas, she promised. Maybe five years was not such a difference. Possibly she'd hung on to her secret virginity too long, and now it would be wasted on men who did not care. Such thoughts weren't helpful.

She dressed in slightly damp underwear and her uniform, didn't bother with shoes, but padded around the room in bare feet. Exercise might help, maybe some music. In a cabinet beneath the TV, she unearthed a selection of CDs and an archaic player to run them. Her favorite salsa tunes were included in the collection. She put one on and danced hard for over an hour, pretending she had a partner big enough to flip her over his shoulder and catch her around the waist, big enough to carry her away from her captivity. Sweaty, she showered again and washed her hair. A few teeth from the cheap comb broke as she forced it through her thick locks.

More movies, more food, more dancing, another shower and to bed. Xochi wished for the voyage to end no matter what the destination.

****

The next day, Xochi roused from a nap to the absence of engine noise and the slapping of waves against the hull. The very stillness woke her. It did not last long. Noise erupted from a very boisterous welcoming party: the shrieks and giggles of women, the hoarse shouts and lewd comments of men that went on for hours. At one point, someone tried to enter her room.

"Beat it!" the cruder of her captors said. "*Es occupado*." The couple searching for a bedroom went on their merry way before she could shout for help, not that they would have heard her above the din of the mariachi band and the singing of drunks.

Xochi felt oddly safe in her locked cabin with a guard outside.

Unfortunately, the door did open as the fiesta wound down, allowing the man with the thin mustache to enter. A swath of red material draped his arm and a pair of the icepick heels like the ones Xochi wished she'd had in the cab dangled from his fingers. His compatriot guarded the exit from the inside now.

"Put these on."

"And if I refuse?" Xochi raised her chin more defiant in attitude than she felt in reality.

"Then, Animal will dress you. That will make him

very happy." El Animal smiled, showing strong, sharp teeth as if he'd like to eat her raw.

She went into the bathroom and considered locking the door until she realized that the mechanism had been removed. No help for it unless she wanted the assistance of the Animal. Xochi shed her business dress and let the cheap, scarlet fabric slide over her underwear, neither mawmaw nor provocative, but she rather wished her bra was not the kind that gave her full breasts a lift. The deep V of the neckline showed off extensive cleavage, and the hem came only to mid-thigh. She sat on the commode to put on the shoes held onto her feet by ankle straps. Standing, Xochi wobbled. One heel appeared to be slightly shorter than the other throwing off her gait. No time to ponder that because the bathroom door flew open.

"*Bueno*. You are dressed at last. Animal, the rest of her costume."

Xochi retreated hard against the shower stall, but could go no farther. "You don't want me to touch you, eh? I am crude and ugly, but he's the one you should fear. They call Diaz *Hijo de Diablo*. You understand?"

"Son of the Devil."

"*Si*." He forced a strip of black silk into her mouth by pinching her jaws until she opened for him. With a hard spin of her shoulders, he turned her around to knot it tight before she could spit it out. Diaz produced a silver mask that descended over her face and was bound to her head by another silky band. As he checked the effect, Xochi viewed herself in the mirror, two terrified brown eyes peering from the slightly slanted, almond-shaped holes, her mouth completed covered by the gleaming, full lips of the mask. The gag appeared to be part of the fasteners.

Both men wore festive embroidered shirts. Diaz donned the mask of a skull and El Animal the vicious likeness of a snarling jaguar. They shoved her from the bathroom. The ship's whistle sounded.

"We go."

"The shoes, I can't walk in them."

"You will not go far." Diaz placed his arm around her neck and the Animal pulled her waist tight against his.

Xochi hobbled along, apparently as drunk as the rest of the crowd, many devils and beasts among them along with tawdry women wearing masks similar to her own, heading for the gangplank where buses waited on the street to take them away. The partiers loaded the vehicles and hung out the windows, many still singing off-color ditties. Xochi stumbled aboard with one man in front and the other behind. They took no special seat, only blended in with the rest of the revelers, Mardi Gras Mexicano style, Xo thought, without a happy ending or even a hangover.

As promised, they did not go far, only to a luxury hotel where apparently the party continued in a ballroom. Only she and her captors and a few other women boarded the elevator to the penthouse floor. Only she, Diaz, and El Animal exited. The rest rode back to the ballroom.

Prodded through a doorway into the suite and across a large room, Xochi came to a halt before a massively ornate silver inlaid desk worthy of the Emperor Maximillian himself. The man behind it on a throne-like chair seemed diminished by its size, but she doubted he realized that. Everything about him had shrunken. Gone the prosperous belly and oily skin of the overly fed. The head of black hair now grew white and wispy above sunken cheeks that made him resemble the skeleton mask. Large yellow teeth gripped the gold holder and grinned at her from behind the glowing red end of a cigarette. The eyes were the same, however—the flat black of a venomous snake.

"Senorita Xochi. *Bienvenido*. Remove her mask and let her speak."

Xochi gazed on the man she had once been tutored to call Don Esteban. She'd hung shyly on her father's leg as he coaxed her to come forward with sweets taken from a pocket. Sometimes, he'd let her ride one of his horses, and she fled to the far end of pasture until her *Papi* ordered her to return and gave her a cuff for avoiding El Jefe. This man had ordered her parents killed.

She licked her dry lips, but looked at him squarely. "Don Esteban, I see you are dying. Perhaps if I am so welcome, you will let me go as a good deed to save your soul."

Chapter Eighteen

El Jefe laughed with a sound like rattling bones. "You have wit as well as your mother's beauty. Her only talent was pleasing a man. But at thirteen, girls have little to say that is worth listening to. Of course, I had her first as soon as her parents sold her to the whorehouse in Laredo. The madam always called me when she had someone young and fresh. Oh, what I taught your mama to do with a man. And when I was done with her, I gave her to your father."

Shifting her weight onto the better heel, Xochi steadied herself with one hand on the back of a chair. No one sat in Don Esteban's presence unless told to do so. She recalled that as well, along with her mother being merry and loving, a young woman who took her child to church and pestered her *Papi* to send her little flower to parochial school. Though the ugly comments the dying man made caused her cheeks to burn, she'd figured out her mother's past fairly easily long ago. How else would a Mexican girl of fourteen have fallen into the hands of Bijou Billodeaux if not through the sex trade?

Xochi did not respond to his baiting. She continued to look into those flat, dead eyes. "I have numerous talents."

"*Si, si*, you know many languages and translate for a living. I have kept track of you for many years. Here."

185

He struggled to open the heavy desk drawer. Diaz leaped to do it for him. "Thank you, *hijo*. A fancy phone, a tablet, no? All your history is here."

He called up photos and ran his yellowed finger over one picture after another of Xochi—playing soccer, dressed in white lace for her first communion on the church steps, graduating from high school, studying abroad and mingling with Spanish friends, receiving her college diploma, summa cum laude in languages, and most recently having her latte and beignets after church services, and walking with Connor in the sculpture garden. Unnerving, all of it, to have been spied upon for so many years. None at the ranch or inside a church, and she took comfort from that. *Mama Pilar and Mother Mary be with me now.*

Xochi looked away from her life flickering by like an old-time movie and regarded El Jefe again. "You have very little time to live, maybe a few days. I can see the dirty brown-green of the cancer inside you engulfing your lungs, your kidneys, your brain, spreading its darkness, becoming one with the blackness of your soul. You are beyond salvation."

Don Esteban raised almost nonexistent brows that wrinkled his lax flesh. "What, a girl so devout she never misses church on Sunday does not believe I can be saved by my last-minute confession to a priest?"

"God is so not easily fooled." Her words sliced like a sacrificial knife. She noticed more about his aura, that the edges appeared to be thinning to smoke, his blackness slowly unraveling. Not long to go at all.

El Jefe slapped his frail hand on the desk. "You, you will give me life again, here on the island sacred to Ix Chel, goddess of birth. The offering of a virgin to her at the time of the full moon will restore me."

"You truly believe that? Or that I am a virgin...an American woman of my age? The cancer has rotted your brain." Xochi matched his laugh now, hers one of scorn.

She bluffed. Her fears had kept her from the ultimate intimacy with men. When her body blossomed so early, casting her into womanhood before her mind could understand its meaning and power, she hunched her shoulders and ran from men who called out to her making suggestive comments and boys her age who just wanted to touch her body. What if she were like her mother—a *puta* in the making, hot-blooded, a natural whore?

The manifestation of her auras rode hard on the tails of that fear. Mama Nell had told her she was her own person, to put her shoulders back, ignore the catcalls, and slap away the gropers, but she could offer no cure for the auras. Help came from Rosemarie Leleux who explained them as gifts from God, one that could protect her from harm and aid others. After seeing them as an asset, relying on them to gauge people, she worried the auras would disappear if she lost her virginity. A silly notion, perhaps, but one she hadn't confided to Miss Rosemarie, unwed and probably still a virgin at her advanced age.

Don Esteban's raspy voice battered through her rambling thoughts. "I know you, Xochi, everything about you. In the clubs, you dance like a wanton woman, but go home alone. When you lived in Spain, you took no lovers among the other students. In college, you only go out in groups of friends. Before that, Joe Billodeaux and your brothers keep the men away."

Xochi straightened her spine and pulled back her shoulders as Mama Nell had taught her. Her posture in the sleazy dress only made her breasts more prominent. El Animal licked his lips, and Diaz's dark eyes glittered at the sight. "I've been in sinful New Orleans for a few years and lived with a man for several weeks recently."

Still bluffing. Even self-involved Stacy did not know her long-time roommate was a virgin. She'd simply assumed that while she carried on with a professor at college, Xochi had done the same with college boys and later experimented some more while abroad. Mooning over Dean and finally connecting with him had taken all Stacy's attention away from anything Xo might be doing.

Again, her bluff did not work. Esteban Miro laughed, his teeth clacking together unpleasantly when he stopped. "That overgrown boy who follows you like a puppy as he has your entire life? I think not. You did not share a room and sent him away not long ago."

How did the drug lord know these things? Being famous, the Billodeauxs were cautious about directional listening devices and long-range cameras. Perhaps, his men had gained access to the electronics store below her and bugged the apartment. Whatever, it did not matter now.

Xochi grasped at a last drifting straw. "What if I told you I was a lesbian? Would that make me ineligible to be a human sacrifice to Ix Chel?"

Don Esteban brought up one more photo—of her kissing Connor by the LOVE sculpture in the park. "All over the internet. But, this doctor has been too occupied to go any farther. Still, you should be more careful of your reputation."

"Why? To save myself for you?" Haughty defiance did not help either, only provoked him.

"Enough! Indio!"

The carved double doors to a master bedroom opened. Beyond it, a bed draped in royal purple waited. Chubby cupids peeped from the intricate design of a golden headboard and giggled atop the bedposts. Seeming out of place beside it stood a man in a white lab coat. He snapped on a pair of rubber gloves from a box sitting on the bow-legged, gilded night table, but it was the man called Indio who came for Xochi.

"Come, Xochitl, warrior queen, you will not be harmed."

"Only Corazon calls me that."

"You should embrace your full Nahuatl name and all it means." He held out an arm thickened by fat to support her.

In the daylight, Xochi took notice of his soft stomach and the lines of age in his broad, sagging face. One swift kick in the gut with the spiked heels, and she could take him. Not as leggy as Alix, but she had her dance moves going for her. Maybe her thoughts showed on her face because the Animal moved behind her and locked her arms with his.

He lifted her half off the ground and bodily moved her into the bedroom. "She kicks," he explained as he tossed her belly down on the bed.

"I will need her face-up, *por favor*," the man in the lab coat said as he held his hands up, keeping them sterile.

"If you think I'm going to cooperate in this you…" Xochi burrowed into the rich coverlet.

"Of course, we do not expect that. Animal, put her

into position," Diaz said, cold, calm and detached.

The Animal put an ungentle hand on her arm, drew it up behind her back, and flipped her before it snapped. She struck out at him with those heels, but he dodged in time.

"Careful. Do not bruise her. Use these as restraints." The Mayan man removed four sets of padded handcuffs from the night table.

The Animal managed to fasten her wrists without help to the bedposts, but when it came to securing her legs spread eagle, he motioned to Diaz to do the work while he laid on top of her calves, pressing her hard into the mattress. Once she was bound, he discarded the shoes, throwing them across the room as if they personally offended him. He shoved the cheap dress above her waist and pulled down the black cotton bikini panties she'd worn to work—how many days ago— stretching them below her knees, her modest bikini wax job exposed for all four men to see. He sniffed her underwear before straightening.

"Good enough, doctor?" El Animal stepped aside, his eyes on her crotch, not Xochi's face as if she were only a cunt to him and not a person.

"*Si*, if you please." The medical man nodded toward a LED light on a headband. Indio fitted it over his gray hair.

Xochi tensed. She could imagine many, many things these men could do to her without taking her virginity. Wasn't she already staked out like a character in a bondage movie? She clung with hope to the Indian's orders—no bruises.

The doctor leaned over and gently parted her labia as if coaxing a pink rosebud to open, nothing more but some close scrutiny. Keeping his fingers in place, he beckoned Indio to come closer with a jerk of his head and aimed the bright light at her vagina again. "*Ella es una virgen.*"

"*Si, Bueno.*"

The doctor rolled off his gloves and tossed them in a wastebasket. Diaz stepped forward to place a wad of hundred-dollar American bills—the preferred currency of Cozumel—into his hands. He left immediately, replaced by El Jefe staring at her privates from the foot of the bed.

"As I thought, the virgin who will restore me to health and allow me to take revenge on Bijou Billodeaux. Once I would have delighted in relieving you of your virginity, would not have hesitated to take you with all these men watching me full of envy. No matter, soon my potency will be restored."

Xochi arched both brows at him. "Bijou is long gone, or have you forgotten? This man, this Indio, is a charlatan after your money. He, too, knows you will not live long enough to turn on him. Your illness has no cure, and your evil is without redemption." She would have spit had her mouth not been so dry.

"Indio is a revered *curandero*, better by far than the old woman you consult. He bears a name in Nahuatl so long and complex that Indio is simply easier. He descends from the royal Mayan priests of old. Indio knows ways to restore a man and bring back his virility—with the sacrifice of a virgin on the night of the full moon to the goddess, Ix Chel." The flat, black eyes of Esteban Miro now held a spark of madness and desperation.

Xochi turned her head to one side to study the face

of the supposed Mayan priest. "While I have no doubt that this man's ancestors sacrificed virgins, he is a fraud and a liar making this up as he goes along. His motive for deceiving you is more than greed, something else personal." Yes, she made the man blink his heavy lids.

Hiding from her gaze, Indio moved away from the bed into a shadow cast by the late afternoon sun. "Your opinion does not matter. To honor your sacrifice, you may request whatever you want to eat, drink, wear, or bring you amusement, but you will remain here alone in this room until it is time to go to the sacred place."

Xochi drew on the attitude of the tough child she'd once been to quell her fear. She peeled back her lips into a snarky grin. "You could start by releasing me, but first I want you, personally, to pull up my panties. Then, I need my clothes from the ship. I hardly think Ix Chel approves of the way I am dressed now."

"Ix Chel is a fertility goddess, not a nun. However, we do as you ask for now. On the night of the event you will have proper attire to honor her." The Indian approached and hooked his fingers in the sides of her panties, drew them up, and let them snap against her skin, a petty punishment for ridiculing him perhaps, but he did not touch her flesh.

The cuffs came off. Xochi sat up and crossed her legs beneath her skirt. "Say, any of you want to rape a virgin, or would a substitute be too hard to find on the island? None of you have a sister or daughter to fill the bill?"

She saw the rage that filled Indio at her mockery. El Animal seemed ready and willing to comply. He rubbed a hand over his crotch. Diaz showed no emotion at her taunt.

"Out, out, all of you! Only I will hold the key." Don Esteban—a man who felt his power waning by the minute and so frail that any of the men might have knocked him down and taken her at will—gestured wildly at the door.

Perhaps, long-term loyalty or the promise of great rewards made them file silently from the bedroom, leaving Xochi alone with the man who'd had her parents killed. Certainly, if one had raped her, she might be killed immediately as useless or be spared to be sold into sexual slavery, both preferable to allowing evil incarnate to have his way.

She lay back on the copious pillows of the bed and exposed her shapely legs to the devil. "I believe I'd like surf and turf for my dinner, baked potato with butter, a fresh green salad, and strawberry-topped cheesecake for dessert. See to it, Esteban." Xochi dropped his honorific and closed her eyes, wondering if he would strike her, bruise her. But no, Esteban Miro left the room without a murmur, leaving her to dream of a lovely meal hopefully served with a steak knife that might be of use later.

Chapter Nineteen

The would-be rescuers steered *Wideout* through the night, the nearly full moon making a pathway on the surface of the sea, as if guiding them to Xochi. Tom explained the guidance system of the boat and showed them all how to hold the course when he rested. They feed themselves with spicy Mexican lasagna, sweet bread pudding, leftover sandwiches from lunch, and handfuls of baby carrots and fruit from the plastic bag. Junior feared they wouldn't get to the island fast enough. The taste of bile filled his mouth, the bitter salt air his nostrils.

They fueled the boat from the cans of gas that made up most of their cargo. *Wideout* possessed a powerful engine. Its owner wouldn't have it any other way, but it did gobble fuel. Thanks to the calculations Dr. Bullock did on his iPad, he got them there with half a can left at a good rate of speed in late afternoon of the third day. Once docked, Tom ceded his leadership to role Tony Ancona who slung the weapons bag over his shoulder and went out to meet the customs officials descending on the boat. Connor lugged the medical bag. As the men rummaged through it, he insisted, "Doctor, el doctor. Supplies for the clinic," improvising on the fly. He showed his passport. Tom and Junior did as well. They received their white tourist cards for a stay on the island.

Tony flashed his badge, let them paw through the firearms he claimed to own, and explained the situation. "We're looking for a kidnapped American girl we believe is on the island. These are friends and relatives who can identify her." He jerked his curly head toward Tom, Connor, and Junior. "Any of you have a picture?"

Tom and Junior instantly moved a hand toward their wallets and flipped them open to a photo of Xochi taken for the college yearbook her senior year, no cap and gown, posed in a simple black drape that the dark waves of her hair cascaded over. "*Muy bonita*" the port officials agreed, but they had not seen her. Tony appropriated Junior's wallet, stuffed with bills for the trip from the ATM at the convenience store in Chapelle. He drew out a reasonable bribe. "Now have you seen her?"

Their heads still shook no, but one added, "Yesterday, so many girls like her come on the ferry to meet *Los Siete Pecados* when she docked. A big fiesta for the men aboard and then all go to one of the hotels on buses to continue the party."

Tony got the name of the place, Casa de Luna, and headed toward a road to hail a taxi. A customs man called after him, "You gonna contact the *policia*, no?"

"*Absolutamente*," Tony said as a cab pulled over, and they crammed inside to place their rumps on bulging springs covered with a Mexican serape.

"Really? We're going to get bogged down with the local cops," Tom complained.

"Nope. Car rental, *por favor*."

On such a small island, nothing was far away. Tony plucked a ten from Tom's wallet, paid, and got out without waiting for change. "I'll get the cars. Look around if you want, but don't go far. And Tom, cover up that red hair. You stand out like a stoplight from a mile away. At least, that sunburn you got helps you to blend in with the other tourists. Not much we can do to disguise Junior, but black jeans and the Sinners tee is good. I like that snarling red devil on the chest. Intimidating. Doc, get a black shirt instead of that yellow Izod thing you got on. You own a pair dark jeans? We might have night work to do."

Connor considered his polo shirt and pressed khakis donned prior to docking as if trying to figure out what he'd done wrong. "Yes, I have jeans with me. I'll buy what is necessary."

"Great, pick up a T-shirt for me, size medium."

All three purchased black caps embroidered with palm trees flanking the word Cozumel, and Connor bought two T-shirts that matched. As Tom shoved his curls beneath the cap, he caught Junior eyeing a poster of a bare-breasted Mayan woman with aggressively protruding nipples. Kneeling, she held a red rose in her hand. Her wavy black locks, crowned by a serpent knotted twice around itself, fell down her back. Everything about her proclaimed sexual fecundity.

"Looks like Xochi," Junior said, the longing in his voice hard to hide from Tom.

"How do you know what Xochi's breasts look like?" Tom snapped.

"I don't, but I have an imagination. I wanted one of these posters when your dad took us on vacation here years ago. My mama wouldn't let me buy one."

"Ah, *senores*, that is our beautiful island goddess, Ix Chel. All of you are old enough to take her home now. Five dollars. We have her on soft, soft velvet for ten," the unctuous store owner tempted as he stroked his hands together.

"No, she's not Ix Chel. This is the real fertility goddess, an old hag with the feet and ears of a jaguar and a snake on her head." Connor passed around his iPad. "See, she's pouring out the water of life from a pot, or maybe it's amniotic fluid considering she oversaw childbirth." He appeared pleased to gross out Tom and Junior.

Jangling two sets of car keys, Tony joined them and took a look. "If I saw that when I came from the womb, I'd crawl back inside. Weapons are stowed in the trunk of my car. Let's get to the hotel, Tom with me, Junior and Doc in the other. Medical kit rides with you two."

They obeyed the pairings, but not happily. Chagrined, Junior slammed his car door. "You really love stomping on other people's dreams, don't you, Connor? I'm getting one of those posters before we go home."

"Boys will be boys, I guess." The doctor put the emphasis on *boys*. "And facts are facts. We have to face them, unpleasant as they might be. We might be too late to save Xochi."

"Tom would feel it—I would feel it if she were gone." He truly believed that. They had a special connection whether Xochi acknowledged it or not.

"Doubtful, but believe what you want. I'll wait and see for myself."

The rivals fell into silence until arrival at the hotel sporting a tasteful Mexican colonial décor with not a single velvet painting of Ix Chel on its walls. Tropical flowers in hammered cooper bowls adorned the tables.

The lobby seemed rather full of loitering single men, but otherwise very nice. Ancona stood in front of the marble counter already speaking to a desk clerk. They moved to stand near him and Tom.

"No, we don't want a room right now. Have you seen this woman?" He nodded for Tom to show Xochi's picture again.

"No, *senor*. But, see the concierge if you want one like her for the night."

Tony automatically put a hand on Tom's arm as if preventing a grenade from going off. "*Policia*." He brought out his badge again. "This U. S. citizen has been abducted and brought to the island. Very bad for Cozumel and this hotel if she's found here without your cooperation."

"So I have heard from the others." The clerk nodded toward the men filling the lobby. "I tell them all the same—many such women are staying here."

"Guests of Esteban Miro?"

"I cannot tell the names of our guests. Jobs are hard to find on a small island." The man, slight of build and making up for that with a huge, slicked back pompadour, shook like a nervous Chihuahua. He lowered his voice to the faintest of whispers and tried to speak without moving his lips. "Some of these men are his. Always stays in the penthouse." Back at full volume, he offered the men a room again. "You will pay in cash?"

"Junior, pay the man for our room."

"Will you not want two?"

Junior forked over the money, which disappeared under the desk. They went through the motions of checking in and getting key cards before settling into ample leather chairs gathered around a small marquetry table with their travel bags at their feet. "Keep your eyes open for any of the guys in the cab with Xochi. Doc, I know you'd recognize Diaz again."

"I think I could identify Miro for you. His face is burned into my brain," Tom offered.

"Doubt it. The NOPD has recent pictures of him. He took chemo for his cancer in Argentina. We hoped he'd try to get into Ochsner so we could nab him, but he's too wily to make that mistake. Anyhow, the chemo really fried him. Looks like a dying old man now—which he is."

Time passed slower than a turtle race. Tony bought a pack of cards at the gift shop and organized a game of gin rummy played for pocket change. Any time an elevator opened or a person entered the lobby, their eyes swung from their hands to the new arrival, never Xochi. Junior, not usually bad at cards, lost hand after hand, many to Connor Bullock. How could the doctor be so unaffected by the situation? As for himself, he wanted to charge the steps that would take him to Xochi, but Tony eyed him every time he started to stand, a silent command to stay put.

One of the conservatively dressed men lurking here and there behind potted palms and in the darker corners of the lobby with their backs to the walls and their eyes on the doors stopped by their seating area and watched the game for a while. "Buy you folks a beer?" he offered.

"No, thanks. We're all recovering alcoholics," Tony lied.

"Look, I can always pick out a fellow lawman. This is an FBI affair. Let us handle it."

"What have you done so far to recover the girl? Miro's men slipped her by you, didn't they?"

"Yes, a clever ruse that party."

"A clever ruse? Who are you, Sherlock Holmes?" Tony wisecracked. "You blew it."

"We couldn't separate her from the crowd, but she's here, you bet, probably in Miro's suite. Neither maids nor room service is allowed inside. And the name is Agent Baldwin."

"Why don't you go and get her!" Tom interrupted.

"Might get her killed if we move in too fast. This is why we don't work with amateurs."

"The way I see it you can always use more eyes. We'll be staying." Tony shuffled the deck for another round of rummy. "We got key cards and a right to sit here all night if we want."

"Just stay out of our way when it goes down."

"Gotcha. Go sit and stop calling attention to us."

The agent offered his card. "In case you get in over your heads." When Tony failed to accept it, Baldwin tucked it into Ancona's jacket pocket and went back to his chair where he picked up a fat Ludlum novel and pretended to read again.

Their group, two by two, took turns getting a light dinner at the hotel restaurant. "Nothing that's gonna give you gas, stay away from the frijoles and cheese. No booze. Remember, this is a stakeout. I'm going for the fish tacos and fries myself," Ancona advised. "Doc, why don't you change into your dark clothes in the restroom after you eat?"

"Why not give me a room key now?"

"Because what we bought was information, not fancy accommodations. I doubt the key cards work."

Connor nodded. He went to dine with Junior, still deeply unhappy about the pairing. Not much conversation over Junior's jumbo shrimp skewers and the doctor's grilled mahi-mahi with rice. When a room service trolley passed filled with domed platters, Junior said, "I hope they're feeding Xochi."

"Not if they want her too weak to resist."

"She will resist, weak or not." Junior felt sure of that.

Connor blotted his lips on a napkin. "That might not be the best idea. I'm going to change now." He returned in dark clothes like most of the men in the lobby. They relieved Tony and Tom to get their plates of fish tacos.

The bulge of his shoulder holster a little more noticeable, Tony came back wearing the black T-shirt under his jacket and a thoughtful look on his Italian face. "Any of you guys have a phone that works on the island?"

Connor held his up. "I have international calling because of the overseas medical conferences I've attended."

Junior, not to be outdone, said, "So do I. Not the medical conferences, but when Xochi studied in Spain, I wanted to keep in touch. I promised my dad I'd work extra hours at the ranch if I could get international calling and I'd pay the bills, so he let me. Believe me, I earned it clearing brush and mucking stalls."

"She couldn't even get away from you in Europe," Connor felt moved to say.

Junior drew back a fist. Both Tony and Tom hung on his arm to stay the blow.

Tony reorganized once the moment passed. "New

partners, then. Doc with me; Tom and Junior together. That way we can keep in touch by phone if we get separated. You good with that?"

"About time," Junior said.

The man who had accosted them earlier strolled by and hissed, "Amateurs," on his way to the restroom. Junior sat down hanging his head for losing his cool as if he'd just been benched for a penalty.

The clock crawled toward eight p.m. like a dying man trying to reach water in the desert. Sunburned tourists returned from snorkeling or a day of scuba diving and went to their rooms. An old Mexican woman toting a large bag from a gift shop hobbled across the lobby around seven-thirty and got into the elevator. A half hour later, she returned without the bag. So much for any action. Getting on their nerves, Tom tapped his foot incessantly. Junior stilled the nervous leg. "Pretend we're at a Sinners game waiting to be called up. Play it cool, Tom."

"Wish I could kick some asses into a net. I'd feel better," he muttered.

The sun set, and the full moon rose in the sky. Junior jumped up when an ambulance screamed to a halt outside the hotel doors. What if her captors had injured Xochi so seriously they'd called for medical assistance, an idea he could not tolerate? Tony flicked him a look, but did not dare tell him to sit again.

Medics unloaded a gurney and dashed for the elevator. Within minutes, they returned with a man, face like a mummy, draped in sheets and moaning pitifully. Diaz, El Animal, and the Indian followed their boss into the emergency vehicle, one of them, Diaz, with a garment bag slung over his shoulder as if El Jefe might need his tuxedo for a formal affair later in the night. Four more of the drug lord's henchmen sitting in the lobby dashed to a van in the parking lot.

"Miro," Tony stated.

"I can't believe that's him," Tom said.

"Believe it. This might be our chance to search the penthouse. I don't care if we have to shoot the lock off the door." Tony rose ready for action, then hung back as Agent Baldwin led his men toward the stairs and elevators.

"Tell you what. Tom and Junior, you follow the ambulance at a safe distance. Xochi could be in there or the van. Take the car with the weapons. I have my own on me." He exchanged keys with Junior. "Doc might need his medical kit if we find her or some of the Feebs get injured. Go, go, go! Bullock stay behind me." They bolted for the elevators—and had to wait for their return from the penthouse floor after delivering the FBI agents.

Tom and Junior extended their long legs and crammed them inside the small car. "Go faster," Tom ordered once they were on the road.

"We can see the ambulance lights from here. If we get too close, they'll notice us."

"Hey, the van is peeling off toward the docks. Maybe Xochi is still on board the yacht, and we could…"

Junior put on his game face; his *I will not be moved* face. "Ancona said to follow the ambulance. He knows what he's doing. We don't. Besides, I am sure the FBI already checked the ship."

"Lots of hiding places aboard, Tony said. Maybe they didn't find the one where Xochi is being held. I vote for the boat."

"This isn't a democracy. It's *Car and Driver*, and I'm the driver. You think we could do better than the FBI?" Junior clung to the steering wheel, his brown knuckles knotted in case Tom tried to take control. He had a hunch, a feeling which vehicle to follow.

A moment later, the ambulance shot by the turn for the medical center and continued on the road that rimmed part of the island. Its emergency lights still blazed, clearing the light traffic in its way. That traffic provided some cover for their small anonymous tourist rental until the vehicle turned onto the Cross-Island Highway that bisected Cozumel. Not much out here to hide them and only one likely destination, the Mayan ruins of San Gervasio, closed for the night. Junior killed the headlights, not really necessary on this night of the full moon, and tried to stay in the dramatic shadows that orb cast over their path.

By the time they approached the entrance to the parking lot of the visitor center, the ambulance passed them in the other lane, its siren no longer blaring, its lights stilled. Tom did not take that well.

"They've dumped her somewhere along here and because you were so cautious, we have no idea where."

"I think we do." Junior parked in the darkness cast by a large tree where taxi drivers often waited for their tourist fares to return. The night guard closed the entrance to the complex as they watched and returned to his post counting a wad of currency.

"Then let's go in!"

"I'm calling Ancona." He dialed Connor's cell. "Did you find Xochi at the hotel?" Junior listened as Tom tried to grab the phone. "Okay, then. I think she's been taken inside the archaeological park. Get here as fast as you can."

"Tell me!" Tom demanded.

"The FBI broke into the penthouse. They found Xochi's uniform dress, her shoes, and a pink and purple scarf I know belongs to her. No blood, just some dark liquid spilled all over the bed. Somehow, they got her out of the room without being seen."

"Shit!"

Junior got out of the car and put his hand on the trunk where the firearms lay. "I know she's here. I feel it like a warm breeze on my face. Do you?"

Tom came to stand beside him, quieted himself, breathed deep. "I think I do."

Chapter Twenty

Xochi stumbled on the moonlit pathway and dragged her feet. Not all of her weakness was feigned. They'd forced enough of that nasty brown liquid down her throat to affect her, though she'd managed to spit out some and let more dribble from the sides of her mouth before Diaz pinched her nose shut and the Animal pried her jaws open for the fake priest. Later, when Indio cut out her still beating heart, she might regret not having taken all of the potion the Mayan said would make the sacrifice painless. The bitter brew contained the same ancient herbs fed to other maidens offered up by their families to the blood hungry gods, Indio claimed.

The drink wasn't the worst of the indignities she'd suffered. At first, she'd enjoyed her surf and turf. Unfortunately, the turf portion arrived rare and thinly sliced, nothing a table knife couldn't cut. The lobster tail was large with lots of melted butter for dipping and extra to pour on the baked potato, and the salad as tasty as salad could be. She'd enjoyed the cheesecake followed by a deep bubble bath, wrapping herself in the hotel's heavy terry robe and watching Mexican TV, which reminded her with a pang of Corazon and Junior. Best of all, near midnight she'd sent Diaz, grinding his teeth, downstairs to fetch hot chocolate and a pastry tray, sure the kitchen would be closed. He did deliver, but it took some time.

In the morning, she'd asked for eggs Benedict and fresh squeezed orange juice only to find herself ignored. "You must fast today," Indio informed her, speaking through a crack in the door. But the room had a coffeemaker, and no one had removed the more than ample pastry tray. She made a pot and ate every last crumb of the sweet rolls and Danish throughout the morning. So much for fasting. Xo hoped that ruined or delayed their plans. No lunch came, nor dinner, no matter how often she made demands. She brewed more coffee and sweetened it heavily with packets of sugar, though she usually took only milk. The more energy she could muster, the better.

The day passed slowly as the sun moved across the sky outlining the pattern of the Spanish grillwork on the windows onto the thick carpeting. Pretty, but they were bars by any other name. Planning to be well rested for whatever came, she napped as much as she was able. At last, the doors opened and in tottered an old woman who could have passed for Corazon's grandmother.

"Take off, take off," she insisted, tugging at the uniform dress Xochi had asked for yesterday. "I brush your beautiful hair and give you something pretty to wear. You will be *una princesa.*"

As she sat there in her underwear feeling the brush gently untangle her often stubborn curls, Xochi closed her eyes, calmed her nerves, and imagined her mother doing the same and after her, Mama Nell, and Corazon, so soothing. She'd kept her hair long no matter how difficult the upkeep in remembrance of Pilar. Mama Nell never insisted she do any different. Bless them all. Unlike her birth mother, she'd fallen gently into the hands of loving women.

The *abuela* finished her work and broke the spell by unhooking Xochi's bra. "What are you doing!"

"Dress you. You stand now."

The fingers bumpy with arthritis peeled down her panties and wrapped a long swath of embroidered fabric around Xochi, high up under her bosom, tucking it in and ending in a notch that allowed her to walk easily. To be sure it stayed in place, a large safety pin was placed carefully out of sight. The granny withdrew a colorful band from the same bag that held the cloth and drew it over Xochi's head and arms until it rested just above her naked breasts. Xo tugged it into place to cover her nipples. Her dresser scolded, "No, no, no" and placed it above her breasts again. "No touch! You a Mayan *princesa*."

Not the kind of royalty she'd wanted to be when her *Papi* brought her a huge sack of American princess clothes and fancy shoes that made her twirl with glee and shout, "*Soy una princesa!*" Of course, he'd stolen them from the Billodeaux twins when he'd robbed Lorena Ranch and taken Tommy as well. Bijou Billodeaux had also stolen some of El Jefe's drugs and paid with his life. All of that had led to this. How could vengeance sustain itself so long in the human heart without eating it entirely away?

The old woman called out that she had finished her task, and the double doors opened. She accepted her payment and scuttled out. The four men entered. Xochi shook her hair over her bosom and covered her naked breasts with her hands. Three of them laughed at her modesty, but Indio dissented. "This is a sign she is a pure and worthy sacrifice."

"Hardly," Xochi said, still hoping to upset their plans. "I've done some really nasty things with men other than have sex with them. Use your imaginations. And I ate breakfast!"

Clearly, the Animal had an excellent imagination from the instant bulge in his pants, but the others remained unmoved, Miro too frail, Diaz too cold, and the Mayan too intent on bringing off this worthless ceremony, breakfast not an issue with him either. Would El Jefe's men kill the priest when it failed to work? His problem, not hers.

Miro gestured to a tall standing closet deeply carved like the bedroom doors. "Let me see her in all the regalia I paid for."

Diaz opened it with a key. Xochi had tried to explore the closet earlier hoping for wire hangers that could be made into weapons, but without a hairpin or nail file on her, she'd failed at beginner's lock picking. He removed a dazzling feathered cloak resplendent in red and yellow. Xo wondered how many small, helpless birds had been murdered to provide the materials as Diaz lifted her hair and settled it on her shoulders. Amazingly light and it covered her breasts, freeing up her hands for a fight. The crown he took from a shelf she could only describe as repulsive. A serpent molded from gold, each scale glittering, reared back showing its fangs while its coils looped twice around its writhing body. They set the monstrosity on her head, and when she attempted to take it off, the Animal cuffed her hands behind her back even though it sent the feathered cloak drifting to the floor.

"*Perfecto*," Indio said. "Remove the crown for now. Cuff her feet and bring me the shoes."

Cautious, the Animal pushed her into a sitting position and grabbed both slender ankles in one hand before she could kick out. He applied the padded cuffs again. Diaz brought the footwear, sandals also made of gold including the straps that held them on. With the Animal restraining her knees, Indio bent reverently to place them on her feet. "As the black Americans say, you will go to paradise in golden slippers."

"I can't walk in these! They'll cut into my feet."

Indio answered her protest mildly. "You will not have to walk far, Xochitl. Now, sip the drink that will ease your pathway to the gods."

He retrieved a bowl from the other room and held it to her lips. Xo clamped them shut and turned her head aside, jostling its contents, spilling a little on the royal purple spread. "This is for the best. You will not feel the knife enter your chest."

The Mayan offered the bowl again. Xochi took a large mouthful and spit it in his face.

"Very well. Restrain her."

Diaz ripped the top sheet from the bed and with the help of the Animal swaddled her body tightly. Better than struggling naked-breasted, Xo thought at first until Diaz pinched her nose and the Animal pried open her jaws. She held her breath as long as she could and when she finally had to swallow pushed some of the potion out the sides of her mouth in a battle she could not win. At last, they let her alone while Indio placed the crown in a garment bag with the cloak, and Miro watched all from a chair, too weak to stand for long. "Make the call," the drug lord ordered in a voice raspy and out of breath.

As the drug numbed her legs and her lips, Xochi

heard the sirens approach. Please God, let that be the police coming to rescue me. No such luck. When the men in white entered the bedroom, she was already bundled knees-to-chin like a Peruvian mummy burial. They dumped her into a sling beneath the bed of the gurney and replaced the top over her. The weight of a body settled above her, too light to be any of them but Esteban Miro. Sheets draped over the gurney hid her from view.

They moved. The ping of an elevator opening, the ride down, another ping as the gurney exited and rolled across the tiles of the lobby floor. She tried to scream but only a moan came out, quickly echoed by Miro above. No need to gag her, the narcotic had taken her voice. Against her will, she dozed as the ambulance drove away from all help, all rescue.

Xochi woke to the light slapping of her cheeks. She sat upright unshackled in the ambulance. The feathered cloak covered her body and the serpent crown sat atop her dark curls. "You must walk now," Indio informed her from where he stood by the open doors. "We go to meet the goddess."

She blinked, trying to focus. Indio had transformed into a figure from the painted walls of his ancestral tombs. He wore a loincloth of spotted jaguar hide, his bare chest covered with an impressive green jade pectoral portraying the head of a screaming man. More of the pelt draped his shoulders, clawed paws dangling. A tall headdress of trailing green plumes sat on his shaved head. He carried a staff similarly crowned with feathers. With his free hand, he offered her help in stepping down. Too weak to do otherwise, Xochi accepted, loathing herself even as she did.

"I will lead and sing the ancient chants of praise to the goddess. Diaz, assist Don Esteban. Animal, you will help the girl to walk." They set off, no one questioning this suddenly regal man. He sang in Nahuatl of which she recognized little except for the name Ix Chel. Diaz held up the tottering Miro. Perhaps her drugged eyes deceived her, but Xochi swore Miro's black aura streamed out behind him like smoke from a piece of coal gradually growing smaller and smaller.

El Animal dragged her along, fondling her breast with one hand hidden under her cloak. Good, that offense helped clear her mind with a burst of anger. She tripped, she dragged the golden sandals cutting into her flesh, she sagged to dead weight, then stiffened again before he decided to carry her. What did the poet say—"Do not go gentle into that good night. Rage, rage against the dying of the light." She had no intention of making her sacrifice easy for them.

Chapter Twenty-One

Junior opened the trunk and took out the weapons bag. He handed Tom a pistol and stuck one of his own in his belt. He yearned to break down the barrier that kept him from Xochi and go after her immediately, but tamped down his emotions. A stupid, impetuous move would not help and might harm. He felt her living presence enough to guide him toward patience.

"What about the assault weapons?" Tom asked with outstretched hand.

"We'll see how Ancona wants to divvy them out."

"Then, give me another pistol. You know Connor won't be able to use one."

Junior complied with that request, adding extra clips, and zipped the bag. "We might as well get the place open in order to move fast when they get here." A giant armed man, he strode toward the guard's hut, and the man came out immediately, not with a challenge but with his hands in the air. He jabbered at Junior in rapid Spanish.

"He doesn't want us to shoot him. He has no money," Junior translated for Tom.

"Yeah, I got that. My Spanish is pretty good. But, he does have money from the bribe he got for aiding and abetting."

"*Si*, yes, I have money. You take it all," said the quaking guard who obviously spoke English well enough. "Not a bribe, *senores*. I am helping a dying man with a last wish to see the temple of Ix Chel on the night of the full moon. His friends, they hire some of the people who meet the cruise ships and pose for pictures to go with them. That is all. No harm to anyone."

"Since the young woman was kidnapped from the United States, harm is intended." Junior repeated the words in Spanish to make sure they had an understanding. "Open the entry for us. We're going in to save her."

No one could have complied faster with that request.

Tom fidgeted, raising on the balls of his feet and fingering the butts of the two pistols in his waistband. "We should go ahead. Let Tony and Connor follow."

"You know Diaz and the other thug will be armed. Maybe the Indian guy, too. If we start a firefight, bullets and debris will be flying everywhere with so much crumbling stone around. Xochi might be hit."

"She could be dead if we wait."

"Then it will be on me." Junior accepted that responsibility with dread. How had his father done things like this for a good part of his life? No wonder he kept himself so locked down. Instead of dwelling on that, he questioned the guard. "How do we get to the temple and what will we find there?"

Yes, they had been here before as children, not paying much attention to the guide, scooting off to chase the iguanas sunbathing on the ancient rock walls, the older boys like Dean and Tom making up stories about the red hand prints found in one of the stone houses—the blood of sacrificed victims, they claimed.

No, no, the guide said, more like a signature of the people who once lived there, paint, not blood. They needed a refresher course.

"Here, a map," the guard handed one over. "Follow the path to the central plaza. Go around and take the way to the left to Ka'na Nah, the tall house, a pyramid where the priests made sacrifices before a big clay statue of Ix Chel. There is a small room on top."

"Thank you for your help," Junior said, though he didn't feel moved to offer any money.

"Let's go," Tom urged again.

This time Junior did not have to hold him back because Ancona and Connor Bullock arrived in a spray of gravel, barely stopping before they charged out to join them. "I have the guns. We enter through the visitor's center. It's unlocked. We're headed for a pyramid with a room at the top for sacrifices. Xochi is still alive. Both Tom and I felt her presence like a warm breeze."

"Sure, you did. We're on a tropical island. All the breezes are warm," Connor sneered. "We'd better get moving."

Their group of rescuers got as far as the first cluster of ruins before Ancona stopped them. "Give the doc one of the automatic weapons. He won't be able to handle anything else. See here, point, pull, and spray side to side. Any two-bit criminal can use one."

He thrust the weapon into Connor's hands, steady enough to perform surgery and also hauling the medical bag. "I understand."

"Great, but try not to fire. We don't want bullets everywhere. One for me, Junior, and you take the other so the hothead doesn't go berserk. Two pistols are enough for him."

Junior disbursed the weapons and extra clips and tossed the bag aside. Tom fumed like a lit fuse. "Are we ready to go now?"

Ancona ignored him. "The plan is we get to this pyramid. I go up first, the doc behind me. If I get cut down, then you fire, Bullock. You guys go around the back and climb from there. We approach quiet as we can. I want you two to create a diversion. Throw some pebbles. Make some noise, but stay out of the way until I shout the hands up police stuff."

"I don't think there will be any hands up with these men," Connor said.

"I'm gonna say it real fast. Junior, if you can grab Xochi and get her out of there, do it. You're the only one strong and fast enough to carry her very far. We good? Enough said. Quiet now."

Junior nodded, but if he had to kill to save her, he would. He'd carry Xochi out of hell on his back if necessary. Or die trying.

They took off at a jog down the stone path white in the moonlight. Iguanas, livelier in the evening, skittered out of their way. The central plaza with its ring of buildings came up fast. No time to sightsee, they skirted its rim and ran on the left-hand path, heavy vegetation pressing in on both sides. A rustling in the bushes and all weapons pointed that way—until a mother peccary with her litter of babies pushed onto the road, thought better of attacking, and took cover on the other side.

"Almost blew it," Connor admitted. "I thought it might be an ambush."

"Of Mexican pigs," Tom said, annoyed because they had stopped.

"Nearly there. You can see the top of the temple from here." Junior pointed.

They approached more cautiously now. As pyramids went, the structure wasn't that impressive, not terribly high, with crumbling steps and twisted trees thrusting out of its base. Might have been nicer in its heyday stuccoed over and painted in a rainbow of bright colors, but not now. Stark and gray, it awaited them. From its peak an eerie chant issued in a language almost as dead as its original speakers. The sound covered their approach.

Ancona started up the precarious steps and waved Junior and Tom around the back. He went slowly, giving them time. Connor trailed him. So far, so good.

At the rear of the building, Junior and Tom climbed in tandem and flattened themselves on either side of entry to the altar of Ix Chel guarded by El Animal engrossed in the ceremony. They meant to wait for Tony, not as in shape as either of them since they'd left him puffing at the base of the pyramid, but the chanting stopped. The outlandish priest facing in their direction spoke to Xochi in English, his words entirely clear. He held a very authentic obsidian knife high above Xochi's naked breasts. They had no choice but to act at once.

Chapter Twenty-Two

Xochi lay on her back, her breasts exposed again, her arms too weak to cover them. She'd been stripped of the ridiculous crown and beautiful feathered cloak. Must not get them bloody. Some sensation returned to her feet, prickling up her legs, allowing her to feel the raw spots where the metallic sandals had rubbed against her ankles and toes. Splayed as she was on the altar stone, any of the men could have raped her. Diaz certainly smirked at her from a corner as if the thought had crossed his mind. She doubted if she would have felt a thing. But no, they needed a virgin—to do what? Oh yes, restore El Jefe's health.

Xo blinked to clear her vision and turned her head. Esteban Miro stood by her shoulder reverently holding his trembling hands cupped as if to receive the sacrament—not a wafer but her beating heart. His aura continued to dissolve, drifting away like the smoke of the small fire the priest had lit in a bowl-shaped depression on one of the stones. Indio had carried a bundle of twigs under his cloak, but lit them with a Bic. The anachronism made her smile as much as she was able, but control of her facial muscles was definitely returning. "Mumbo jumbo," she managed to say. "Fr-Fraud." She should have felt terror, but only a weak defiance surfaced, the drug perhaps suppressing her true emotions.

"Do not fear, Don Esteban. Soon she will carry our request for your restoration to Ix Chel."

"Won't," Xochi vowed.

"She will have no choice. She is our virgin sacrifice. You will live again, and she will pay for the death of my son, Miguel, killed by the man who adopted her. Let him feel the pain of losing a child." The obsidian knife he drew from a sheath at his waist rose high into the air to gain power from its downward thrust on its way to cut out her heart.

Xochi wished she were sleeping, but did she dream? Some mighty force shoved the Animal from the doorway and sent him facedown onto the stone floor. Junior filled one of the small entries to the sacrificial chamber. Not bare-chested, not wearing a bandoleer, but gripping a weapon in his hands. His deep violet aura clothed his entire body as he rested a heavy foot on the back of the thug.

"My father killed Miguel, not hers!" All eyes turned his way. The leering red devil on his shirt grinned in the moonlight, the rest of him dark in the night to all eyes except hers.

At her shoulder, Xochi heard Esteban Miro whisper, "El Diablo."

His cupped hands broke open. The last of his aura evaporated. Xochi swore she saw a final flash of red in his eyes before the man crumpled to the floor of the temple. Let him ask Ix Chel for his own favors!

His darkness was replaced by the blazing yellow light of Tom's aura as her brother ducked under Junior's arm and fired at the priest's hand as the knife moved downward. Shards of the jade breastplate filled the air. The tip of the sacrificial knife broke off, propelled by the bullet toward Indio's eyes where it lodged, blinding the man. Yet, the lethal obsidian blade continued to descend. Junior discharged his pistol. Xochi believed he hit the man dead center where the mouth of the screaming man on the pectoral created a perfect O of a target. Junior walked over El Animal, moved into the chamber, scooped her from the altar, and threw her over one broad shoulder before he pivoted and darted toward the way out.

El Animal rolled over and raised his weapon to destroy them both. Tony Ancona took him out with a shot to the head. The man fell back like the dead beast he was. That left only Diaz alive, either fleeing or in pursuit, spraying bullets at Tom to gain exit. Had any hit her brother, extinguished his brilliant light? Xochi lost sight of him as Junior took three of the precarious steps at a time, gripping the gnarled trees at the side of the pyramid for balance. He jumped to the ground and hit the pathway running, the greatest speed trial of his life. His great heart pumped hard against her breasts. His lungs heaved beneath her ribs as he zigzagged down the path. Xochi felt the warmth, the connection between them, overcoming any numbness, any fear.

With her head lolling over Junior's shoulder, Xochi watched him put distance between them and Diaz. Still the man fired at them, coming amazingly close to Junior's feet and aiming higher. One bullet glanced off the automatic weapon he had strapped over his shoulder. Junior bucked but kept running as if he carried an intercepted ball toward the goal line. Nothing stopped his strides, not even the peccary in the road clacking its tusks in defense of its young. He vaulted over the pig. Diaz gunned the animals down to clear his way, but their fallen corpses scattered across the pathway slowed him and made the stones treacherous with their blood. He slipped, scrambled, regained his balance.

Junior reached the plaza where the road curved slightly, putting the bulk of the ruins between them and the gunman, but they could hear his running footsteps gaining as Junior slowed. "The ruin with the red hands, remember?" Xochi whispered in Junior's ear. His breath coming hard, he nodded against her hair. "A little house with two rooms sits behind it. Go there. Hide us. He might have more men waiting to meet him at the entrance."

"No, I can do this, keep running until you are safe."

"Junior, we need to hide. Please listen to me. You are running on adrenaline and going to crash."

Without breaking stride, Junior veered off on a little side path and stooped inside the building. He laid her tenderly on what Xochi knew to be another altar. Doubled over, his hands on his knees, Junior gasped for air. Diaz's footsteps passed and headed for the visitor's center where he might summon reinforcements of his own kind.

"If he doubles back, I'll stand in the doorway and shoot."

"No, I want you to take me." Xochi found she could sit up on her own as the herbal potion wore off helped along by her own adrenaline rush.

"Take you where?"

"No, Junior, take *me*. They wanted a virgin. I refuse to be one any longer. I will not die a virgin."

"Any other time, Xo, but not here, not like this. A virgin, I didn't know. I'd have to be more careful."

"Junior, come here and put your hands on my breasts."

Laying his weapons aside, he moved to stand between her legs and obeyed. His hands were big and hot on her skin. He massaged gently, making her nipples press against his palms. His eyes closed as if he'd dreamed of this forever. She thought perhaps he had.

"Now kiss me."

He did. Again, their lips fit perfectly, sealing with mutual passion. She licked the salt of his sweat from them. Xochi felt the warmth rising in her loins, spreading from a central core. She lay back against the stone of the altar taking Junior with her, pleased to feel his arousal in this most dangerous of situations. One of his hands deserted a breast and probed into the V of her skirt. She opened wide for him as he tested her with a broad thumb that sent bolts of pleasure through her body. "Hurry," she said, arching for him.

"Soon."

He continued the delicious torment of the thumb and inserted one broad finger inside of her, stretching her, trying to make this easier for her she knew, spreading the wetness he found around her opening. He paused, fumbling with the stubborn zipper of his jeans.

"Just do it, please, Junior!"

He gave one tremendous thrust of his pelvis and pushed through her virgin's membrane. She'd felt worse pain when she skinned her knees playing soccer as a child. This was more of an extraordinary fullness that made her move her hips beneath his, seeking comfort.

"This is going to be fast, sorry. Later, I'll make it

up to you. I promise." Junior pulled back and thrust again, two, three times. He kept that thumb in place, though, bearing down, and Xochi felt the surge of completion other women talked about, but new to her. She clawed at his back in excitement. He flinched and withdrew. Her right hand came away bloody.

"You're wounded, and yet you did this for me."

"I would do anything for you. Take a bullet. Well, I guess I did." With nothing to see him by but the moonlight of the goddess, Ix Chel, his smile still charmed her.

Footsteps approached. Their friends or Miro's men? Junior tucked himself in, drew up the zipper, and grasped the automatic. "Get down behind the altar."

Xochi pulled the embroidered band across her breasts, covering what she could, and crouched, but the running steps and heavy breathing passed to be followed a bit later by a more measured tread and Tom's voice complaining, "Jesus, Connor, I can walk by myself."

Calm and self-possessed, the doctor answered, "I've heard more than one man say that and then collapse. Accept the aid."

"Here, in here!" Xochi shouted. "Junior needs help." She crowded up behind her savior, trying to leave the small sanctuary and bring him assistance. Junior did not move. Blocking the doorway, he remained ready to fight. The conversation stopped, and the footsteps turned their way.

Xo saw the somewhat muted glow of Tom's aura through Junior's akimbo arms as her brother entered the first room of the shelter. He had a startling white sling on one arm and an equally pristine bandage on a bicep where his shirt had been torn away revealing a pressure pad on his shoulder. His attitude, not scared, but grouchy.

"Put that weapon down, Junior. You are damned intimidating when armed. Tony went ahead to pursue Diaz. He's called in the FBI, too. Big mess to clean up back at the temple. Miro is dead—of natural causes, Connor says. El Animal and the Indian, they died of gunshot wounds. Tony took out the Animal. I fired on the priest, but I think Junior did the kill shot."

Connor crowded in still toting the medical kit and the automatic weapon on his shoulder. "I only had to use one of these, and Tom is exceedingly ungrateful as well as lucky. A graze on the upper arm, and a bullet that passed clear through his shoulder without hitting anything major. Junior, let me take a look."

"A bullet in his back. He's been bleeding all this time, and I might have made it worse," Xochi confessed. "Junior, take off your shirt and show him."

"I'm fine. Just leave it, Xo. It felt like a bee sting."

"Adrenaline kicked in just as it does when you are making a big play."

"Yeah, I know that."

"Right now, the bullet is plugging the wound, preventing too much bleeding. Now, give Tom the gun and show me your back—or I can just go around you if you stop blocking the way." Connor waited with exasperated patience.

Xochi pressed hard against Junior's hip trying to turn him like a stubborn revolving door. Finally, he yielded and passed his weapon to Tom while Xo stripped him of his red devil T-shirt and gathered the bloody shirt against her chest.

Connor took a flashlight from his bag and examined the wound. "Some scratches that don't amount to much, and a bullet hole that needs to be probed somewhere with better light and much more sanitary conditions. I suggest we go to the clinic. It doesn't look as if it's embedded deeply, possibly a ricochet. On the whole, you are fortunate to have the musculature of an ox, Junior."

"Gosh, thanks. I worked hard for my— musculature."

They filed out, Tom and Connor and Junior. Xochi held back a moment. She'd left the goddess an offering of a small, brown stain on her altar. As she passed the wall of the red hands, she pressed her bloodied palm firmly against the stucco, then drew the T-shirt over her head to hide any accidental nakedness if the band should slip. They'd been here that imprint proclaimed, Xochi Billodeaux and Junior Polk, the man she loved.

Chapter Twenty-Three

Junior Polk only winced as Dr. Bullock captured the bullet in his back and tugged it free. The slug made a metallic sound, clanking into a metal pan at the clinic. The rest wasn't so bad. Even if it had been, he would never give the doc the satisfaction of hearing him scream or let Xochi know how badly he might have been hurt. Bullock closed the wound with the help of a local anesthetic, slapped on a dressing, and administered a huge dose of antibiotics into Junior's round, brown hind cheek. He wondered if the pants-down humiliation was necessary since Xochi stayed by his side, holding his hand, lending her warmth, as he lay on his stomach on the examination table.

Connor offered her a lab coat as a coverall, but Xochi refused to relinquish the bloody T-shirt. "I'm fine, not a scratch on me. I had to be kept perfect for the goddess. Lucky me." She dropped Junior's hand and hugged her arms tight around herself.

"Except for your feet, obviously."

Xo wiggled her toes inside a pair of paper slippers, now washed clean and coated with antibiotic ointment. Ordinary stick-on bandages covered the shallow cuts on her ankles. "Those sandals did kill my feet. Being a human sacrifice is no picnic."

Connor eyed her stance. "You should also see a psychiatrist for PTSD. Not only soldiers suffer from it."

"I'll see someone."

"Someone better than a *traiteur*."

"That's up to me."

Tony Ancona slouched in and propped himself up against a counter. He'd shed his jacket and wore the tight, black T-shirt and his shoulder holster, gun at the ready. *Mucho macho*, Junior thought.

Folding his arms across his chest, Ancona reported, "Diaz got away. The Feebs probably passed him on the road. That security guard hunkered down behind a counter as soon as he heard shots fired and left the entrance open. He said Diaz got into a white van with a bunch of other men. There must have been a plan to escape after the sacrifice and make for the yacht. The agents watching the ship couldn't stop them. The *Siete Pecados* was all stoked to go and left without permission. She almost rammed several harbor patrol boats on her way out."

"Where's Tom?" Xo asked him.

"Calling Alix and your folks to tell them everyone is okay. I'm bushed. I really need to take up jogging again," the police officer said as Junior pulled up his pants, shooting the athlete's firm behind a look of envy. "I barely made it up that pyramid when Junior jumps into the doorway to say his daddy killed this Miguel, Miro's right hand Mayan man years ago. By the way, a diversion is a few thrown pebbles, not baring your chest to a room full of gunmen. Maybe you'd go running with me, Xo, once your feet heal, to give me some encouragement."

Xochi stared intently at the man, and Junior wondered what she saw as he had so often. "Tony, you believe strongly in what you do protecting the citizens of New Orleans and taking down the bad guys, but the work is already staining your soul. I see small black spots in your…never mind. I couldn't live with what you do every day of the week. Take care not to go too far over the edge of darkness."

"Yes, I never did hear you shout, *Police*," Connor said.

Ancona shrugged. "Must have been too much noise with all the shooting going on." He turned his attention back to Xochi. "Are you trying to tell me we don't have a future together, Xo?"

"You will always be a hero to me. You and Tom, Connor and Junior who came so far to rescue me, but I intend to return to Chapelle and pursue my studies in— folklore."

Junior inhaled, expanding his chest, and felt a slight twinge in his back. One rival down and one to go for Xochi's affections.

"Mumbo jumbo," the doctor said.

Xo stared at him with a sharp obsidian edge to her glance. "As for you, Connor. You have great confidence and self-esteem and will go far in your field, but I won't be going along with you. You have no respect for things you do not understand."

The remark hit home, and for a brief moment, his green eyes betrayed disappointment, quickly gone. He fell back on his medical training, detached and clinical. "I suppose that's settled then. Tom and Junior, no kicking, no pumping iron until those wounds heal."

"Hey," Tom protested. "I kick with my feet, not my shoulder."

"But you do when you analyze it. Check with your trainers."

"Okay, fine, but I really wish I could kick a few balls into the net right now and pretend they are the head of Esteban Miro."

"Actually, the ancients often played ball games with the heads of their enemies," Connor elucidated as he packed his supplies. "I'd suggest a few day's rest before we take *Wideout* home."

"Sounds good," Junior agreed. He had no desire to draw Xochi's attention to himself since she'd already dispatched two suitors as neatly as Bullock probably performed amputations. He knew what she'd asked of him back in the ruins was a favor, not a promise of love to come. Much as he wanted to take her into his arms this minute, he had to allow her to stand there in his bloody T-shirt hugging herself.

****

As it happened, they were required to stay in Cozumel until Agent Baldwin sorted out the situation. Choosing a different hotel from the one where Xochi had been imprisoned, Connor footed the bill for himself and Tony. Junior picked up the tab for himself and Tom while Tom paid for Xo's room adjacent to theirs. "Just a scream away," he jested, but his sister did not smile.

Following hot showers, sponge baths for Tom and Junior, and precious little sleep, the day progressed from sheer horror to the annoyance of long, separate interviews, to a mundane shopping trip amid the boutiques of Cozumel. Xochi begged for her underwear, purple dress and scarf and exchanged them as evidence for the Mayan garb she'd been forced to wear for the sacrifice. Junior offered to go first into the interrogation room as Xochi dressed and partook of a light continental breakfast with as much milky coffee as she wanted charged to her room.

While Tony, Connor, and Tom did their depositions, Junior took Xo out to look for clothing. He waited at shop after shop with the patience of a loyal St. Bernard, roving only once to buy a certain poster he carried around in a cardboard tube. His credit cards were at her disposal as she had no means to pay, but Xochi did not take advantage.

Her first purchase consisted of a pair of flip-flops bearing bands with tiny seashells from the hotel gift shop as her pumps hurt her scraped toes. After that, she bought a pair of jeans, not cheap on the island, and a variety of bright, often embroidered cotton tops, which were. She decided on a long, gauzy blue skirt that floated around her ankles simply because Junior liked it. "I'll pay you back, I swear," she said.

"No, you won't. I'd buy you the world, and you know that."

Instead of arguing or asking him not to say such things, her cheeks suffused with dusky rose. "Thank you," she said and glanced away.

He thought that might be progress, remembering how she'd fought off his buying her anything at the Riverwalk only weeks ago. While she debated whether to get a simple knit shift in her favorite hot pink color, Junior slipped into a *farmacia* and made another small purchase that fit in his hip pocket. She shed her purple uniform in the fitting room and wore the pink dress with her scarf instead. Bending over and giving Junior a wonderful view of the fabric stretched over her rounded bottom, Xochi stood and flung her long black hair into place, letting it curl wildly around her shoulders.

"There, that's the best I've felt in days. Free. If I

had my pink tote, I'd be complete. I guess I'll never see it again since it was in the cab when they took me."

If he had Xochi, he'd be complete. Junior answered, "The police have it. If you can't get it back, I'll buy you another."

Her answer was a squeeze to his bicep that as usual filled him with warmth and maybe a little lust this time. She let him carry her bags. Xo leaned in against him as they walked along, and he slipped his free arm around her waist. They enjoyed a brief, relaxed lunch in a taco joint near the plaza and picked up ice cream cones on the way back to the hotel where Agent Baldwin waited, impatience marring his stern face. "Your turn, Miss Billodeaux."

Baldwin kept her in the interview room until dinnertime and released her looking worn and shaky after such a long interrogation. Junior waited nearby as he had all afternoon to take her hand.

"I kept telling them and telling them I saw only the four men they already knew about. This had nothing to do with drug running or ransom, only revenge and the delusion that sacrificing me would gain Miro a new lease on life. I strongly suspect that the priest only led him along to get the resources to seize me and avenge his son in a spectacular and gruesome way in order to hurt Daddy Joe."

"I think you're right."

"They were also peeved that I didn't report being followed earlier. I can imagine it now. These men with black auras are stalking me. I see them everywhere. Open the file for crazies and insert Xochi Billodeaux."

"Tom believed you. So did I. Forget about it. Almost dinnertime. Let me treat you to lobster. I know you love it."

"Lobster was supposed to be my last meal. They feed sacrificial victims fairly well until the day of. I'd rather have something simpler. Where are the rest of the guys?"

"The Feds picked up Ancona again. Not happy about how he got involved in this operation after being warned off. I'm not sure what they can do to him."

Junior felt the surge of anger as Xochi said, "Over my dead body—and I would have been dead without his help. I'll ask Dad to assist Tony all he can. What about the others?"

"Went to the beach."

"Should Tom be doing that with his injuries?"

Junior shrugged and felt that twinge in his back again reminding him to go easy on himself as well. "He has his doctor with him, so he should be okay. I suspect they'll eat at one of the bars in the area. That leaves just you and me. Connor loaned me his iPad, wonder of wonders, because he is as attached to that as a limb to his body. I scoped out a few places while I waited. How about *El Viejo y la Mar*? It's a fisherman's cooperative and should have really fresh seafood."

"Okay, I love the name, *The Old Man and the Sea*. Just let me get my purse. Oh right, no purse. I guess I'm ready."

They sat in the rustic open-air dining area of the restaurant, started with seafood ceviche and moved on to whole fried fish, got a bottle of wine to share and linger over until closing at eight. On a slow walk back to the hotel, Junior bought churros from a street vendor for their dessert. He shared the sticks of fried dough well coated in cinnamon sugar with Xochi as the blue hour before dusk set in.

"There are places we could go dancing," Junior suggested, trying to extend the evening.

"Considering the condition of my toes, that is a no. You should rest. I should rest."

They found Tom and Connor in the hotel lobby— Connor a little peeved as he held out his hand for the iPad. Junior, affable and still one-upping the man, said, "Thanks for the loan. We found a great place to eat. Xo wants to rest now."

"Nice of you to wait for us. We're starving," Tom complained.

"Tommy, you are always starving. Good thing you married a woman who likes to cook." Xochi gave her brother a careful but affectionate hug, not only because of his wounded shoulder, but also to avoid putting any pressure on a ferocious sunburn. "We thought you'd eat at one of the places along the beach."

"Right," said Connor, full of skepticism. "It's you and me, Tom. Let's find a nice restaurant and a cold beer."

Junior escorted Xochi to her door and gave her a kiss he put his heart and soul into, but she didn't invite him inside. "Leave the connecting door unlocked. Shout out if you need anything," he said.

"I plan to sleep and sleep and sleep." Still, she ran her fingers down the side of his face in a way that seemed to say one day she might want more, but not tonight.

Chapter Twenty-Four

She woke screaming in a strange room in a foreign land. Xochi pressed the top sheet against her lips to stop more cries from escaping, but Junior barreled through the unlocked connecting door and scanned the area for the source of her terror much as he might search for a ball carrier to bring down.

"It's nothing, only a bad dream. You can go back to bed. I hope I didn't wake Tom, too."

"Only eleven p.m. He and Connor are still out on the town."

Junior did not leave. He moved to the bed and sat beside her, not taking her word that all was well. Now she knew he slept in boxer briefs, not naked like her for lack of buying a nightie when they shopped. Somehow, she couldn't allow him to purchase lingerie for her, but that would have been better than trembling entirely nude beneath a sheet, not wanting him to go, but not brave enough to say so.

He put his arm around her, as sturdy and broad as the limbs of the live oak trees they climbed in childhood, and held her close. "Remember when I was around ten and you found me crying behind the barn because the men were trying to toughen me up, and I was still a pudgy kid and didn't think I could do it?"

"Yes." She nodded against his chest, breathing in that lime scent of his, knowing he had taken the time to trim his beard that morning to look his best for her despite the wound in his back and the trial they'd all gone through. Her trembling eased, but she knew he'd felt it.

"You had the breasts of a woman, so soft and warm and comforting, but not one dirty thought passed through my mind."

"You were still a child with the sweetest heart."

"I felt your belief in me, that I could succeed, and I wanted to for you. Men made remarks about your body, and I thought one day I'd punch them in the mouth."

"Also the reaction of a child, but I thank you for the thought. I learned to cope, and when the other girls caught up, I didn't stand out so much anymore. And look at you, so big and strong no one wants to take you on. I am sure that is why Diaz and his men backed off when you were with me."

"That didn't help you in the end. I'll bet you did not cry."

"No, I used wisecracks as my defense. Sent Diaz on foolish errands to get a little back. Inside I was terrified, always searching for a way to escape or defend myself like a cat shoved into a sack and trying to claw its way out. Really, I didn't stand a chance against them."

Junior shook his head. She felt his chin brushing across the top of her head in denial. "I know you. You were brave, always brave. Now, tell me about your nightmare. I know you've had them for years about the killing of your parents. Same one?"

He finger-combed her curls, snarled and damp from the nightmare. His touch was so gentle, Xochi wanted to nod off in his embrace, but she answered.

"No. With Esteban Miro dead, I think that dream might be exorcized. We'll see. Now I have a new demon, Diaz, standing over me with a sacrificial knife scooping out my beating heart and no handy gris-gris bag to fend off the terrors."

"I'm staying the night. I'll lie here beside you ready to fight off that dream and for no other reason."

Xochi ran her fingers over the thin lines of his close-cut beard and across his upper lip, which made him smile when it tickled. "Back in the ruins, you said you didn't want to take me like this. How did you plan to be with me?"

"What we did there was just getting the job done. I wanted to give you a gradual seduction, a day together, a nice dinner, wine, a retreat to a luxurious room with a large bed waiting for us. Slow loving, but I didn't know you were a virgin. That changes everything."

"I'm not anymore, and we just had that day, Junior. Despite everything that happened, it was lovely being with you. One thing about nearly dying is it puts things into perspective, what matters, what doesn't. I tried to fall in love Connor with because he seemed appropriate, a little older than me, good career, friend of the family, all the right reasons, and we never would have made it together. I let our age difference stand in the way of seeing you as the man I loved."

She did not expect his reaction, his next words. Junior pulled away a little, and said, "Are you sure this isn't because I was your first and now you feel obligated to stay with me? I know how devout you are, but I mean—you don't have to."

He made her laugh. After these last few awful days, she could actually laugh. Junior drew farther away, hurt and offended. "I was trying to be considerate, not funny."

Feeling suddenly playful, Xochi grasped his ears and pulled him back into an embrace. "I might be devout, but I'd never stay with a man I didn't love. I do love you, Junior Polk. That's what I learned on Ix Chel's altars, both of them."

"I've always loved you, Xo."

"Then what are we waiting for? We had a nice day together. We are sitting on a big bed in a pretty room. Come under the covers with me."

"Give me a minute." Junior made a fast dash to the other bedroom and returned with the purchase of condoms in his hand. He bolted the adjoining door and came to the bed, slipping beneath the covers to press his heated body against her naked form.

"I think we can get rid of these. They're only in the way." Xochi slid her hands inside his briefs and lowered them to his knees. He kicked them off. Her hands remained where they had been, cupping him, stroking his shaft grown hard. "Impressive," she said.

"Not something I expected to hear from a recent virgin." She felt his grin go wide against her cheek.

"I have lots of brothers who forget to lock bathroom doors—and more than one man has shown me his whether I wanted to see it or not. Sex is not a mystery to me, Junior. I always stopped short of their goal. Last night, you showed me the rest. From what others have told me, I had a way better than average first time."

"All the adrenaline in our systems, I guess."

"Don't short change yourself. I came my very first time." She drew his head closer for more kissing and less conversation.

He did kiss her, but started with an ear lobe briefly sucked, working his way along her cheek before he got to her lips, inviting her into his mouth for the tongue play they'd done before. Junior left her lips to kiss his way down her throat into the cleavage of her breasts, emerging to lick each nipple to a sensitive peak.

"I'm ready now," she moaned.

"Not by half." His kisses wandered over her body, his tongue circling her navel before moving on to travel down one thigh and up the other until he reached the hard pearl at the top of her cleft and sucked again. Xochi's hips raised off the bed. Her hands held him in place until the sparks flying through her caught fire and ignited with a huge burst. She sank back quivering as he left her. "No, no, no!"

"Hush. We're going for two the right way."

The condom wrapper crinkled as he ripped it with his teeth, a flash of white in the dark room. Understanding, she took it from his hand and sheathed him as he towered over her. Covers kicked to the floor, Junior mounted between her legs, probed cautiously, asked, "Are you too sore?"

She answered by wrapping her legs around his hips and urging him to take her again. Invitation accepted, he drove into her hard and picked up his rhythm, going for distance, still teasing her clit with a thumb until Xochi spasmed and he reached completion. After a moment of recuperation, he took his weight off of her, rolling to one side and lying on his back. She rested her head on his chest, listening to the rapid thud of his heart against her ear as it returned to his natural steady beat. He slept—and snored a little, the same rhythmic sound she'd become familiar with when he inhabited her guestroom. Smiling, she reached down and relieved him of the condom, setting it carefully aside on a hotel notepad, restored the covers, and burrowed in beside him sure he had defeated the bad dreams for the night.

Xochi came instantly awake when the adjoining door rattled at two a.m. She clutched Junior's arm hard enough to rouse him from a heavy sleep. "What?"

"Listen."

Then, Tom's voice projected at great volume. "I guess Junior went out on the town after all. Good thing I'm a sound sleeper. He won't wake me when he comes in."

"Who do you think he's talking to?" Junior whispered. "Connor?"

"No. I believe he's talking to himself. He knows you are here with me. My brother just gave us his blessing."

"In that case since we're both awake I have another condom. We can practice making loving love very, very quietly."

"Suit up. If I know Tom, he'll be out cold in five minutes—and we can start the foreplay now."

Chapter Twenty-Five

"Man, I didn't get much sleep last night," Tom groused.

They were having the full Mexican breakfast, *huevos rancheros* with warm tortillas, while sitting on a terrace with an ocean view, not a day to be unhappy. Xochi knew she beamed, and Junior kept smiling for no reason at all. He broke open the yolk of one of his three fried eggs and let it mingle with the chili sauce and black beans before scooping the mixture up with a tortilla.

Full of contentment, Xo sipped her *café con leche* and watched the waves roll in as timeless as love.

Connor raised an eyebrow. "If you'd let me treat that sunburn, you would have had a better rest. And you, Junior, you've been overdoing it. More ooze from that wound than I like to see when I change a dressing."

Tom raised his red brows. "I doubt anything you could have given would have helped me sleep." He attacked his own breakfast only slightly smaller than Junior's plateful.

"Here." A little apologetic, Xochi twisted in her chair and pinched several succulent leaves off an aloe vera plant growing in a clay pot near their table. "Shirt off, redheaded brother of mine." She squeezed the thick sap onto his scarlet back and spread it on his skin.

"Gooey! Cool. Nice."

"I could have written you a prescription for something better," Connor said.

"Aloe vera has been a treatment for skin disorders for thousands of years, and it's free. Also good for constipation, too, if that's your problem this morning, Tom," Xochi tweaked her brother.

"With all this Mexican chow I've been eating, hell no! I only want to get home to my wife."

Tony Ancona sauntered over to their table. "I have the power to grant that wish." He spread his arms wide. "The Feebs said you three are free to go. Guess I'll be flying home later."

"Oh, Tony, with all the help you gave us you shouldn't be in trouble. Sit, have some breakfast." Xochi patted a spare chair.

"I had what our government would pay for earlier. Only came to tell you *Wideout* is cleared for passage. I guess I won't be seeing you around the station anymore, Xo. Best wishes to you—and Junior." Either more observant of a couple whose arms touched on the table or a better loser than Connor who frowned, he pecked her cheek and shook Junior's hand. "Connor, thanks for picking up my tab. Tom, have a great season."

"You're welcome to stay in the room as long as you need it," Connor replied, not as sour as the previous remark made him.

"I never worked with a more generous bunch. See you guys around." Tony turned his back on the new dawn and returned to the business of dealing with darkness.

"I'm getting him a season ticket," Tom said. "Only one of us who knew what to do. Let's finish up here and pack." He got unanimous agreement on that.

****

Loaded with fuel and some fresh groceries Xochi insisted upon, *Wideout* went to sea again. They traveled more slowly this time, stopping at sunset, dipping a line from Riley's stock of rods and reels into the Gulf waters and pulling up a small tuna and some redfish. Junior grilled the tuna steaks and breaded the redfish fillets with the crumbs of crushed Fritos. Xochi put together a fruit salad from the edible remains in the plastic bag. They drank the beers the men had left untouched in their race to save a woman they all cared about in one way or another.

"I think I could live this way forever," she said.

"Not me. I miss my Bundt cake." Tom checked Junior's phone for bars as he did every few miles. Possibly, he had more than a desire for baked goods.

"I have patients whose surgery has been delayed," Connor added.

Junior stretched out his legs and put his hands behind his head to keep them off Xochi. "I think I'm going to have to buy a boat, one with a bigger galley." *Wideout* slept four but in too close a proximity for him to act on his urges now that Xochi had accepted him as her lover, only the first part of his plans for their life together. Marriage. House. Children. A fine restaurant in Chapelle.

"I'd like that," Xo said as if she read his thoughts, all his thoughts, not simply his immediate needs. "But I suppose we must go home sometime."

Junior suspected she knew what awaited. Not only Alix lurked at the dock, outdistancing everyone in the crowd with her long legs to run into Tom' arms, but every Billodeaux who could get there to hug and kiss and carry on with Cajun excitement over their safe return.

The Rev engulfed Connor in his huge embrace while his mother attempted to wrap her arms around them both. "Hey, I didn't know you were that worried about getting your medical kit back. I left some of the supplies at the local clinic since they were a little low."

"A charitable gesture, we'll send more if they need it, a little thank offering for your safe return," his father answered.

"I'll build them an entirely new clinic and go down there once a year to see to the needs of the people on the island," his mother vowed.

"Not too big a sacrifice there. It's a lovely place when no one is trying to kill a childhood friend." Junior heard and acknowledged that Connor had accepted that he'd lost Xochi as anything more.

Mack had deemed to return from Dallas to be among them, but appeared to remain in competition with Junior when he strolled over and said, "Wish I'd been there to shoot a few of those kidnappers. Pow! Pow!" He gave his older sister a squeeze. "Next time, call me before you take off to become heroes."

"No time," Junior said, thinking he'd killed a man out of necessity and how it hadn't felt good at all in the end.

Unfortunately, the press and the paparazzi had gotten wind of the situation. Knox Polk, Sr. saw they kept their distance from his weeping wife with Xochi in her embrace. Junior joined his father to help force a way open to a long line of waiting vehicles, losing Xo in the process to ride with her family in the big van that had once transported the Billodeaux children and himself to school. He rode in the double cab truck with his parents, his mom alternating between Spanish and English, sharing her fears for him and Xochi, beaming at the happy outcome. When they let her down at the kitchen door of Lorena Ranch, Junior stayed in the truck as his father went to park it.

"Dad," he said before they got out. "I zigzagged like you said. Still, I took a bullet in the back, but I saved Xochi from a man with an automatic weapon. He got away because I couldn't stop to make a stand. I had to go into hiding with her."

"That's okay. You lived to fight another day. I'm glad of that."

"The FBI confiscated the guns I took. I doubt you'll get them back."

"I can always buy more guns. I have my only son back. That's what counts."

"I killed a Mayan priest, a shot to the center of the chest to prevent Xochi's murder. I don't want to kill again unless I must. I haven't got it in me to do what you did for so many years."

Knox studied his son with unreadable eyes before he spoke. "I pushed you toward the service, but you have your mother's warm heart. I hope you never have to kill again. Still, I know if you must take a stand, you will. I'm proud of you, Junior, so very proud."

After that statement, because his dad was Knox Polk, Sr., the older man simply got out of truck and walked to the big house beside him.

****

Junior sat at the kitchen table while his mother cut a huge piece of cake and tipped it onto a plate. She set it before him. "I make *Tres Leches* cake for you and Xochi, no one else. You are wounded and must build your strength, *hijo*."

"I had a doctor with me. Connor patched me up and changed my dressing every day on the way home. I'll be fine."

"You stay here now. Let your mama take care of you." Corazon helped herself to cake and sat down with a cup of coffee, hands wrapped around it as if warming herself. "Miss Nell, she wants Xochi to live at the ranch now."

"Ah, Ma, we both have to go back to New Orleans to straighten out a few things. Xo needs to sublet the apartment. She promised to help me pick out furniture for my condo before she starts her *traiteur* training."

His mama's thick eyebrows raised, and her smile could have outshone the Mexican sun on a hot day in July. "Buying furniture together. That is good, next step to getting married where I come from."

"Maybe. I need to give her some space to pursue her goals, but yes, I think so."

His mother's dark eyes suddenly streamed with tears as if her joy needed watering. She set down her coffee and leaned over her cake to embrace him again. "I am so happy, Junior."

No need to tell his dad the situation. His mama would fill his ears with her elation when they sat side by side in the cozy two room cottage where he'd grown up, a game of some sort on the TV, her hands busy letting out the seams and the hems of the clothes her son kept outgrowing. He and Xochi would find a house nearby and keep them in their lives.

"Where is everyone else? Where's Xo?"

"Everybody, they pick up shrimp off the boats at Intracoastal City while we wait. We gonna have a big boil with the corn and the little red potatoes out of doors. Is good time for it since the campers went home this morning, and the new ones do not come until tomorrow afternoon when the maids finish the cleaning. Mr. Joe is in the pavilion getting the pots ready with all of them drinking beer, waiting for the food. Not so much work for me or Miss Nell. I make two big sheet cakes for dessert. My work, it is done. I eat with the family tonight."

"And Xochi?"

"Up in her old room with her mama, Nurse Shammy, and Miss Rosemarie. They checking her body, brain, and soul, I think. Xochi, she is strong. She be all right."

Junior hoped so. He knew he'd have to sleep in his childhood bed this evening, no matter that it no longer fit him. Though he had the door codes, he wouldn't be able to hear Xo's screams if the dream woke her in the night. Nell would be the one to run to her and hold her tight until the terror passed. For a while, he'd have to live with that.

****

Sitting on the bed of her childhood with its sunny yellow spread and rose-shaped cushions, Xochi faced her well-meaning interrogation squad. "I wasn't raped, Nurse Shammy, so no need for an internal exam."

She wasn't sure if the resident and somewhat elderly nurse who had taken care of the premature Billodeaux babies and seen to all the cuts and scratches a family of twelve children and the Camp Love Letter kids generated would be able to tell that she'd had sex recently and often, but regretfully, not since Cozumel. A former nun and married to Brinsley at an advanced age, what did she know about it? Still, Nurse Shammy had taken a bullet for the Billodeauxs just like Junior, and was hard to deny.

"Let me check those toes at least."

"I had an orthopedic surgeon taking care of them."

"Exactly, a surgeon. What does Connor Bullock know about scraped toes?"

Xochi gave up and stuck out her feet for examination. Satisfied with placing new bandages and antibiotic cream on them, Nurse Shammy gave way to Mama Nell.

Nell had gathered her four oldest daughters around and given them the birds and bees talk at a young age, especially when Xochi developed early. This had been followed later by a more candid teen sex talk about self-respect, waiting for the right man, and taking precautions about pregnancy and STDs. The girls suspected Mama Nell hadn't followed these rules early in her life and so knew whereof she spoke which gave her major creds.

"Sometimes, the man who seems right won't be. Don't worry about that, just take care and don't sleep around casually. Yes, sex feels good, but there is far more to it than that for women." Sound advice from their mom, the psychologist, but all the girls left for college as virgins thanks to an overly protective father and fierce older brothers. After that, Nell did not inquire about the status of their purity and had no idea Xochi held onto hers for so long. Ironic that only Don Esteban guessed her closely held secret.

"Do you want to talk about your ordeal, dear?"

Nell sat beside Xochi on the bed and held her hand.

"Not particularly after all the times I had to tell the tale to the FBI over and over again, but basically, Esteban Miro's men kidnapped me to be a human sacrifice in the mistaken belief that an offering to the goddess Ix Chel would cure him of cancer. I saw immediately he stood at death's door, but a man called Indio who claimed to be a Mayan priest convinced him otherwise. We believe that Indio wanted revenge against Dad for the death of his son many years ago when he went to rescue Tom. I was treated fairly well until the time of the sacrifice, then drugged and taken to a temple. Four of the best young men I know rescued me. All the others involved are dead except the man named Diaz."

"That must concern you."

"Sure, scary guy, maybe Esteban's son, but he isn't likely to come here with so many searching for him."

Nell patted her hand and let go. "Any time you want to talk, I'll listen."

"Always."

Rosemarie Leleux, waiting at the gates of the ranch when the cortege of Billodeaux vehicles arrived leaking ice water out the backs from the sloshing coolers full of shrimp, studied Xochi's face and especially her eyes. The *traiteur* claimed not to have her grandmother's second sight, but she knew how to read people very well. Xo had seen her in action ferreting out what really bothered her clients before giving a cure.

"A terrible event like this changes a person. You will need a new gris-gris bag to ward off the dreams. I'll give it some thought and make one for you. In the meantime, let me seal this room from bad thoughts."

Rosemarie walked the four corners of the bedroom murmuring prayers and leaving small pinches of herbs in each corner. Nurse Shammy and Mama Nell might not believe in her efforts, but wouldn't object considering that the *traiteur* had given Xochi rest from night terrors before and helped her cope with the auras. "There, that should do it. Stop by my place before you return to New Orleans, and I'll have the new bag ready."

Xochi stood and beckoned the women to her in a group hug. "Thank all of you for taking such good care of me for most of my life. Go enjoy our welcome home party. I'll be down as soon as I change into something less grubby than my boat clothes."

"I wouldn't mind a cold beer," Rosemarie admitted.

"I think a stiff drink is in order. Brinsley makes a mean martini. Sometimes we have them for a nightcap," Nurse Shammy said.

What you didn't know about the people who surrounded you. Finally, the dear women left her in peace. She changed into the gauzy azure skirt and a scoop-necked blouse embroidered with red and blue posies, still wearing the seashell flip-flops. As she brushed out her long curls, Xochi faced herself squarely in the mirror. No glancing aside.

Losing her virginity had not taken away her gift of seeing auras. The pale green peridot glow of a healer still confronted her, but she had changed. Now it bore spikes of violet, Junior's color, the color of love.

She went downstairs and outside to run the gauntlet of family and friends. Mawmaw Nadine grasped her in an iron squeeze despite the woman's age. "We prayed for you, my baby, we prayed day and night for your safe return."

"So did I. Must have worked." Xochi searched for Junior and found him amid the men standing by the boiling pots. He stood out, big, brown, and sturdy. Now, to escape Mawmaw.

"I see where your eyes are roving, Xochi Billodeaux. He's a tee-tiny bit young, but a good Cat'lic boy. You got my blessing." Within the family, Mawmaw's opinion really counted for something. She could make a boyfriend she didn't care for shrivel to dust and disappear with the wind using her sharp tongue and had applied her censure more than once. But, she knew Junior—and approved. Her grip loosened. "Now you go on and give him a nice big kiss for bringing you home safe with the help of Mother Mary."

Xochi did exactly that, declaring them a couple before the whole clan and quite a few friends. Her dad and Knox Polk shook hands, Joe with a big Cajun grin on his face and Knox with a more reserved smile, good as it could get. She and Junior might have a hard time escaping from Lorena Ranch tomorrow, but would make the effort to return to New Orleans and that condo with the great big bed.

Chapter Twenty-Six

Xo and Junior rose early, but not early enough to evade a hearty breakfast prepared by Corazon, and coffee with Mama Nell and Daddy Joe. They laid out their plans to pack Xochi's belongings and shop for furniture for Junior's condo, promising to return in a day or so to the safety of the ranch. Junior decided to work out there before training camp started and allow Nurse Shammy to fuss over his wound, which didn't bother him at all. Xo, however, meant to take up residence on the edge of the swamp with Nestor Leleux. She held up a hand to indicate no arguments could persuade her to change her mind.

Leaving, they picked up a tail of a couple of sleepy paparazzi who should have known better. The Billodeaux family had issued a statement to the press giving most of the credit to the efforts of the FBI in saving their daughter with some help from her brother, Tom, and three good friends. Intervention occurred when Xochi's life had been threatened. Three of the four kidnappers died in the struggle. Expressions of gratitude for all who prayed for Xochi's safe return. End of story. No mention of human sacrifice. The press should have known they would get no more from the Billodeauxs, but were undoubtedly spreading cash like chum around Cozumel hoping to lure those whose information could be bought.

A short stop at Rosemarie's house did result in a confrontation with two members of the yellow press who blocked their way when they exited the cottage with the statue of the Virgin Mary in her bathtub shell.

"Move." Junior held out both arms as if he meant to throw them to the ground. They moved, and the newly minted couple managed to escape Chapelle for the big city.

In Xochi's apartment, they packed her clothes and boxed her personal items. Most of the contents would remain for the next occupant to use. As it turned out, that person was Annie Billodeaux. As Junior cleared the top shelf of Xo's closet, she stuffed clothes and shoes into garbage bags once her suitcases filled.

"Nice that Annie is coming to live here since the Ochsner Medical Center offered her that neonatal nurse practitioner position. She told me at the shrimp boil she needed a place to live. Saves me from subletting to a stranger."

Junior dumped a jumble of purses and hats onto the bed. "Yeah, that's great, but I thought the twins would never cut the cord between them, close as they are."

With a cock of her head, Xochi considered his statement. "Close yes, but not the same. They look very much alike but aren't identical. Annie's aura is green like mine. Jude burns orange. She's always been the dominant one, leading the way, telling Annie what to do. Now, I think they've come to a parting place. Jude keeps climbing the nursing ladder higher and higher. Annie has found her happiness in caring for the most vulnerable of infants. She likes the peace of the nursery at night, helping the parents learn to handle their fragile babies and love them. It is time Jude and Annie went separate ways."

"I'd bet Jude wasn't happy."

"Nope, but keeping Jude happy shouldn't be Annie's purpose in life."

"I think I found mine in making you happy." Junior stooped to kiss her neck. "The closet is cleaned out. Anything else we need to get?"

"No, I won't need much at Nestor Leleux's place, and those things are in my big suitcase. Most of this stuff I'll leave at the ranch."

"Or how about my place? I have three empty bedrooms. Heck, I have an empty living room and kitchen, too."

"Once you finish unpacking all that cookware, the kitchen won't be empty." She referred to the mountain of boxes they'd found waiting at his place ordered online or from local restaurant supply businesses. Opening them had been like Christmas, or maybe a bridal shower described it better: heavy duty pots and pans, plates thick and white with a thin blue line of a border, substantial mugs, chunky glasses, and oversized stainless steel dinnerware with a nice beaded design on the handles.

In his defense, Junior said, "A man needs a good blender that can make both smoothies and frozen margaritas."

"And a deluxe food processor, a convection oven, and a toaster with six adjustable slots. I'm surprised you didn't get a bread machine."

"All those other items save time, but bread should be handmade."

"Right. Better you than me. But okay, let's haul my belongings to one of your bedrooms and then go furniture shopping."

They managed the transfer from Junior's SUV to the condo easily enough with the help of a platform dolly supplied by Arturo the doorman to lessen the trips to and fro and his intervention with the tabloid reporters begging to speak to the pair. "Is Miss Xochi moving in should anyone ask after her?" he inquired politely. Heaven only knew how many women he'd seen staying with Sinners players.

"No, I'm just storing her stuff for a while—but I wish she would." If very large men could look wistful, Junior managed to do so.

"Someday," Xochi promised. "Now push that cart to the elevator."

Unloaded, they headed for the furniture store and barely set foot inside when a sharp clicking of high heels like the claws on a predator approached. Junior offered a wide grin to the woman clad in a leopard print that clung to her rounded breasts and rear. "Hi, Glorious, I came back to look for a dining room set and living room furniture."

She placed a hand with an LSU-themed manicure on his arm. Xochi thought it clashed with her clingy dress. "I've been giving your needs a lot of thought, Junior. Let me show you what I've picked out."

Glorious led the way with a sway to her hips entirely unnecessary in a furniture store salesperson in Xochi's eyes. Glorious had the orange aura so common to the ambitious, and it became her dark skin and long, black, straightened, and extended hair. Ambitious to sell furniture—or find a rich husband? Unfortunately, her taste in furnishings was spot on for Junior.

She ran her hands over a vast sofa almost as if she

touched his body. "This is chocolate brown microfiber, but we could order it in the same suede fabric used for your headboard. Recliners at either end and a large, tufted hassock that can serve as a coffee table and has storage within."

"Tom has built-in recliners like that," Junior answered with enthusiasm.

"I think two self-standing recliners might be better. Then, they could be moved around." Xo put in her two cents, all the while wishing she weren't wearing old jeans, sneakers, and a T-shirt so large her breasts were buried in it.

"This is a modular unit. The recliners can easily be removed to be free standing."

"That's great, Glorious!"

A bit more excitement than Xo felt furniture deserved. "What about throw pillows?" she asked, knowing Junior and most men disliked them.

"We have a wide selection, but I think Junior would prefer large floor cushions, perhaps in a gold fabric that could be stacked in a corner when not in use."

Damn, this woman knew her stuff. "Sounds good," Xochi conceded.

"As for the dining room, I thought this would do." Glorious with her outrageous sway took them to another side of the store. She pointed to a large table in dark wood, matte finish, not glossy at all, with heavy benches on both sides and two end chairs very square, cushioned, and quite capable of holding Junior or any of his large friends. Xochi thought she'd need a booster seat to buoy herself to table level, but Junior loved it along with a matching sideboard. Everything approved,

255

he went to sign the paperwork with Xo trailing behind.

As they sat in the cubicle belonging to Glorious, their salesperson made an offer. "I could choose some accessories for the walls and flat surfaces, bring them over, and place them for your approval at any convenient time."

Xochi felt a flare within and knew it for jealousy so intense she wanted to rip out the woman's hair extensions. Rachelle's flirtation with Junior had mildly irritated her along with the clerk in the handbag shop, but what she experienced now was volcanic. She erupted from her chair. "I don't think so! We can manage."

Glorious raised her plucked eyebrows as if taking real note of Xochi for the first time. "Are you Mrs. Polk?"

Junior answered. "Not yet. She's my *girlfriend.*" He said the word as if he'd never used it before. "I should have introduced you earlier. Glorious Hamilton, meet Xochi Billodeaux."

"*The* Xochi Billodeaux, adopted daughter of millionaire quarterback, Joe Billodeaux, the girl who went missing? I thought you'd be more—more…"

Xochi filled in mental blanks: attractive, taller, built, stylishly dressed? "I've been clearing out my apartment and moving my things to Junior's today." That inner child who once punched out bullies clenched her hand, but she used her words, as Mama Nell liked to say. She'd told the truth. Let Glorious believe what she wanted.

The woman cleared her throat. "I am happy for your safe return. That takes care of the paperwork. The sofa will take a few weeks because of the change in fabric, but we can deliver the table, chairs, and sideboard tomorrow." She didn't walk her customers to the door.

Outside in the insane heat of a July day in New Orleans, Junior said, "I think we made some real progress."

Had he noticed her jealousy and been pleased about it, or did he simply refer to the furniture? From his wide shit-eating grin, she thought the former. "That woman was hitting on you right in front of me!"

"Yeah." No doubt he was pleased. "This is the first time you didn't try to shove me off on another woman."

"Never again. Junior, *te amo,*" she whispered in his ear and tugged his face down for a kiss.

They were definitely having a moment—interrupted by a paparazzo who shouted from across the street, "Hey, Xochi, how about your side of the kidnapping story?"

"You and Junior a couple now?" another inquiring mind wanted to know.

"Let's get in the car, go back to the condo, and try out the memory foam," Xochi suggested.

****

"So, what did you think?" Junior asked as he moved off of Xo's hot body and sank in beside her on the new bed.

"I think you didn't get the same sexual advice from Daddy Joe as the girls got from Mama Nell."

"I doubt it. His went something like 'when it comes to football and sex, do it well. That takes practice, practice, practice. Never forget to suit up'."

Xochi smothered down more jealousy over women she did not know and would never meet. "I guess you practiced a lot."

"Not nearly as much as I did for football. All your brothers dipped their wicks in high school except maybe Teddy in the wheelchair and little T-Rex, but his day is coming fast."

She buried her face in his chest. "I must seem fumbling and inexperienced to you."

"You are all I hoped for and a fast learner. You were in college. I was in high school. I believed I'd have to compete with fraternity boys. If I'd known, I would have waited. But, I was really asking about the memory foam mattress."

Xochi flung herself back into his arms and laughed out loud, her hot chocolate laugh that often turned heads her way. "It sort of sucks you in and keeps you from moving as much as you'd like."

"Good back support, right? I know I'm a big guy, and while you aren't tiny like the twins, I don't want to hurt you."

She propped her chin on a hand in order to look him right in the abashed brown puppy dog eyes. "No complaints here, but you need to experience the wonder of memory foam. Next time, I want to be on top."

They split the experience evenly, twice with her on top and twice with her on bottom. Xo enjoyed the ride. She'd been an excellent rider on horseback in her teens. Dancing kept her thighs and her grip firm. She enjoyed the view of the vast planes of Junior's body beneath her, the way his eyes tracked the bobbing of her brown breasts before he reached out and captured them in both hands. His hips pushed out of the foam to meet her. He seized the flying locks of her hair and used them as reins to pull her closer into his embrace, to his lips for a kiss, against his chest to excite more erotic friction. She leaped the final fence at last, and Junior followed her over.

Ensconced in memory foam, they slept in late the next morning. Junior rolled out to made his fantastic coffee and bring it to the bed, but Xo insisted he go fetch croissants from the coffee shop instead of slaving over a breakfast for her. He returned with a half a dozen assorted and a tabloid from the newsstand tucked under his arm. Holding it out to Xochi, he said, "Could be a lot worse."

There they were smooching in front of the furniture store under a headline reading *Xochi Housekeeping with her Hero?* She threw it down on the night table in disgust and ripped open the bag of croissants.

Junior shoved one of his new plates under her selection, chocolate of course. "You get crumbs in the bed, you have to be on the bottom again."

"Yes, sir, all right with me." She sighed, took a big bite and caught the flaky crumbs on the plate. "Sex makes a person hungry," she observed.

"I have noticed that." Junior put three croissants on his plate before she ate them all.

"It's only a matter of time before the press gets wind of the human sacrifice angle. That guard at the temple site is a very weak link. I want to be away from here right after the furniture arrives. Let them try to track me down at Nestor Leleux's place."

Junior lost interest in his croissants. "I wish it were true, that we were setting up housekeeping together. Once training camp starts, and then the season, I won't be able to get to Chapelle very often to see you."

"I should be the one to worry. Women are going to

be all over you. You might decide you want the freedom to roam."

"Done that. Done with it." Still, worry creased his usually broad, smooth brow. "I won't be able to protect you there."

"I'll be fine. I'm sure Nestor has said the appropriate prayers to keep snakes of all kinds out of his yard. Let's make the most of our time together." Xochi lowered his head to her lips and made sure he tasted the chocolate essence of her mouth.

Chapter Twenty-Seven

The bright yellow Jeep bounced along the dirt road with potholes big enough to fry a turkey. Xochi now understood the reason for the vehicle Daddy Joe chose for her, handing over the keys and remarking that he'd been to Nestor's place more than once. She and Junior followed the lane lined with tall longleaf pines, utility poles, and weekend camps for fishing and hunting.

Nestor's cabin at the very end of the way rested on stout wooden pillars and hung out halfway over the water with a couple of boats tethered in the back and an ancient pickup truck parked in front of a low fence concocted from odd boards, driftwood, and tree stumps. The barrier surrounded a dirt yard almost as pitted as the road. A tall pole to one side guided electric and phone lines into the house.

A small plantation bell stood mounted at the gate along with several homemade signs pounded into a board and a rusted mailbox sitting atop a post. The signs read *Ring Bell before Entering After Dark* and *Louisiana Yard Dogs* with a crude green gator painted below the lettering, an old joke. Tourists bought mottoes like that all the time at the gift shops in town. A raised board walkway with railings on the sides led to a deep front porch, also railed, that held a swing and couple of sagging cane-seated rockers. Xochi's favorite plant, aloe vera, stretched its fleshy arms out of a plain

261

clay pot by the door. It appeared to be benefiting from the condensation dripping off a rattling window air conditioner.

Junior wrinkled his broad nose. "Kind of stinks around here."

"No one promised the swamp would smell good."

"I don't think it's the water, Xo. Maybe those hides drying on the walls."

The sun hadn't yet lowered itself behind the cypress trees dotting the waters of the marsh beyond the house, but they rang the bell regardless. Its peal brought Nestor Leleux shambling through the door. He held out wide hands with no hint of a tremor considering his age. His white hair snaked down his back in a tight braid yellowed on the end. A wispy beard framed his mouth and flowed across his chest. The skin left exposed was weathered and brown from an outdoor life, but a perfect smile, most likely dentures, welcomed his guests.

"Come, come, my new 'prentice." Xochi crossed the boardwalk and took his open hands in hers. "*Mais oui,* you da one." Nestor gripped her fingers and raised his bushy eyebrows. "I got an early supper on da table. Put her bag in da front bedroom, you," he said to Junior.

"That's Junior, Junior Polk. He'll be playing for the Sinners in the fall," Xo said. That pronouncement got a curt nod from the *traiteur*. "I watch da games."

Junior hefted Xo's big suitcase under his arm and clattered up the boardwalk bending beneath his weight. Inside the cabin smelled better—of spicy food and dried herbs hanging from open rafters that let the heat rise and the feeble A/C cool. The cottage might have belonged to the fairytale bears since three mismatched wooden chairs sat around a cable spool table holding three bowls and three large spoons. Nestor ladled chili over clumps of white rice, not porridge, from a cast iron pot sitting in its middle.

Junior could tell the chili had some bite to it simply by smelling the aroma. He spotted strings of dried red peppers and braids of garlic among the herbs and guessed Nestor made liberal use of both. A loaf of homemade sliced bread on a board sat surrounded by a stick of butter on a chipped plate, a pot of strawberry jam—both the pot and the jam Rosemarie's handiwork—and a squeezable honey bear. Nestor had the iced tea poured, sweet, sweet.

They dipped their spoons into the deep red gravy lumpy with chunks of meat and kidney beans. "Not too spicy for you, eh?" the old man asked.

"My mom is Mexican, and Xo is a Cajun Mexican blend. We can take the heat," Junior assured him, whisking away the beads of sweat that formed on his mustache with a finger. "I'm interested in cooking, especially local dishes. Would you share your recipe?" Of course, he'd have to cool it down for tourists.

Nestor ran through a list of ingredients until he got to the meat. "The real secret is I make my chili with nutra rat what I trap. Get five dollars a tail for protecting the levees from da vermin. Ain't much market for da hides, but I tan dem anyhow. People is prejudiced against eatin' it, but it tastes jus' fine, no?"

The old man waited for their reaction. Neither of his guests flinched. Judging by his wide grin, they passed the test. Junior gained extra credit points by asking for seconds. Nestor, pleased with himself, slathered his bread with butter and wiped his bowl clean of the gravy. Xo, possibly soothing her mouth, ate hers with honey. Junior, really not bothered by the heat of the meal, piled on strawberry preserves, making his thick slice into dessert. Nestor had strong coffee ready to be poured and offered around brown sugar as a sweetener. When Xochi asked for milk, he punctured a can of condensed and set it by her place.

"Let me wash the dishes since you cooked tonight," she said.

"Jus' put dem in the sink for now. Da sun is settin'. I show you somet'ing, me."

Nestor led them to his back porch and opened a cooler filled with reeking carcasses. Beside it, nutria tails filled a plastic bucket and their orange buckteeth lay in a basket. "Some likes to make jewelry from dem big, ugly teet'," he explained. Then, he clapped his hands and made noises suitable for calling hogs to dinner, only alligators answered his summons not pigs. The big reptiles arrowed toward the deck, their strong tails propelling them through the murky water. Nestor began chucking the skinned nutria into their gaping, toothy maws.

"Can't eat dem all and don't like to waste. See dat one dere? I call him Big Ben after da quarterback, Roethlisberger. Maybe you gonna meet up with the real t'ing this season."

Junior nodded. "I probably will since I play defense, but I don't think the man will be quite as scary."

Nestor chuckled into his beard. "Now, son, when we done here you better get going. Some of my pets like to stay around and digest under da house. No foolin' about my yard dog sign, so don't you come tomcatting after dis little girl at night, you hear?"

Junior heard but didn't like it. Xochi walked him to the front porch and stood on her toes to kiss him goodbye.

"Xo, I don't want to leave you here." He held her tight against him.

"I'll be fine. Meet me at church on Sunday, and I'll tell you all my adventures. Now, go before the gators get you." She patted his rear and he went, thinking of just how flimsy that boardwalk felt beneath his feet.

****

To say her days were enchanting would not have been using the right word. That first night alone with Nestor and the gators grunting under the floorboards, he gallantly let her use the tiny bathroom first because sometimes the hot water ran out. "No need to worry 'bout snakes coming up da plumbing," he added.

"Did you pray them away from your yard?"

"*Mais*, no. Da gators eat dem."

Hmmm, comforting? After a very quick shower, Xochi wrapped in a terry robe and asked whether he'd mind if she plugged in her laptop.

"Mind, you can keep in touch with dat big beau of yours, but nuttin' I teach you can be written down. *Comprendre?*"

"Yes, I understand."

Xochi used the early evening hours to check her e-mail. She received documents to interpret or translate from loyal business customers who trusted her work. Her greatest talent, being able to translate Spanish and English documents into Portuguese for Brazilian clients, paid the best. She returned the finished work with an invoice and instructions for a direct deposit into her account. Income was way down, of course, but her needs were few living with Nestor, only gas for the Jeep and chipping in for groceries the swamp couldn't provide.

At night, the one thing that gave her comfort was the new gris-gris bag made of deep violet velvet that probably came from a Crown Royal sack. She swore it had the heft and softness of Junior's scrotum and gave off a hint of lime whenever she squeezed it. Miss Rosemarie had citrus trees in her yard and must have used some dried zest in her formula. Regardless, she slept well with it tucked next to her cheek.

As it turned out all the healing prayers were in French, but she had a facility with languages and an excellent memory even if the French she'd learned in high school and college didn't always coincide with the Cajun dialect Nestor spoke. Nestor taught them as they puttered along in his boat, rising at dawn before the temperature soared too high in order to check the traps for nutria, do some fishing and herb gathering if he found anything interesting, though the heat had shriveled a lot of the plants to the ground.

Generally, his gators followed the boat for a while hoping for another easy meal, then gave up and peeled away. "Where do they spent the day, Nestor?" Xochi asked.

"Oh, dey go over by where da swamp tour boats pass to get anodder handout. Las' year one of dem guides teased a gator, holding a chicken up high to make him jump—and dey can jump. Took da man's hand right off along wit' da chicken. You should never tease a gator."

He showed her his mayhaw grove where he kept bee hives to produce honey and knocked the ripe red fruit into his boat in late spring for Rosemarie's jelly making. "You can close a wound and keep it clean wit' honey. Spider webs are good for stopping blood," Nestor said as they passed beneath a giant, communal web of large banana spiders.

Xochi nodded. "Have you always lived like this? Do many patients come out here to see you?"

Whap! Nestor brained a nutria only half dead and chucked it into the bottom of the boat to keep company with the others and a pail of catfish he'd caught along the way. "No, I come to live here after my wife passed. Me, I'm done wit' haircuts and shaving, and young priests who got no respect for what I do. Mostly, I gather herbs for Rosemarie and let her handle the town folks. Seven kids, four daughters, and not one interested in receiving my gift. The best of the lot went to be a nurse. I'm eighty-two and need to do this now."

Xochi absorbed as much about living off the swamp as she did about healing. In the evening, she made cornbread from a mix while Nestor skinned the catfish and removed the mud vein that tainted the flesh of wild caught fish. He fried them whole, heads off, and dressed up a can of green beans with bacon and a dash cayenne for a side. Dessert? Usually canned peaches in heavy syrup or jars of syrupy figs grateful clients left on his doorstep and always, sweet tea and black, black coffee.

When Xochi made a run into town, she supplemented their diet with fresh fruit, filling a tupelo bowl Nestor had carved with grapes, peaches, oranges, plums, and bananas. Sometimes, she picked up a pint of vanilla ice cream, about all the tiny freezer had space for besides ice trays, and made sundaes with the fig syrup. Nestor enjoyed that. He seemed very hale for his age and the radiated the jolly pink aura of a man happy with his life. Still, she saw patches of that khaki color denoting disease, perhaps only the ills of a very old man, but hard to tell when he denied any infirmities.

Most of the week, Tall Pines Lane lay deserted, but come the weekend, the cabins that lined the road filled with families getting out of town to their camps for fishing and crabbing or simply lazing in a hammock strung between two trees. Miles and miles of bad road away from a pharmacy or a hospital, Nestor's business picked up on Saturday and Sunday.

Xochi witnessed him revive a boy who had played too hard in the hot sun and collapsed by lying the child down on his bed, placing the kid's hands into cold water, and praying mighty hard. He asked her to join in, and she did, stroking the hot, dry forehead, lending strength. In a short time, the child opened his eyes, ready to play again, but Nestor advised a nice, cold pop in the shade might be a better idea. Later, he found a fifth of whiskey on his doorstep.

He often complained about loud music disturbing his peace and four-wheelers churning up the dust, but he never turned away a person who came to seek his help. A distraught young mother with a howling baby on her hip made her way to his door. "My husband says if I can't shut him up, we'll have to go home where he can watch his Braves game in another room. Jordy is teething, and nothing seems to help."

Xochi watched as Nestor took a shiny dime from a roll on his work counter, a piece of rough split cypress with four legs pounded into it. Using a small auger, he drilled a hole in the coin, ran a safety pin through it, and pinned it to the baby's slobber-wet shirt. The bemused infant stopped whining and focused on the new object within his range. He made a few grabs for it. Xochi cupped the baby's chubby cheeks and kissed the top of his sweat-soaked head. Jordy offered her a smile with the tiny chips of new teeth shining through his pink gums.

"Oh, thank you!" his mother said to both of them.

Nestor held up a hand. "No t'anks, never. I share my gift. Now if he start up again, give him a half teaspoon of dis lizard tail tea."

Xochi envisioned Nestor collecting the snapped tails of the green anole lizards that walked up his walls and sunned on the tree stumps. Why not eye of newt, too? Her skeptical expression gave her away.

"Not dat kind of lizard tail, da plant we find in da swamp. I show you next time we go out."

A person with a bad cough showed up on the porch. "I'm scaring off the fish," he claimed.

Nestor took the red seeds of the mamou plant—also known as coral bean—that grew along his fence, its scarlet flowers long turned to black pods splitting open with a free home remedy. He boiled a few in a half cup of water, drained the tea into a mason jar, and added a dollop of his honey, lemon juice, and a good slug of whiskey from the gift bottle. "Dat should do you. Keep it cold."

The fellow, a regular customer, offered no thanks, but brought by a string of bass he caught later. A batch of dense chocolate brownies on a paper plate covered with a napkin to keep the flies off appeared on the porch swing. They ate well on Saturday night. Nestor topped off his coffee with a shot of the whiskey, but Xo declined.

Xochi learned to concoct mamou cough syrup and other remedies: elderberry buds for headache, fever, chills, and eye washes, the weird brown fruits of the pawpaw tree for constipation. All interesting and possibly effective, but what worked best for her was the laying on of hands as she prayed. She doubted she would ever tell anyone about the warmth that flowed from her body and into another person to comfort them, and certainly would never claim to be able to heal, but as Nestor said, word got around. He thought she could most likely heal from a distance with her prayers as long as no water came between her and the patient. "Stay on dis side of da bayou," he directed, not joking at all.

Learning as much as she could as fast as she could, still, Xochi lived for Sundays, her day off. She offered Nestor a ride to church, but he declined. "A man old as me ain't got much left to confess. Besides, I have my own ride. Dat old truck don't look like much, but I worked as a mechanic for Aldus Thibodeaux at his gas station years and years. Her engine, she is good if I want to go to town."

A little relieved that she wouldn't have to transport Nestor back and forth, cutting into her time spent with Junior, she went off to meet him and the Catholic branch of the Billodeaux family for early Mass. She held hands with Junior under the cover of a prayer book, but Mawmaw Nadine looked at them with knowing eyes whose white brows rose if both of them didn't get up to take communion.

Beignets and coffee at Pommier's Bakery followed, then Sunday dinner of pork roast and gravy or prime beef with the Episcopalians of the clan later. Under the pretext of taking in a matinee at the theater in Broussard, conveniently located near a couple of chain hotels, they got a room for some afternoon delight. If the movie showed again at four, they actually went, filling up on nachos and hot dogs for dinner and getting Xochi back to Nestor's before the alligator brigade took up residence in the yard. When she went for groceries on Monday, she stopped by Ste. Jeanne de Arc for confession. Obviously, Junior didn't always do the same.

July raced toward August training camp for him, this year held in the kinder summer climate of West Virginia at a luxury resort, too far away for visits home. After that, preseason games started where Junior had to prove himself, Tom and Alix kicked, and Dean played a quarter or two before turning it over to his backups. During the regular season when Junior would be working out in New Orleans, on the road, playing Sundays, he wasn't likely to get the time to drive the six-hour round trip to Chapelle. How she would miss him, this man of many talents she'd tried to push away simply for being a few years younger than herself. His absence would be unbearable.

Chapter Twenty-Eight

The rusty chains of the porch swing creaked as Junior and Xochi spent their last afternoon together before he caught a redeye flight to West Virginia, reporting on Monday for the grueling two-a-day exercises. The weekend campers loaded their pickups and SUVs and headed out. A motorboat still on the water purred by, and the flock of snowy egrets with a rookery in the area circled in the air before roosting for the night.

They rocked slowly back and forth with the slight breeze keeping off the mosquitoes. After executing their movie ploy, they returned to the cabin to have a dinner of nutra rat spaghetti with the meatballs finely ground and covered in tomato sauce sopped up by French bread soaked in garlic butter. Xochi joked a good thing they'd both had the same meal as she shared a few kisses with Junior before nestling against his great chest, trying to live in the moment and forget he would be gone for a long time after Nestor called the gators.

Beneath her ear, his heart ticked up a few beats as Junior shifted on the swing. "Everything all right? If you need the bathroom after that meal, I can swear snakes don't come up through the toilet." She tried to keep things light, but what if he thought they should break up or cool it for the season in order to take advantage of the freedom she'd once stupidly offered him. But no, his aura still shone with the deep violet of his love.

"Good to know about the absence of snakes in the john, but I have to stand up for a minute and get something out of my pocket." He withdrew a ring box, not from LeClerc's in town, and sat down beside her again. "I want to give this to you before I leave. I know you might not be as ready to commit as I am since I've been ready for years, but I'd like you to wear this as sort of a promise ring."

He flipped open the box with one of his big thumbs. An amethyst of deepest purple nested in a unique setting glowing against white satin. Golden blossoms surrounded the stone, each with a center of a tiny white diamond. "A jeweler in Lafayette makes rings to order. An amethyst is supposed to help with healing, bring good dreams, and protect from evil, or so he told me—since I won't be around for a while."

"So, it can't be an engagement ring?" she asked, looking deeply into the most sincere brown eyes a man could possess.

How he brightened. "It could! Unless you want a diamond, which I would totally get for you."

"No, this is thoughtful, wonderful, and unique— very much like you, Junior. Put it on my finger, and I will promise to marry you."

His smile was broad, and she loved that little gap in his front teeth all over again and the way his huge hand trembled a little when he slipped it on. In the background, Nestor called the alligators with grunts and *sooeys* and *here, gator, gator, gator*. Junior frowned. "This isn't the way it's supposed to be. We should have had a candlelight dinner and soft music playing in the background, not nutria spaghetti and hog calls."

"You said something like that to me in Cozumel, but it makes no difference to me. We are officially engaged. Proving we think alike, I have something for you, too." Xochi reached into the pocket of her gaily flowered Sunday dress and held out a chain. A shard of amethyst dangled from the end of it. "Also good for staving off drunkenness and keeping a man faithful." She hung it around his neck.

"I don't have a problem with either, but I'll wear it always. *Te amo*, Xochi."

"*Te amo*, Junior."

As they leaned in for a kiss, a sharp ping sounded near Junior's head. The rusty chain severed and dumped them onto the porch. From underneath his body, Xochi said, "I should have known that old swing wouldn't hold both our weight."

Junior knew better. The sounds of the fight in Cozumel came back to him. With Diaz still on the loose, he moved to put his body between the shooter and Xochi. If he died doing so, at least she had accepted his ring and made him the happiest man alive however briefly.

"Not the swing, Xo. A bullet. Belly toward the door beside me. Let me cover this side."

They began a desperate crawl across the aged cypress deck. Another slug sent splinters of gray wood into the air. The door flew open almost in their faces.

His hands still covered in nutria blood from the feeding, Nestor stood there with a double-barreled shotgun, the one he took along in his boat and propped in a corner each night. "Stay away from my gators, you!" he shouted into the on-coming dusk. Their forms louche and dark, a few of his pets slithered into the yard. "You t'ink dey easy pickings? Take dis!" He let loose with a blast.

Junior urged Xo inside the cabin. Nestor took a step forward to let him pass and emptied the other chamber in the general direction of the next shot, which lodged in the doorframe. Junior pulled the old man inside and slammed the door. "He isn't after your gators, Nestor."

"How you know? Won't be da first time someone t'ink they can take a gator wit'out getting a tag or going into da swamp." Beneath the house, some of those gators disturbed by the ruckus splashed into the water.

"Because he aimed at us. Xo, call 9-1-1."

She made her way carefully to a black wall phone Nestor must have brought from his last home. "Shots fired on Tall Pines Road, Nestor Leleux's house, the last on the lane. Please hurry!" She blurted out her name and the telephone number. Another pane of glass shattered.

"Now, I'm mad. Glass costs good money, no?" Nestor said. He chambered two more shells from a carton on the spool table.

"You got any other weapons I could use?" Junior asked.

"Deer rifle in my bedroom closet and some sharp, sharp skinning knives on da work table."

Before Junior could find the rifle, running footsteps sounded hollowly on the boardwalk as the gloom of night deepened. He grabbed a knife. Their attacker kicked in a door that had never known a lock. Dressed in black, his boots muddy from traversing the edge of the swamp, Diaz stood before them. He gripped an assault rifle and fanned its muzzle across the three of them without pulling the trigger. Holding the knife down and close to his side, Junior moved in front of Xochi

"*Viejo*, put down the gun. No need for you to die. I come for the girl to complete my father's last wish, that she have her heart cut out, and the big one stands in my way."

"Don't listen to him, Nestor. He is the son of the devil and will kill you in the end," she said.

Unconcerned, Diaz shrugged. "Take your chances."

Nestor did. He pulled the trigger of the shotgun, but this time his knees buckled with its kick, and he drooped to the floor, his aim skewing upward toward the ceiling. A few bits of buckshot bounced off the assailant's armored chest as he twisted away. A couple scored his cheek., sending rivulets of blood down his face. The rest dug into the rafters and sent fragments of herbs raining down like autumn leaves.

Junior took advantage of the distraction and did what he did best, went in low for the tackle, thrusting forward so powerfully he knocked Diaz out the doorway, across the porch, through the flimsy railing, and down into the alligator pit. He lay there on top of the flailing Diaz, slightly stunned by hitting his head on the edge of the porch.

Not all the gators had abandoned Nestor's yard. Big Ben snapped at an arm coming within his range, not Junior's. Like all the kids at the ranch, he'd been schooled not to wave a limb around gators who were mostly attracted to motion. That zigzag running, no good. Just run fast as you can. He shook his head, trying to clear it, as the distracted gator jerked Diaz's arm hard enough to dislodge him from beneath Junior. The man attempted to discharge his weapon into Big Ben, but the gator already had him in a roll. The bullets clattered into Nestor's makeshift fence. Unconcerned, the giant gator worked on ripping that arm from the socket. It succeeded with a fierce shaking of its clenched jaws and a crunching noise as the bone and sinew severed.

Diaz screamed, making Junior's ears ring, but the man did not surrender. He ran for the gate, leaving as the gator tilted his head and wolfed down the arm. Instinctively, Junior pushed up to pursue him—and drew the attention of Big Ben ready for another snack. Chomp into the meat of his bicep. The only thing to do when a gator got your arm was to hold tight and roll with it while trying to get at its eyes. They tumbled around, once, twice, three times, the gator unable to get a better grip as Junior hugged the scaly belly of the beast against his chest.

He caught a flash of color on the porch. Xochi fired the shotgun, but the pellets bounced off the reptile's horny plated back. More annoyed than hurt, Big Ben loosened his grip. Junior broke free and drove the knife clutched in his other hand into one murderous yellow eye. The gator backed off, made an amazingly agile turn with a flick of his mighty tail, and retreated under the house. They heard the splash of his huge thousand-pound body entering the water, then momentary silence after the chaos.

Gradually, the cricket frogs began to chirp. Far off, sirens sounded. Junior pressed himself over the edge of the porch to find Xochi gone. Inside the cabin, he discovered her kneeling by Nestor and performing CPR, her hands pressing over his heart, her lips giving the old man breath. The smile of his dentures lay beside him on the floor. Of course, she knew CPR. Anyone who'd served as a Camp Love Letter lifeguard knew the drill.

She looked up at Junior. "Heart attack, I think."

"I'll take a turn when you get tired."

"You're bleeding again."

Junior regarded his arm. "A little bit. Didn't even feel it with the adrenaline rush."

"You will. Press a towel around your wounds and sit down for heaven's sake."

The cacophony of emergency vehicles entered the lane. A familiar voice shouted, "Police! We're coming in." Tony Ancona appeared in the doorway going low while Officer Chauvin went high. Both wore the same uniform.

"Tony? Diaz is gone. He ran into the woods minus an arm thanks to Nestor's yard dog who got a taste of me, too." Junior lifted a blood-soaked towel from his arm.

"But Nestor needs an ambulance." Xochi continued to pump the old man's heart. Her patient opened his eyes a tad, turned his head, and vomited nutra rat spaghetti out the side of his mouth. "Oh, good," she said.

"Yeah. We have an ambulance with us out at the end of the road and a fire engine. You never know in these situations. Chauvin, you want to track the perp or stay here?"

Officer Chauvin eyed the stinking puddle on the

floor and opted to search for Diaz with the night growing deeper. He took the flashlight off his utility belt but kept his gun handy. "We might have to call in the dogs."

"He left a blood trail, a big one," Junior assured him. "I can go with you. Make sure we get him."

"No, you won't." Xochi raised Nestor's head and lovingly put a folded towel from the kitchen under it. She turned to the refrigerator, clattered around in there, filled a dishrag, and plopped it on Junior's head.

"A magic potion?" he asked

"Ice," she answered, "but I can whip up a poultice to take down the swelling if you want."

"Uh, no. A kiss would make me feel better."

Xochi removed the ice pack, cupped Junior's face, and applied her lips to the lump on his forehead. Nothing amazing happened, at least externally, but Junior smiled. "That cleared my head."

"Right. You just wanted a kiss the way you did in childhood." Xo replaced the ice.

"I was *canaille* about getting you to kiss me even then." His grin reassured her.

"Xochi," Nestor said, feeble as a baby. She came to sit beside him. "Your gift is in your hands. I could feel you making my heart beat, praying for me."

"Only mentally. What you heard was me keeping the count for the CPR. Here comes the gurney. I hope the medics can get it up the ramp."

"Makes no never mind how you done it. You got da gift already. Anyt'ing you want to learn, I teach you once I come back here, but *cher*, you don't need it. We each heal in our own way."

The EMTs asked her to step aside, and she did after

a quick squeeze of his hand, but Nestor's fussed. "My tee't. I can't go to no hospital wit'out my tee't." Xochi placed his dentures in a zip lock bag and handed them over. Soon, he'd be in a sterile environment getting the help he needed and hating every minute of it.

Officer Chavin waited until the gurney passed to report in. "Found him. Bled out in a patch of palmettos not far from a rented boat. Minus an arm like you said."

"Call in the coroner and another ambulance to take him away." Tony shook his head. "Sorry, you have seniority, Chavin."

"*Mais*, yeah, but you passed the dectective's exam down in New Orleans. I'll take care of it."

Xochi beamed at her favorite cop. "You did? That's wonderful, Tony."

"For all the good it did me. After a review, the department cut me loose for my *vigilante* actions in Cozumel. Someone put in a good word for me with the sheriff here. Back in uniform. My former buddies are calling me Barney Fife now."

"Probably Daddy Joe spoke to the sheriff. As for your old pals, ignore them. Your aura is already healing."

"My what?"

"Never mind. You will be healthier now. I can feel it."

"Whatever you say, Xo, but my heart is still broken." He thumped a hand against his chest. "I see that fancy ring on your finger. So, you and Junior are…"

"Engaged. Yes. Actually, you are the very first to know. We didn't even have time to tell Nestor or call the family before Diaz struck."

"Looks like he won't be bothering you again."

"No, Big Ben took care of him for me, but I don't want you to harm that gator trying to get the arm back. Let Diaz go to his grave without it. The next ambulance goes to Junior. The corpse can wait."

"No arguments from me. Junior might feel differently."

Junior shook his head. "Say, that didn't hurt at all. No, Big Ben was only doing what gators do. We got in his space, and he grabbed what he could. Honestly, I don't need an ambulance." Xochi filled a basin with water and brought it bubbling to the table to fuss over his wounds. Junior winced. "What is that stuff?"

"Soap and water, only soap and water. You need stitches, antibiotics, and a tetanus booster."

"Plus a special prayer?"

"I've been doing that all along." Xochi kissed the clean skin of his upper arm, then wiped it away with a dab of her cloth.

"I swear I'm healing from the inside out right this minute." No more chubby, smitten boy, but the man Xochi Billodeaux loved answered.

Chapter Twenty-Nine

Junior sat in one of Joe's oversized leather recliners in the vast den where most of the important decisions the Billodeaux family made took place. His parents and Xochi's plus a good number of her siblings gathered around to listen to him explain to Coach Buck why he'd be late for training camp.

"No, sir, not holding out for more money. If you'd let me explain..."

Blistering and salty language shouted loud enough for the closest to hear issued from the phone Junior held away from his face. Mama Nell made little Edie and T-Rex cover their ears. Both kids rolled their eyes—as if they'd never heard curse words on the ranch.

Junior tried again. "No, sir, it's not the bullet I took in Cozumel. That's all healed up. An alligator bit me and..."

"Dumbest excuse I ever heard," blasted from the phone for the listening audience.

"But true. I have a bunch of stitches in my upper left arm. No, I wasn't alligator wrestling, though I guess I did accidentally. I was trying to save Xochi, yes, again, and fell into a gator pit."

Simmering, Joe Billodeaux ripped the phone from Junior's hand. "You listen to me, you. If my future son-in-law says he was bitten by an alligator saving Xochi, den he was. Sure, I'll tell him dat. Coach says he's putting a no alligator wrestling clause into your contract. Dumb, no?"

Mama Nell pried the phone from her husband's fingers before he made matters worse, and gave it to Xochi who perched on the side of the recliner. "Nestor said you could probably heal over the phone. Have a go."

"Coach Buck, I promise you, Junior won't do anything more dangerous than get married next offseason. Why, thank you. Of course, you are invited. Probably May here in Chapelle at the church of Ste. Jeanne d'Arc with a reception at the ranch. Good, now I want you to close your eyes and let your blood pressure go down. Listen to this little prayer for your health." Xochi whispered into the phone so quietly not even Junior overheard. "Feel better? Good. Here's Junior."

"I'll fly up tomorrow and accept any fines levied. The trainers can take a look at my arm and decide how much I can do. I don't want to fail you or the Sinners. Great, thanks. No, I won't use that excuse again." Junior disconnected. "He sure calmed down."

"Age must be catching up with him," Joe said. "Glad you are off his shit list."

T-Rex mouthed shit list at his sister, and Mama Nell said, "I do not want those words to come out of your mouths ever!"

Corazon interrupted. "But you do not see the month is set for the wedding, and we have the reception here. We must start to plan today!"

Chapter Thirty

Xochi Billodeaux's wedding wasn't perfect, and she didn't care at all. So what if her wedding gown very much resembled a *quinceanera* dress with its many flounces gathered in places by red silk roses. Corazon had made it with love over many months. A white lace mantilla sent by Junior's family in Mexico crowned her dark hair.

Elderly Fr. Ardoin performed the nuptial Mass as Xo requested. She'd hoped Nestor would attend if he didn't have to confront the young priest. He had, accompanied by his niece Rosemarie. He lived in her white cottage now. Better for his gators if they stopped coming around his place, he said. Rosemarie said better for him, too. Xochi sent her mentor a special smile as she walked down the aisle on Daddy Joe's arm and a consoling one to Connor Bullock who sat with his family and still appeared disapproving.

Choice of bridesmaids is no problem when a girl has five sisters and a sister-in-law. Edie as the youngest proclaimed herself too old to be a flower girl anymore. Wynn filled in admirably strewing flower petals with abandon. Xochi handed her bouquet of roses over to Stacy who looked uncomfortable in the much more tailored scarlet dresses the bridesmaids wore. Xo suspected she worried her breasts might leak because her baby, Dean Joseph Billodeaux, Jr. securely held in

Mawmaw Nadine's arms, fretted in the first row. Mawmaw corked his cries with a bottle. Crisis averted.

When Ilsa showed up late leading with her pregnant belly and dragging Beck and her daughter, Princess, down the aisle to push into the second row—not Xochi's problem. She pitied the woman Prince Dobbs now said he'd never marry unless she gave him a son of own, and this one was another girl.

Junior stood, a big handsome man first in the row of handsome men that made up the six Billodeaux brothers. He couldn't seem to wipe the grin off his face despite the solemnity of the occasion, and Xochi loved him all the more for that. Tom, acting as best man, held the ring box containing a gold circlet of flowers with diamond centers to match her engagement ring despite Stacy saying it clashed with all the red. Hey, she'd let Stacy talk her out of bouquets of yellow daisies for the bridesmaids and allowed them to carry a single long-stemmed rose, but no way would she give up wearing the ring Junior had made only for her. Tom seemed more nervous about dropping the wedding band than Junior did about marriage. As her groom said, he'd wanted this for a long, long time.

They reached the point in the ceremony where Stacy plucked a rose from the bouquet for Xochi to lay at the feet of the statue of the Virgin Mary tucked into her own special grotto. As Xo completed the veneration, she murmured another prayer for her long dead mother, for the good mother she had now, and for the mother she hoped to become. Vows and communion completed, she and Junior burst from the sanctuary running the length of spectators who couldn't fit in the church and showered them with more flower petals. A few paparazzi pushed to the front. She ignored them. Her day, not theirs. They piled into Dean's black Mustang convertible and peeled out with a police escort, the rest of the wedding party following in limousines. Yes, she'd asked for Tony to provide security.

Plenty of time to take pictures once through the secure gates at the ranch where a reception, half-formal, half-casual awaited: linen-covered tables under white tents, a bouncy house and pony rides for the kids, a buffet full of catered delicacies and pans of Mawmaw's tender brisket and Corazon's taquitos, lots of champagne and even more beer. A lot like the Billodeaux family, this way, that way, all ways, Xo thought, loving being a part of it all.

The music started out formal with nimble Daddy Joe twirling her around a dance floor laid for the occasion. Knox Polk, Sr. steered her stiffly, clearly worrying about the security placed in Tony's hands. She worked her way through brothers, whirling with Teddy in his wheelchair, and half the Sinners team, eventually getting back to where she wanted to be—in Junior's arms.

Xochi disappeared into the house after a while and returned wearing the inexpensive coral dress she'd bought at the mall a year ago, back in the days when she'd tried so hard to throw away true love. She and Junior, Stacy and Dean showed the guests what salsa dancing was all about to huge applause. Rachelle pulled Joe into the mix. Tom danced with his wife the way he always did—with enthusiasm but not well, and Xochi adored him for it. They ended with Cajun two-steps and chank-a-chank the older relatives appreciated. Nestor requested the honor of a dance with the bride and did another with Mawmaw Nadine. All so perfectly imperfect.

They left the land of Louisiana where a one-eyed gator still waited for the swamp tour guides to throw him a chicken for a honeymoon anywhere but Cozumel, Junior's choice. She did not care because she would be with him. Long before Junior made the pro bowl numerous times and brought home injured players for her healing touch and those with psychological problems in need of a gris-gris bag earning Xochi the title of the *Sinners' Traiteur*, before the birth of Pilar Corazon Polk and their other children, before a house of their own in Chapelle and Junior's restaurant, Xochi knew one thing for sure: when Junior entered their bedroom, they made magic together.

A word about the author...

Once a librarian, now a writer of romance, Lynn Shurr grew up in Pennsylvania Dutch country. She attended a state college and earned a very impractical B.A. in English Literature. Her first job out of school really was working as a cashier in a burger joint. Moving from one humble job to another, she traveled to North Carolina, then Germany, then California where she buckled down and studied for an M.A. in Librarianship.

New degree in hand, she found her first reference job in the Heart of Cajun Country, Lafayette, Louisiana. For her, the old saying, "Once you've tasted bayou water, you will always stay here" came true. She raised three children not far from the Bayou Teche and lives there still with her astronomer husband.

When not writing, Lynn likes to paint, cheer for the New Orleans Saints and LSU Tigers, and take long road trips nearly anywhere. Her love of the bayou country, its history and customs, often shows in the background for her books.

You may contact Lynn at www.lynnshurr.com or visit her blog—lynnshurr.blogspot.com.

****

Don't miss:

The Sinners Series: *Goals for a Sinner, Wish for a Sinner, Kicks for a Sinner, Paradise for a Sinner, Love Letter for a Sinner*

A Sinner's Legacy Series: *Son of a Sinner, She's a Sinner*

The Mardi Gras Series: *Queen of the Mardi Gras Ball, Mardi Gras Madness, Courir de Mardi Gras*

The Roses Series: *The Convent Rose, A Wild Red Rose, Always Yellow Roses*

Single Titles*: A Trashy Affair, An Ashy Affair, A Will of her Own*

www.ingramcontent.com/pod-product-compliance
Lightning Source LLC
Chambersburg PA
CBHW051524260626
47170CB00003B/768